B.J.
NEW YORK TIMES BESTSELLING AUTHOR
DANIELS

At the
CROSSROADS

HQN

ISBN-13: 978-1-335-62100-9

Recycling programs
for this product may
not exist in your area.

At the Crossroads

Copyright © 2021 by Barbara Heinlein

This edition published by arrangement with Harlequin Books S.A.

For questions and comments about the quality of this book,
please contact us at CustomerService@Harlequin.com.

HQN
22 Adelaide St. West, 41st Floor
Toronto, Ontario M5H 4E3, Canada
www.Harlequin.com

Printed and bound in Barcelona, Spain by CPI Black Print

I had no idea how much my life was going to change for the better when I asked Christie Conlee if she would be my assistant. I smile as I write this because she doesn't just brighten my day; the readers love her, too. I've never met anyone with so much energy— not to mention her innovative ideas, cheerfulness and efficiency. Never has she said, "I can't do that." Nor has she ever complained. She told me she would make my life easier. Boy howdy.

This book is for Christie, who isn't just a friend. She feels like part of the family now. Thanks for coming into my life.

At the
CROSSROADS

CHAPTER ONE

BOBBY BRADEN WIPED the blood off his fingers, noticing that he'd smeared some on the steering wheel. He pulled his shirtsleeve down and cleaned the streak of red away, the van swerving as he did.

"Hey, watch it!" In the passenger seat, Gene Donaldson checked his side mirror. "All we need is for a cop to pull us over," he said in his deep, gravelly voice. It reminded Bobby of the grind of a chain saw. "If one of them sees you driving crazy—"

"I got it," he grumbled. "Go back to sleep," he said under his breath as he checked his rearview mirror. The black line of highway behind them was as empty as the highway in front of them. There was no one out here in the middle of Montana on a Sunday this early in the morning—especially this time of year, with Christmas only weeks away. He really doubted there would be a cop or highway patrol. But he wasn't about to argue. He knew that would be his last mistake.

He stared ahead at the narrow strip of blacktop, wondering why Gene had been so insistent on them coming this way. Shouldn't they try to cross into Canada? If Gene had a plan, he hadn't shared it. Same with the bank job that Gene said would be a piece of cake. Unless an off-duty cop just happened to be in there cashing his check—and armed.

Concentrating on staying between the lines, Bobby took

a breath and let it out slowly. He could smell the blood and the sweat and the fresh clean scent that rose from his shirt he and the others had stolen off a clothesline somewhere near the border. The shirt was too big, but he'd liked the color. Blue like his eyes. It bothered him that he'd gotten blood on the sleeve. The smear kept catching his eye, distracting him.

At a sound behind him, he glanced in the rearview mirror and saw Eric's anxious face. Bobby regretted letting Eric talk him into this, but he'd needed to get out of the state for a while. Now here he was back in Montana.

"How's Gus?" he asked, keeping his voice down. He could hear Gene snoring but not his usual foghorn sound. Which meant he wasn't completely out yet. Or he could be faking it.

Eric moved closer, pulling himself up with a hand on Bobby's seat as he leaned forward and dropped his voice. "He's not going to make it."

Bobby met his gaze in the rearview for a moment, a silent understanding between them. They both knew what would happen if Gene's younger brother died.

"We aren't leaving Gus behind," Gene said without opening his eyes. "He'll pull through. He's strong." He opened his eyes and looked around. "Where the hell are we?"

"According to the last sign I saw, just outside Buckhorn, Montana," Bobby said.

"Good. There's a café in town. Go there," Gene said, making Bobby realize that had been the man's plan all along. "We'll get food and medical supplies for Gus and dump this van for a different ride." He pulled the pistol from beneath his belt and checked to make sure the clip was full before tucking it under the cotton jacket he'd gotten off the line.

Bobby met Eric's gaze again in the mirror. Things were about to get a whole lot worse.

CHAPTER TWO

AT THE CAFÉ counter in Buckhorn, Culhane Travis rubbed the back of his neck impatiently as he watched the distracted, skinny male cook. This was taking way too long and making him nervous. He could hear the drone of Christmas music on a radio turned low in the kitchen and smell bacon frying unattended.

For the third time in the past fifteen minutes, the cook looked at the clock on the wall, then at his phone lying on the counter next to the grill. Leo Vernon, a parolee who'd only recently been released from Montana State Prison, had a rap sheet as long as his tattooed arm.

But Culhane was only interested in his latest crime. He'd been waiting for the short-order cook to take a smoke break out back rather than confronting him in the kitchen in front of all these people. He didn't want to call any more attention to himself than he had to.

But if Leo didn't take his break soon… Why was the man staying in the kitchen? Had the cook seen him and still thought he was with the sheriff's department? Or was Leo waiting for something? For a text? For some important news? Waiting for someone?

Whatever it was, the cook's mind wasn't on cooking, Culhane thought as he watched his breakfast beginning to burn on the grill. When Leo picked up the spatula, his hand was shaking.

With a start, Culhane realized that the man wasn't just distracted, he was scared. He felt his pulse bump up as he sensed the man's tension even from the counter where he sat watching him through the pass-through.

The bell over the front door of the café jangled, making them both start. Leo's gaze shot to the door. All the color bled from his face.

Feeling a gust of Montana fall air, Culhane turned to see three men come in. As a former sheriff's deputy, he knew the look too well. Trouble had just walked in the door. He swore under his breath. With a warrant out for his arrest, he had more than enough trouble already. He picked up his Stetson from the counter and pulled it low, watching the men out of the corner of his eye.

The older man of the three had a lined face, buzz-cut gray hair and old prison tattoos that showed at his neck and forearms where he'd rolled up his shirtsleeves. He gave the other two no more than a glance. They were much younger, both looking nervous compared to the all-business demeanor of the obvious leader of the bunch. Novice criminals, he thought and felt the earlier tension spark like the first hint of an electrical storm. He knew instinctively that the three men weren't here just for breakfast.

The locals in the café watched the three enter but lost interest—just as they had when he'd come in. Buckhorn, Montana, must see enough tourists that locals were immune to strangers passing through, he thought.

He wanted no part of whatever trouble these three were peddling and reached for his wallet. He'd leave the cost of his breakfast he wasn't going to get to eat on the counter and clear out. He had enough problems without buying more. He'd just have to catch Leo after whatever was going down here was over.

He shot a glance at the cook. Leo looked as if he wanted to make a break for the back door. Culhane swore under his breath. There was no doubt. The arrival of these men was what Leo had been waiting for. It made Culhane hesitate. Given the fear on the cook's face, this was about to get ugly.

Reminding himself of all the reasons he didn't want to get involved in this, whatever it was, he still hesitated. He just needed to talk to Leo, but it appeared so did these men. He groaned inwardly, cursing the way his luck was going.

As badly as he needed information from the cook, Culhane knew that the best thing he could do was hightail it out of there. This wasn't his fight. Worse, trouble would bring cops, and that was the last thing he needed right now. Once these men finished their business with Leo…

As he started to push to his feet, he heard the bell over the door jangle again. In the plastic of the pie display case, he caught the woman's reflection. His heart plummeted. With a curse, he slowly lowered himself back onto the stool as Alexis Brand entered the café.

Her timing couldn't have been worse. Of course she would come after him. He shook his head, remembering how he'd left her bed last night like a thief in the night. It wouldn't matter that he'd only done it to keep her out of the trouble dogging him right now. Not that she would understand even if now were the best time to explain. He'd left so many of the details out about his life before her. Now thanks to the BOLO for him, she knew the worst of it.

He and everyone else in the café had turned to see her standing in the doorway. Her short dark curly hair framed a striking face with its large brown eyes and thick lashes and that full sensual mouth that he'd never tire of kissing. In a T-shirt, jeans, boots and a denim jacket, Alexis turned heads. She wasn't just cute. She was sexy as hell, even though she played it down.

Everything about the way she carried herself said that she wanted to be taken seriously. He definitely took her seriously—especially right now with that look in her eye and that gun in the shoulder holster under her jean jacket. She'd come to take him in—one way or the other.

In the pie display he saw her make a beeline for him—the bounty hunter totally unaware of the trouble that had just preceded her in the door.

ALEXIS HAD ACTUALLY hesitated in the café's doorway at the sight of Culhane sitting bigger than life at the counter. Finding him had been too easy. She didn't trust it any more than she did dumb luck. So what was he still doing here? He'd had a good head start since he'd learned about the BOLO—a lot quicker than she had. He had to know she would be on his tail. It wasn't like him to let her catch him, and that worried her.

But then maybe she didn't know this cowboy as well as she thought she did. After this morning, she questioned if she ever had really known him. When she'd spotted his pickup out in front of the cafe, she'd thought for sure that he'd ditched it and gotten himself another ride. For a man on the run, he sure didn't look anxious to get anywhere.

After finding her bed empty this morning, she'd showered and turned on the news. Culhane wanted for *murder*? But that wasn't the real shocker. He was wanted for the murder of his *wife*. "Murder? *Wife*?" she'd repeated, sounding like a parrot before she'd called Al Shaw, a deputy she and Culhane used to work with—before they'd both been fired six months ago by the new sheriff.

"Tell me what's going on, Al."

"They haven't found the body yet, but there was sufficient blood at the scene…The marriage was over seven years ago. Her name is Jana Redfield…Travis."

"That's all nice, but where has he gone?" She knew Culhane—or at least she'd thought she had. He would be on any lead he could turn up to try and clear his name. There was no way he'd killed anyone. Let alone his…*wife*?

That was the part that astounded her. Wouldn't a wife have come up in conversation over the past year that she and Culhane had been lovers? Even an ex-wife. The man had a whole lot of explaining to do. She'd sworn that she would find him and bring him in.

"Where's he gone, Al? I know he would have called you."

"You're really putting me on the spot here, Alexis. He'll have my hide for this."

"So will I, Al, if you don't tell me right now."

With a sigh, Al had finally weakened, since Alexis knew when push came to shove, he was probably more afraid of her than Culhane. "He's gone to Buckhorn to talk to a parolee by the name of Leo Vernon. He's a cook at the café there. He has some connection to Culhane's wife, Jana."

Culhane's *wife*. The words made her grind her teeth. So when she'd found Culhane sitting calmly in the café as if about to have breakfast, it was all she could do not to pull her gun and shoot him right there. But then, she wouldn't have the satisfaction of seeing him behind bars—after she got the answers he owed her.

As she headed toward him, all she could think about was the two of them last night in her big bed and all the other nights they'd spent together over the past year. Oh yeah, she had a lot of questions.

She took the stool next to him at the counter. "Culhane," she said quietly, calmly. "Hope I didn't miss breakfast."

He didn't look at her. "We need to take this outside," he said, his voice low.

The urgency in his tone made her frown. As he made a motion to get up, she put her hand on his arm and felt his muscles tense as he looked over at her.

Just in case he'd forgotten, she reached with her other hand inside her jacket. His eyes narrowed. He knew from experience that she had a gun tucked in there. She doubted he wanted her to pull it here in the café with all these people.

"Alexis," he said, but she interrupted him. Surely he didn't think he could sweet-talk her into stepping outside with him. So he could get the jump on her?

She saw that he hadn't eaten yet. "I'm hungry," she said, looking around for the waitress. Catching her eye, she motioned the teen over to them. "A stack of pancakes and bacon," she told her. "And coffee, please."

"You need to trust me on this, Alex," he whispered as the waitress left. A knot formed in her stomach at the use of his nickname for her. It conjured up images of the two of them in bed, the sheets twisted around them, a breeze cooling their naked bodies. But that was back when she'd thought she knew this man and trusted him with more than the left side of her bed. Hard to believe that that was just yesterday.

"Trust you?" She chuckled and held his gaze with a fierce one of her own. Sometimes she forgot how damned handsome he was, especially when he smiled at her like that. She could have drowned in those bottomless blue eyes of his. Perhaps he was thinking about them being together just last night. It gave her little satisfaction. Taking him in, though, would make her feel better.

"Just look where trusting you has gotten me. So I don't think so," she said and lowered her voice. "And Culhane? If you give me any trouble, I'm taking you down right here."

She had pepper spray and handcuffs in her purse and a Glock in her holster under her jacket. This wasn't her first rodeo, and he knew it.

FIFTY-SEVEN-YEAR-OLD Bessie Walker could smell her cinnamon rolls she'd made baking in the café's oven. Earlier, she'd told herself that they might be her last ever here in her native Buckhorn. She'd been thinking about leaving. Maybe just for the winter. Maybe for good. On the radio in the kitchen, a Christmas song came on. She'd forgotten all about the holiday this year. She hadn't even gotten a tree. Her heart just wasn't in it.

"Bessie?" She'd smiled in spite of herself as she'd heard Earl Ray call her name. "Bessie, did you notice that one of those cinnamon rolls had my name on it?"

"This center-cut one that I'll slather with extra icing?" she'd called back from the kitchen and heard that low chuckle she'd come to love. She knew the way to Earl Ray's heart. The problem was the overcrowding when she got there. He was still in love with his wife, who'd been dead for years.

Grabbing the coffeepot, she'd gone out front. Some locals had gotten up early this morning, knowing it was cinnamon-roll day—and the last of the season. It was that time of year. The tourists had cleared out. Buckhorn was about to become a near ghost town, with shops and residences boarded up as winter set in.

She'd refilled coffee cups, including the cowboy's at

the counter who'd given her a nod of thanks, before she'd moved to people she'd known all her life. Today had felt bittersweet. She'd closed her bakery at the edge of town for the season, likely for good, but few people knew that.

Normally she moved her baking down to the café for the winter months. But last winter had been brutal. She'd been thinking about following some of the other Buckhorn residents south for some time now. She'd never thought she'd be a snowbird, but lately she'd realized she would be on her own for the rest of her life. At her age, she could kid herself that she had all the time in the world. But in truth she was almost sixty and all alone.

Deep in these kinds of thoughts, she'd handed off the coffeepot to Cheri, the teenage waitress, after refilling Earl Ray's cup and joining him this morning in his booth. The ex-military hero was the heart of Buckhorn. Her own age, he had dark blue eyes that she swore twinkled and this great smile. His great love had been his wife, Victoria "Tory" Crenshaw Caulfield.

But when Earl Ray smiled at Bessie, it made her as weak in the knees as if she were a schoolgirl. She'd been in love with this man for years. Looking at his open, honest face, she'd wondered if she could live without the sight of him for even a few months this winter—let alone the rest of her life.

Earl Ray had said he couldn't live without her baking. Maybe it was time to find out if that were true. She would miss him horribly, but it could be the best thing for both of them, since she knew Earl Ray would never go south in the winter. Just as he would never leave his house that he'd shared with his late wife. Just as there would never be another love for him—no matter how much he adored Bessie and her baking.

"Did you hear on the news this morning?" Earl Ray had

asked when she'd joined him in his booth only minutes before the three men had walked in. "Big snowstorm coming."
Montanans joked that there were only two seasons, winter
for nine months, and spring, summer and fall for three…if
they were lucky and winter didn't hang on—or start early.

"I'm thinking I might go down to Arizona," she'd blurted
out, not looking at him.

Earl Ray had laughed. "You'd hate it."

"I'm not so sure about that," she'd argued, finally settling
her gaze on him. There was such warmth and generosity
and compassion in his eyes. Maybe even love.

"You're serious?" He'd seemed more than a little surprised.

"I've looked into it. I can rent a place down there on the
Colorado River near Parker, Arizona. Do some fishing. Or
maybe just sit by the water and daydream if I feel like it."

His gaze had been so intense that she'd had to fight not
turning away. "Do I get a vote?"

The question had taken her by surprise. "Why would
you? It isn't like…" What was their relationship? She saw
Earl Ray every morning, every noon, every evening. He
never missed a day that the café or bakery was open. They'd
often sit and visit for long periods of time. Then he would
go home to the house he had shared with Tory, and she
would go to her small house. Both would be alone.

"Like we're best friends?" he'd asked. "Like seeing you
is my reason for getting up every day? Not to mention how
I feel about your baking."

"How do you feel about *me*, though, Earl Ray?" she'd
asked, her voice breaking as she'd lowered it and leaned toward him. She'd never asked. She'd always been too afraid.
At that moment as she saw his expression, she'd wished
she hadn't.

Her face burning with shame, she'd shot to her feet, but Earl Ray had caught her arm. She'd seen the battle going on in his expression. "You and I…" He shook his head. There were unshed tears in his eyes. "You can't leave. We've been friends for too long."

Bessie had shaken her head and pulled free. On the way to the restroom, she'd dabbed at her tears with the corner of her apron before anyone saw them.

When the café door jangled, she hadn't seen the three men who'd walked in. Men who were about to change her life forever.

CULHANE SAW BESSIE come out of the ladies' room. He could tell that she'd been crying as she picked up the fresh pot of coffee the waitress had just made and started around the room, refilling cups.

"We have a problem here," he said under his breath to Alexis.

Her snort was like an arrow to his heart. "You could say that."

Culhane hated that he'd left out what he now realized was some crucial information about himself. He swore that if he ever got the chance to make things right… But he couldn't let himself go down that particular winding trail of thought right now. Now wasn't the time. He had to get Alexis out of here before all hell broke loose.

He could see that she was angry and with good reason. But seeing him had thrown her off her game because of the history between them. That and the way he'd left things last night. He suspected all of that was what had her so determined to take him to jail that she hadn't picked up on the tension inside the café yet.

They'd met when they were both sheriff's deputies in

Gallatin County. Then Willy Garwood had taken over as sheriff, and six months later they were both out of a job. Alexis had opted to start her own business as a bounty hunter because she was still determined to bring in the bad guys. That's why, come hell or high water, she would take him back to stand trial for murder. But had she not been so intent, she would have sensed the danger in the air.

There was a lot he needed to tell her, but first they needed to get out of here. As he watched the three men out of the corner of his eye, he debated how to make that happen without causing the kind of disturbance that would bring out the weapons the men were clearly carrying.

He heard the older of the three say, "Take a seat," to his companions as he moved down the hallway toward the rest-rooms and the door into the kitchen.

Glancing over his shoulder, Culhane saw the younger men take a booth sitting across from each other. When he turned back, the older man had stepped into the kitchen— just as he'd expected—and was now confronting the cook. Clearly, the two knew each other, and from what Culhane could see, it wasn't congenial, as the older man grabbed Leo by the throat.

"Alexis, I can explain everything once we're out of here," Culhane whispered. Glancing over at her, he saw that she was watching the two men in the kitchen. They were keep-ing their voices down but were clearly arguing. He heard something about a vehicle and saw Leo shaking his head and talking fast as if trying to explain. On the grill, smoke was rising from Culhane's breakfast.

"Gene, listen," the cook kept saying, pleading in his voice as the man backed him up against the counter next to the grill. Pots and pans rattled as Gene slammed Leo against the counter hard, but no one in the café seemed to have noticed what was going on. Like most people, they had their own concerns. Unfortunately, Culhane feared their concerns were about to change.

He told himself that he and Alexis would be more help once they were outside and had called the cops. Unfortunately, the nearest law enforcement was an hour away in either direction. But at least outside they could decide how to handle this. Otherwise...

"Please just come with me without any gunplay, Alex," Culhane whispered. He saw that she had assessed the trouble in the kitchen and, like him, expected it to escalate. But she didn't know about the two in the booth behind them, both with weapons under their shirts. He lowered his voice to a whisper. "There are two armed men in the booth to your right as we leave."

As he started to rise, the deafening report of a gunshot filled the air.

CHAPTER THREE

VIVIAN "VI" MULLEN had been sitting in the round café booth and simmering all morning, her breakfast now roiling in her stomach. "The nerve of Lars to bring that woman in here," she said to her daughter.

"Mother." Tina tucked the soft baby blanket around her infant daughter sleeping in her carrier on the booth seat between them. "Please don't make a scene. Lars and Shirley have every right to be in here as much as we—"

"I can't believe you've put up with this for *months*," Vi said, her voice rising. "You even invited her to your baby shower!"

"Mother, please," Tina reproached her again as she glanced across the café to where Lars Olson was sitting with Shirley Langer. Even from here, she could see that the two were arguing. She didn't have to guess about what. Lars had been spending more time with Tina and the baby. "You should see how good he is with Chloe."

Vi harrumphed. "He won't even acknowledge that she's his child." She'd been looking for a fight, and Lars and Shirley were a favorite trigger. Not that her head of steam hadn't been building for months.

"We should go," Tina said in that submissive voice that Vi hated.

"And let them think they ran us out of the only café in town?" she demanded. "Not a chance." She'd been glaring across the room when the bell over the front door jangled and three men had come into the café, passing in front of her view. She'd paid them no mind, too angry to notice.

For months, her daughter's live-in boyfriend and father of her child had been sneaking over to that sleazy motel to do God-knew-what with that twice-divorced woman. Everyone in town had known about it. Worse, Lars had been telling anyone who would listen that the baby wasn't his.

Vi had wanted to fire him, since he worked for the Mullen family, but her husband, Axel, had insisted she stay out of it. She couldn't understand her daughter putting up with this.

"Do you love Lars that much?" she'd demanded of Tina at one point.

"It's my life, Mother. Let me live it."

"You didn't answer my question. You couldn't possibly love this man after the way he's treated you."

"It's between Lars and me. And yes, I love him. So please, leave it alone. He's really good with the baby and—"

"What? While he tells everyone in town that you don't want him to take a paternity test?" She'd seen her daughter look away and had felt her heart drop. "The baby is his, right?"

"Mother." Tina had closed her eyes. "Stay. Out. Of. It. You'll only make matters worse."

"I can't see how," Vi had snapped.

Now Lars and Shirley were sitting over there flaunting their immoral behavior. Vi felt sick to her stomach. She'd been through so much recently and now this. Why didn't Lars just leave town with Shirley so they never had to see him again?

She glanced at her daughter looking lovingly down at the sleeping Chloe. She couldn't bear the thought of Lars breaking Tina's heart. She went back to glaring at the two across the café.

Only when she heard the gunshot did she look up startled and wondered what she'd missed.

CULHANE SWORE AS the gunshot reverberated through the small café. He quickly put his hand on Alexis's arm as he saw her start to reach for her weapon. In the kitchen, the cook was looking down at his chest, his white apron blossoming bright red with blood.

In the seating area, a cacophony of screams and curses exploded along with the shuffling of feet as people started to rise from their seats to see what was going on. The baby, startled awake, began to wail.

The other two gunmen had shot to their feet in surprise and drawn their guns.

"Everyone shut up and stay right where you are!" Gene yelled as he came out of the kitchen brandishing his weapon.

Culhane watched the cook slowly slide to the floor as he heard the commotion behind him. All three men now had their weapons out.

"What the hell, Gene?" the thinner of the two men with him demanded. "I thought we were just getting something to eat?"

"Shut up, Eric," Gene snapped and glanced at the other man. "Bobby, lock the front door and turn the sign to *Closed*." The café erupted in a roar again with crying, screaming and the baby bawling as Bobby, waving his gun around, rushed to the door. An older couple near the door had gotten up and had been trying to leave but were pushed back into their seats at a booth.

"*Everyone* shut up and sit down!" Gene bellowed. A second gunshot boomed in the small café. The bullet that lodged in the ceiling brought down dust and debris and resulted in more sobbing. The older couple who'd started to leave were holding each other and weeping openly.

Culhane saw how quickly this could go even further south. He looked at the others in the place. He'd only given the customers a passing glance earlier as he'd come in. But now he considered each of them, seeing the fear and trying to decide who was apt to overreact and get them killed before this ended.

Apparently the locals had gathered for a Sunday-morning breakfast before the holidays. When he'd walked in earlier he'd noticed most plates were empty and diners were just sitting around finishing their coffee and visiting.

He recalled that the young waitress had been admiring the baby. The baby's mother had been sitting in the booth with an older woman with a rigid thin face and lips to match. She was the one who'd been staring daggers at the younger couple sitting on the opposite side of the room. The couple, in their mid-to-late thirties, had been facing each other in a booth, having what had looked like a lovers' quarrel.

There was the older couple near the door in another booth and what appeared to be a man and his twentysomething either employee or son at the only other booth. Both were wearing blue overalls. Culhane couldn't make out the logo but guessed it was the local garage and gas station he'd seen at the edge of town.

The younger of the two had a tough look about him and was now smirking as if enjoying this. He's the one, Culhane decided. He's the one who will do something stupid and get himself and others killed.

Then he spotted the teenage waitress frantically keying something into the cell phone she'd pulled from her pocket. Calling 9-1-1? Or her boyfriend? Or a parent?

Just as Culhane had feared, Gene saw her, too. The gunman took two quick, long strides, snatched the phone out of her hands and backhanded her. She let out a cry of surprise and pain and covered her face with her hands as he smashed her phone under his boot heel.

"Gather up all of their cell phones!" Gene ordered. Neither Eric nor Bobby moved for a moment. "Now!"

Bobby grabbed a wicker basket from the Christmas window display, dumped out the collection of carolers made out of plastic soda containers and began to fill the basket with phones as he worked his way around the room.

Culhane saw him stop at the table with the two men in garage overalls and felt his stomach knot.

FRED DURHAM SAW the young man coming to collect their phones and pulled out his own with trembling fingers. The man called Bobby didn't look that much older than his own son, Tyrell. He was silently telling himself that he should have gone with the vanload of residents to the next town for church services like he normally did.

But he'd been having so much trouble with Tyrell lately that he thought maybe a nice Sunday breakfast and a talk was in order.

"Your cell phone," Bobby demanded, sounding impatient and clearly upset.

Fred looked over at his son, saw the stubborn expression on his face and swore under his breath. "Give the man your phone, Tyrell."

His son met his gaze and held it a few moments too long before he said, "I forgot it at home." An obvious lie, since Tyrell had been on his phone at the table earlier. Fred had told him to put it away, and his son had been surly ever since.

The man considered Tyrell for a moment before he ordered, "Stand up!"

For a moment, Fred worried that his son was going to refuse. His heart was hammering. Why did Tyrell always have to cause a problem? He realized that he was past being tired of it. He was going to fire him from the garage. It was time for his son to find another job. He'd carried him long enough. Tyrell needed to find out what it was like out in the world. The young man had a rude awakening ahead of him.

Not that Fred wanted to kick him out of his life. He'd thought the garage would one day be Durham and Son and at some point he could retire and let Tyrell take over the business.

He just hadn't anticipated the problems. Tyrell often came to work late or didn't show at all. He didn't even try to be responsible. He pushed and pushed as if testing Fred, pushing him to his limit and beyond. Fred had come to see that he'd spent his life making excuses for his motherless child, but minutes ago, he'd realized that he was through. He'd decided to tell his son to pack up and leave as soon as breakfast was over. Now this incident with these gunmen had happened.

"I said stand up," Bobby ordered and touched the gun tucked in the front of his jeans.

"Son, stand up." Fred thought if Tyrell didn't get up right now, he'd grab him and throw him out of the booth himself.

Tyrell rose with that insolent way of his, a smirk on his face as the gunman checked his pockets and then shoved him back down.

Satisfaction flashed in Tyrell's eyes, and Fred held his breath, expecting him to do something that would get him killed. And over what? Nothing really. A stupid phone.

But Bobby moved on, bored with the impudent young

man. Had it been the other man, the one he'd heard called Eric, Fred feared it would have gone much differently.

"Are you just trying to get yourself killed?" he whispered hoarsely across the table once Bobby was out of earshot.

Tyrell merely smirked and glanced toward the two armed men as if he thought he was so much smarter than them. Fred saw him reach between the seats and fish out his cell phone. He wanted to scream as his son touched the screen and then surreptitiously pointed it in the direction of the two men who were still busy collecting phones. He realized that Tyrell was recording all of this with that self-satisfied look on his face that Fred had come to hate—and fear.

CULHANE SAW WHAT the punk was doing but quickly turned away. It confirmed what he'd already suspected. The fool was going to get himself killed—and possibly all of the people here with him, including himself and Alexis.

Maybe Tyrell hadn't noticed, but Culhane had seen Gene watching them all to make sure no one tried to call the cops before the phones were gathered. Gene hadn't seen what Tyrell was doing. Yet.

As Bobby approached, Culhane saw the blood on Bobby's sleeve. The shirt was too big for him. In fact they all looked as if they were dressed in someone else's clothing. Whatever had happened that they had to get rid of their own clothes was something he didn't want to know.

He pulled his phone from his pocket and slid it down the counter before turning to Alexis. She handed hers over, and he slid it down as well. Bobby stared at him for a moment before scooping up both phones without a word. But as he walked away, Culhane realized that he'd seen Bobby somewhere before. Recently, but the memory eluded him.

"We just need food and medical attention for a gunshot wound," Gene yelled over the racket. "Then we'll be on our way." That seemed to lessen the clamor a little.

"Eric, make sure no one moves." Gene shifted his gaze to Bobby. "See about getting us some food to go."

"How am I supposed to do that? You killed the damned cook. It isn't like I can boil water," Bobby whined. Gene turned the gun on him, making the younger man pale.

"I can cook," Culhane said and shoved to his feet. He knew he had a better chance of defusing this situation on his feet. He heard Alexis let out a sigh as if not surprised he would volunteer.

As he turned to face the three, he could see that Gene was eyeing him with suspicion. "I believe those are my eggs back there burning to a crisp on the grill," Culhane said as he took off his Stetson, laid it carefully on the counter and raked a hand through his thick dishwater-blond hair. He hoped his boy-next-door appearance made him look as harmless as any aw-shucks cowboy fresh off the ranch— and not a former deputy or a gun-toting criminal wanted by the law.

Bobby stood frozen in place as if waiting to see if Gene was going to shoot him—and turn the gun on Culhane as well. It took a moment before the older man lowered his weapon and gave a sharp, still-pissed-off nod.

The baby's crying reached an earsplitting level as Culhane headed for the kitchen. He could see that it was starting to get under Gene's skin.

"Somebody shut up that squalling kid!" Gene yelled. "Or I'll shut it up!"

OF COURSE CULHANE had volunteered to cook, Alexis thought. It was so like him to put himself into even more danger, but at least now he could move around—which she was sure was his plan.

Not that she'd ever known Culhane to have a plan. In all the time she'd known him—about three years—he'd scoffed at plans.

"What would be the point?" he'd told her one time when they'd both been on the same deputy assignment. "We make a plan, it doesn't work, we're screwed." He'd shrugged. "I just go with my instincts—wherever they lead me—and see what happens."

She couldn't imagine anyone living his life like that, and yet it seemed to work for Culhane. From what she could tell, he had few roots, had done a lot of other things before getting into law enforcement and never seemed to concern himself with the future.

"Do you really not have a five-year plan?" she'd asked soon after they'd met. The question had made him howl with laughter.

"Five years?" He made it sound as if that was so far off in the future that he found it incomprehensible.

"It's not that unusual for a person to consider where they'd like to be five years from now," she'd said, smarting a little. She'd always had a plan. Had one from the moment she awoke in the morning until she went to bed at night.

"So I'm going out on a limb here," Culhane had said, "but I'm guessing you have a five-year plan. Where is it you see yourself in five years? Sheriff? Mayor? Governor?"

She'd waved the question off. "None of your business."

He'd let it go, and she'd been glad since she'd wished she hadn't brought it up.

Now she watched Culhane make his way into the kitchen and wondered if he had any idea what he was doing. Fortunately, he had good instincts—most of the time. But given that the man was now wanted for the murder of a wife Alexis hadn't known existed, she had to question those instincts that had him now in the kitchen cooking for killers.

She tried to breathe. Since she'd awakened in bed alone this morning, she'd hurriedly packed an overnight bag and gone after Culhane. She'd feared she was on a fool's errand. He would never let her take him to jail without a fight. Not to mention, she didn't like the idea of turning him over to the sheriff who'd fired them. Culhane was in the middle of a wrongful-discharge lawsuit against the sheriff and his department. Could she really put him in the hands of a man like "Willy" Garwood? Would Culhane even last a night in jail?

She told herself that she was just her doing her job. She would hate for him to think this was payback for him leaving last night without even a goodbye. Or for him not bothering to even mention a wife and the murder charge.

He had to know that waking up alone in that big bed and finding out that he was now wanted by the law had left her more than shaken. She'd thought she knew him. Thought she knew his heart as well as she knew his body.

Why had he kept all of this from her? Just the thought made her sick to her stomach, something that had been happening a lot lately. He should have trusted her. He should have told her everything. He should also have known that she'd come after him. Just not for the reason he thought.

She had to take him in, get him locked up and safe. If not in Sheriff Garwood's cell, then one where it would buy her time. As long as he was running loose, he was in danger—and not just from Garwood. Right now he was considered armed and dangerous. She couldn't let some trigger-happy cop kill him.

But taking him in had been her plan before everything

had gone sideways in this café in the middle of nowhere. She tried to slow her pounding pulse. There'd been times when she'd been fearful with good reason as a deputy—whenever she'd walked into a situation without knowing what was really going on.

But this time, she could see where this was headed. This time, she had even more reason to be afraid, she thought as she watched Culhane. Her hand went protectively to her stomach. She could lose everything today.

CHAPTER FOUR

EARL RAY CAULFIELD had recognized Culhane Travis when he walked in. Just that morning, he'd heard all about him on the police scanner he kept by his bed. Former sheriff's deputy. Armed and dangerous. Wanted for the murder of his wife. He'd jotted down the man's description and the make and model of his pickup along with the license-plate number—as he often did, though never expecting that they'd cross paths. Montana was a huge state.

When the cowboy had walked into the café, Earl Ray had looked out front to the pickup the man had been driving. Years of working in a special division of the military had honed his skills. Earl Ray had seen that Culhane had a gun under his shirt, and he'd considered what to do about it.

He liked to think himself a good judge of character. In his line of work in the military, he'd had only seconds to assess a situation before acting. While he might have slowed some with age, he still believed he hadn't lost a lot of those ingrained abilities that had made him good at his job.

He'd watched Culhane Travis take a seat at the counter. He'd picked up on the cowboy's interest in recently paroled part-time criminal Leo Vernon, who'd just gotten back after spending the past eighteen months as a guest at Montana State Prison.

He'd decided to just watch him, pretty sure there

wouldn't be any trouble inside the café. The cowboy seemed to be waiting for Leo to take a smoke break outside, something Leo usually did by now.

But that was before the three armed men had walked in. At first Earl Ray had thought the men were looking for Culhane Travis. Instead, their leader went straight back to the kitchen after Leo. Earl Ray saw the former sheriff's deputy take in the men and start to leave, only changing his mind when the woman came in.

He had no idea who she was—just that she also was armed and seemed to be here because of the cowboy. As she took a seat next to Culhane, there was no doubt in Earl Ray's mind that the two knew each other—and well.

That much firepower in this small space made him more than nervous. He had been thinking about how to get everyone out of there before there was trouble, when he heard the gunshot.

The situation had gone downhill from there and was about to get worse. He just hoped the cowboy and his lady friend bided their time for an opening. There were too many people at risk in this café for more gunplay.

He looked over at Bessie. What she'd told him earlier about wanting to move to Arizona had shaken his world. He couldn't let her do that. Yet, he also knew he couldn't stop her once her mind was made up.

"It's going to be all right," he said now, voicing his hope as he took Bessie's hand and squeezed it. "We're all just going to stay calm."

She looked at him with such admiration, such trust, that it hurt his heart. He had to swallow, feeling the weight of everyone's life balanced on his aging shoulders, especially Bessie's.

"You are so full of bull, Earl Ray Caulfield," she said with a chuckle. But she squeezed his hand for a long moment before letting go.

SMOKE WAS RISING from the grill. Culhane stepped over the dead body on the floor and, taking off his jean jacket, furtively pulled his weapon from the waistband of his jeans and hid it on a high shelf next to the grill. As he pulled on a clean white apron, he glanced toward the counter where he'd left Alexis.

Damn but she was beautiful. It was a stray crazy thought that made him realize what he had to lose. It was one thing for him to get himself killed. But he couldn't bear the thought of anything happening to her. She wouldn't be here right now if it weren't for him. True, he'd tried to warn her, and she hadn't trusted him. Not that he blamed her. Why would she trust him, given what all he'd kept from her—and she didn't know the half of it?

But his...so-called wife, Jana Redfield, was the least of his problems right now, he told himself as he cleaned off the grill and got it ready to get serious about cooking. Yet at the back of his mind, he was trying to figure out how to get Alexis out of this mess, along with the innocent residents who'd thought they were just going to a quiet Sunday-morning breakfast.

SHIRLEY LANGER HAD been sitting in the booth across from Lars, wishing she'd never agreed to breakfast or anything else.

"It's over between Tina and me and has been for a long time," Lars had been saying, keeping his voice down. His living with Tina Mullen while sneaking out and seeing her had been a sticking point for months.

Shirley remembered the night he'd shown up half-drunk at her apartment behind the Sleepy Pine, the motel that she managed on the edge of Buckhorn. It wasn't like she hadn't known that he liked her and was interested, but he'd been with Tina for several years, worked for her parents and lived in Tina's house. He had always seemed comfortable with that arrangement.

Until that night when she'd opened the door to him, and he'd poured his heart out to her. "Tina's pregnant," he'd said a year ago on her doorstep, upset and angry. "That baby she's carrying, it can't be mine. We'd been having problems for a while. No way is that baby mine, and she knows it."

Shirley had comforted him, feeling badly for him because he was so hurt and confused. It made it worse that he had both work and residential ties to Tina's family. Tina had begged him to stay at least until the baby was born. Lars had agreed grudgingly and begun spending more illicit time with Shirley.

Now the baby was two months old. Shirley had been waiting to see what would happen once the baby was born. Nothing had—until this morning when Lars had shown up at her apartment. He'd wanted to take her to breakfast. He'd said he was sick of hiding how he felt about her.

"I told Tina that I'm moving out," Lars had said. "I thought you and I could stay in your place at the motel until we decide where we want to go, what we want to do."

She'd said nothing—even now sitting here with him telling her over and over how he felt about her. She still stung from the looks they'd gotten from the locals when they'd walked in together. Everyone had to have known about their love affair, and yet this was the first time they'd come out together—only to find Tina, the baby and her mother Vi here in the café having breakfast.

Shirley had wanted to turn around and leave, but Lars wouldn't hear of it.

Since they'd walked in together, Vi had been glaring holes into her. It hadn't been that hard to ignore the woman. Tina and the baby, though, had been another matter. Tina had always been kind to her. She'd even invited her to her baby shower, although Shirley was pretty sure that was just to rub her face in it.

"You still don't know for certain that the baby isn't yours," she'd said.

"Not you, too," Lars had groaned. "I told you. I don't need a DNA test. It's why Tina doesn't want me to take one, because she also knows the baby isn't mine." His voice had risen, and several people had turned to look at them.

He'd leaned across the table toward her and spoken more softly. "Shirley, I thought this was what you wanted. Do you still want a life with me or not?"

She'd been thinking about that when the three men had come in. She'd hardly noticed them. Instead, she'd felt the cold fall air rush in with them and yearned to get up and walk out of the establishment, leaving Buckhorn, leaving Lars Olson and this mess behind. She was sick of being the other woman.

Up until she'd heard the first gunshot, Shirley had been thinking that the only question was whether or not she had the strength to leave town, to start over, to go off on her own, to leave Lars.

As THE INFANT screamed at the top of her lungs, Tina Mullen fumbled with the straps that held Chloe in the removable car seat, feeling her panic growing. She didn't know what to do. The baby had been sleeping peacefully but had startled awake with a shriek at the sound of the first gun-shot and only gotten louder with the second.

Her hands were shaking. She had to quiet her baby. She could hear the man called Gene approaching her booth. He'd already killed the cook, someone had said. If he got his hands on her precious little baby girl—

"Shut that damned baby up!" Gene yelled again, loom-ing over the booth.

Tina finally got the straps undone and awkwardly picked up her daughter. She was all thumbs with the in-fant and had been since Chloe's birth.

She felt out of her depth. The baby was so tiny, so frag-ile, so demanding. Nothing Tina did seemed to make Chloe happy. "I'm a terrible mother," she'd wailed to her own mother recently.

Vi had pooh-poohed even the idea. "It's just all new and different than carrying her around in your womb where you don't have to do anything. Wait until she's two. What am I saying? It's not like there is a magic year when sud-denly you're finished raising your child. You're a perfect example."

Tina had groaned at what had sounded like the begin-ning of another lecture on having a baby out of wedlock. "Lars and I are practically married, Mother."

"You're a single mother," Vi had snapped. "You might as well get used to it. Lars won't be sticking around, which is just as well. He has no interest in being a father, and you knew that even before you got yourself pregnant."

"You make it sound as if I used a turkey baster."

"You'd have been better off if you had with some stranger," Vi had said and then huffed. "Give me the baby. You act like she's made of glass." Her mother had taken Chloe roughly, but the baby hadn't even whimpered. That her daughter preferred Vi over her didn't help and seemed to say it all.

Like now. Chloe continued to scream no matter how Tina tried to soothe her. "Please, baby, please," she said, shushing her. "Please stop crying."

BEFORE THE FIRST GUNSHOT, Lars had been professing his undying love to Shirley. But once the baby had started crying, he'd been distracted. When he heard the gunman threaten the baby, Shirley had seen the look on his face.

"Lars is like a baby whisperer," one of her friends had told her. "Tina says when she's at her wits' end, he will take little Chloe, and the baby quiets right down."

Here in the small café, the baby continued to scream. Shirley saw the panic on Tina's face as the armed man headed for her and the baby, fury reddening his face.

He was almost to the table when one of the men with him yelled, "Hey, Gene, come on. It's just a baby."

Gene didn't seem to hear. As he reached the circular booth's table where Tina sat with her baby and mother, Vi jumped up to stop him.

"Get the hell out of the way, old woman," the man bellowed, knocking her back into the booth. Tina frantically tried to get Chloe to stop squalling, but the infant seemed to wail even louder.

"You should go to her," Shirley said, turning to Lars. She had no doubt what the gunman might do if he got his hands on the baby. Lars looked at her as if he misunderstood. "She needs you. Tina and the baby need you. Go!"

"Shirley?" But Lars was already on his feet and rushing toward Tina and the baby as Vi struggled to right herself in the booth.

Gene was reaching for the baby again when Lars rushed

up to the booth. "I can quiet her," he said and stepped between Gene and Tina to hold out his arms for Chloe.

Shirley watched with her heart in her throat. Had she just sent Lars to his death? "Give him the baby, Tina," she said under her breath like a prayer. The woman was going to get them all killed if she didn't hand over the screeching child.

"Tina," she heard Lars say, desperation in his voice as the baby continued to scream. "Give her to me."

From across the room, Shirley held her breath. She hadn't seen Lars and Tina together for months. She couldn't help being curious about their relationship. Had Tina thought he'd marry her once the baby was born? Why stop Lars from getting a paternity test? Because she knew Chloe wasn't his?

After a few heart-thundering moments, Tina finally handed over the crying baby. The moment the infant was in Lars's arms, she choked back her sobs and began to still. Shirley couldn't believe it, even though she'd heard it was true. The baby quit crying. Lars really did have the magic touch.

Tina leaned back in the booth and began to cry, her body racked with sobs of obvious relief. As they began to subside, Shirley heard Tina say through gritted teeth, "Don't say anything, Mother. Not a word."

Vi harrumphed but didn't speak for once.

For a moment, Shirley thought the danger was over, until she realized that Gene was still standing there with his gun pointed at Lars's back. In the tense silence that followed, the only sound was Tina's sniffles.

Gene seemed to be making up his mind about shooting Lars. Finally, he growled, "Sit down."

Lars, the baby in his arms, turned to look at the man. What surprised her was the challenge in Lars's expression.

She saw something that she'd already feared. Lars would die for that baby.

For a moment, the café went deathly quiet as the two men stared each other down. Then Lars slowly sat down in the booth next to Tina. Gene still seemed to consider shooting him but finally lowered the gun with a curse.

As he turned away, Shirley tried to catch her breath. Across the room, Lars was looking down at the now-quiet baby and smiling. Shirley had to look away.

CULHANE FELT HIS pulse drop a notch. He knew this moment of peace wouldn't last, couldn't last. He saw Gene run a hand over his face. He looked exhausted and possibly coming off something.

"I heard you have a retired doctor in town?" Gene asked the café crowd in general.

"He died this spring," someone said, making Gene swear. He no longer looked calm. His nerves were fraying. He looked like a man who could go off at any moment and empty the clip in that gun into anyone who breathed.

"I have some first-aid experience," said a man with salt and pepper short hair from one of the booths. He was an older, late-fifties or early-sixties gentleman, with an ex-military look. The woman of about the same age who'd been sitting with him grabbed his arm and tried to stop him as he rose to his feet.

"Earl Ray, no," she said, but he gently peeled her fingers off his forearm.

"It's okay," he assured her before turning to Gene. "I'd be happy to help, if I can. I've had some experience with gunshot wounds." As he started to move toward the kitchen, Gene stopped him.

"Not Leo," he said of the cook. "He's dead. In the van outside."

Earl Ray glanced toward the front of the café to the older-model gray van parked outside, his expression resolved. He seemed to know how badly this could end with all these people trapped there with these men. He started toward the front door.

Over his shoulder, he said, "Bessie, it smells like your cinnamon rolls should be coming out of the oven about now. Best see to them. I'll want one when I come back in." He sounded so composed that the tension in the room dropped slightly. Clearly, the locals seemed relieved that Earl Ray was taking charge.

The waitress, a girl of no more than fifteen, had dissolved into sobs in the corner of the booth Earl Ray had left. "Turn off the waterworks, Cheri. *Now*," the woman Earl Ray had called Bessie said, rising. "Stop now."

The girl choked back a couple of sobs, her eyes wide with fear.

"Sit here and stay. I mean it. We don't need your histrionics right now." She straightened to her full height and looked around at the customers. "Everyone just sit tight. We can get through this."

Culhane hoped she was right about that as he left the grill to walk back out into the dining area. "What would you like to eat?" he asked Bobby and Eric, who were leaning against the end of an empty booth, their weapons still in their hands.

When the men had come in, he'd seen trouble in every line of their bodies. He'd noticed at once that they were armed, but he hadn't really looked at their faces. Now he studied Bobby. Where had he seen him before? The memory teased at the back of his brain. He couldn't shake the feeling that it was important. He'd seen Bobby somewhere recently.

"What can you make?" Eric asked, sizing him up and finding him unthreatening, apparently.

"Whatever you want," Culhane said.

Eric turned to look back at Bobby. "What sounds good to you?"

Bobby stretched out his long legs, the gun resting on his thigh as he watched the others in the café to make sure no one made a sudden move. "Pancakes, egg, bacon, hash browns."

Eric shook his head as his gaze came back to Culhane. "Make enough for three."

"The guy outside said you wanted it to go?" he asked.

Eric's gaze narrowed in warning. "You just tend to the cooking. We'll go when we're ready. Get too cocky and you'll end up like that poor slob on the kitchen floor."

Eric turned back to Bobby and the others. Culhane's gaze went to Alexis as he tried to reassure her as he headed into the kitchen again. But she was no fool. He saw the worry and fear in her eyes. He knew she was thinking the same thing he was. They couldn't just stand by and do nothing.

He gave a small shake of his head as he met her gaze. He could see no easy way to defuse this situation without getting people killed. The three men weren't leaving until they got what they'd come for. All the rest of them could do was wait.

Shooting her what he hoped was a reassuring grin, he told himself that he'd do what he could to protect her. He knew this woman. Alexis would be right in the middle of anything that went down. No shrinking violet this one, he thought as he leaned through the pass-through and said to her, "Your pancakes and bacon are coming right up, too."

"What are you doing?" she whispered as if feeling the heat of his gaze on skin. It had always been like this between them. A connection that was both sexual and cerebral. Half the time he feared that she could tell what he was thinking. Often he sensed what she wanted, what she needed, especially in bed—or on the job when they were deputies.

"Just admiring the view," he whispered and grinned.

She shook her head, her smile brief. "Save it, Culhane," she whispered back, but he saw color rise to her cheeks and something spark in those golden-brown eyes. She hadn't forgotten how good they were together. Maybe in time she could forgive him for not telling her everything about his past. If they lived that long.

But right now he had a murder charge hanging over him and was trapped in a small-town café with three killers and a room full of locals. Including a baby that could start crying again at any moment.

The atmosphere in the room was tense. They knew there was a bomb ticking in there and that it wouldn't take much for it to go off and kill them all.

CHAPTER FIVE

BESSIE HURRIED INTO the kitchen, stopping at the sight of Leo lying in his own blood, dead on the floor—and the cowboy who'd been sitting at the counter. She didn't have to check the cinnamon rolls to know that they weren't quite ready. Earl Ray had only wanted to keep her busy so she didn't worry. *Ha,* she thought as she got flatware, napkins, cups and a pot of coffee for the men who'd come in. Truth was that if she didn't keep busy, she'd lose her mind. She'd waitressed her share over the years, and Cheri was in no shape to help. Better for the girl to stay huddled in a corner making herself invisible.

Bessie tried not to think about all the people held in there or Earl Ray being out in that van with a dangerous, armed man. She rued the ultimatum she'd given him this morning. They were probably all going to die today, anyway. She couldn't miss the irony of it. Earlier her only problem had been being in love with a man who was still in love with his long-deceased wife. Hard to compete with the perfect late wife.

She put everything down on the table next to the man called Bobby, making a point not to look at the other one, Eric. There was something about him that turned her blood to ice water. Of the three, it was hard to tell who was the most dangerous. Definitely the man who had Earl Ray outside. But Eric was one worth watching.

Back to the kitchen, she also avoided looking into the expectant faces of those sitting at the tables. They were people she'd known her whole life. She knew that they were all looking at her as if she was going to save them. With what? A spatula?

All she could do was give them all cinnamon rolls when they came out of the oven. They'd all probably lost their appetites—if not still full from breakfast. But it would give them something to do while they all waited to see what was going to happen. The tension in the room was palpable. She knew it would take only one tiny spark for the whole place to go up.

Earl Ray was really the one everyone was depending on, just as they always had, as she always had. Her heart ached at the thought of him out there with a killer. She hoped he could do something for the man who'd been shot. But as knowledgeable as Earl Ray was, he wasn't a miracle worker. What would happen if the man died?

She feared she already knew that answer. It gutted her to think that she might lose Earl Ray. Not that she'd ever had him, really. But since his wife Tory died, she and Earl Ray had become almost inseparable. Except for those lonely nights.

Just the thought of losing him… It was one thing to move to Arizona knowing he was alive and well in Montana. It was another to know she'd never see that smile of his again. Tears blurred her vision as she walked back into the kitchen and pulled down an oven mitt to check the cinnamon rolls.

That's when she saw the gun.

Her gaze shifted to the cowboy working at the grill. "Don't get these people killed," Bessie whispered, not looking at him.

FROM THE CORNER of his eye, Culhane could see the set of Bessie's jaw. He thought about telling her that he was a former deputy. He didn't want her thinking he was one of these fools out there with guns, but then again, he now found himself a wanted man on the wrong side of the law.

Otherwise he wouldn't be wanted for murder with bounty hunter Alexis Brand after him and now trapped with him in this café. That part hurt the most. He hadn't wanted her involved in his mess, and yet here she was, both of them risking their lives because of his bad decision seven years ago.

"I'll do my best," he said quietly to Bessie.

"I need to get my cinnamon rolls out of the oven," she said as the timer went off. Her voice broke, and she cringed at the sight of the cook lying dead on the floor. She bit her lower lip as if to hold back tears and lifted her chin. The woman was a trooper, he could see that. He wondered about the older man who'd gone outside with Gene, wondered about their relationship, and hoped Earl Ray knew what he was doing.

Culhane lowered his voice. "Take your time. You're better off in here than out there."

She studied him for a moment before glancing out the pass-through. He knew she was looking at the gray van parked out front. He'd already seen that the side door was open and only Gene was visible, standing outside no doubt supervising.

"Those customers out there," she said quietly. "I've known them all my life. They're like family. A dysfunctional family, I'll admit, but they're mine."

He met her gaze and nodded. "I understand."

She glanced from him to Alexis. "Maybe you do." She

sighed. "If you need more of anything, there's the walk-in out back."

"Thanks," he said, seeing how nervous and upset she was but trying hard to keep it in because of the others. He watched her as she put on the oven mitt, opened the oven door and took out a large tray. The kitchen filled with the smell of hot, fresh cinnamon rolls with that underlying hint of blood and gunpowder.

He saw her start to put the mitt back on the shelf to hide the gun—and hesitate. He shook his head slowly. She held his gaze for a long moment before she dropped the mitt back over the gun and reached for a knife to cut the cinnamon rolls.

Culhane went to work cooking. When he was sixteen, he'd left home and ended up working as a wrangler packing hunters into the mountains. He got the job because he'd told the man he could cook. Turned out he was terrible at it, but after getting insults and even more painful objects thrown at him, he'd gotten the hang of it. If he could cook over a campfire, he should be able to cook on a grill.

On the radio, a Christmas song finished, and the news come on. The top story was about a bank robbery by three masked men in Idaho that had ended with the deaths of two bystanders and a guard. One of the robbers had been wounded. He quickly reached up and turned off the radio as the announcer began to give descriptions of the men.

ALEXIS SAW THE man Gene had called Eric move to the end of the counter and look in her direction. She could feel the hair on the back of her neck rise as goose bumps raced across her skin. She willed herself to ignore him as she picked up her coffee cup and took a sip. Her hand was steady, just like her resolve. She'd faced down men like this one before.

But this time, the stakes were much higher with a building full of innocent people—and Culhane. Not that she could consider him innocent even on a good day. But he had a target on his back already. She didn't want these men—whoever they were—to keep her from taking him back to jail.

She still believed in justice, even though she and Culhane had gotten little when the new sheriff had used them both as scapegoats, leading to their terminations. She'd taken it better than he had. Not that she didn't want to see Sheriff Willy Garwood get what he had coming to him.

"At least you've never been one to hold a grudge," she'd joked sarcastically at the time. Not only was he in the middle of a wrongful discharge lawsuit with the sheriff's department, he wanted to see Willy fired and put behind bars.

Culhane had laughed and leaned back, looking as if he hadn't had a care in the world. "Willy will get what's coming to him one way or another."

She'd looked over at him from where she lay naked in his bed. She'd thought they were on the same side. "You aren't talking about taking justice into your own hands, are you?"

"There is no justice—at least not the kind you're talking about. You should know that by now, Alex."

She'd been upset with him and his attitude. Admittedly, it was one reason she'd become a bounty hunter. She did believe in justice, and damned if she wouldn't get it. She'd just never imagined that she'd be hunting Culhane—especially for murder. Not to even mention that he had a *wife*. How was that possible?

As the scent of cinnamon rolls wafted throughout, Eric

said, "I want one of those. How about you, pretty lady? You want one?"

Alexis knew he was talking to her but pretended otherwise. She heard the man take a step toward her. She could smell the sweat on him and something else: desperation. It set her pulse pounding. In a couple more feet, he would grab her roughly, and she would pull her gun. Once he did, she'd have to shoot Eric and the other one leaning against his booth before he could shoot her.

She was wondering how long it would take the man outside to come running in and if she could depend on Culhane to stop him.

The bell over the door dinged, and she felt a gust of fall Montana air rush in.

"Bessie Walker makes the best cinnamon rolls in the county—heck, the entire state," the man she'd heard called Earl Ray said as he came in. He looked right at her as if seeing what Eric was up to.

Eric turned away from her as his boss followed Earl Ray inside. But Alexis had felt Eric's eyes on her, felt the meanness and the need pouring out of his pores. He'd be back.

THE SMELL OF Bessie's cinnamon rolls turned Earl Ray's stomach as he pushed open the café's front door. Gene prodded him from behind with the barrel end of his gun, a reminder of how on edge the man was becoming.

He took a whiff of the cinnamon and yeast and wondered if he would ever love that amazing scent again or if it would always remind him of this day—a day he feared a lot of innocent people were about to die. He had been anxious before in his life, but nothing like he was right now.

He'd learned over the years that bad luck came in threes. When Bessie told him this morning that she was leaving, he'd felt the bottom fall out of his world. Leave Buckhorn forever? She couldn't have meant it, and yet, he knew she had. Just as he knew why. He had only himself to blame. She was leaving because of him, because he couldn't love her the way she needed and deserved, because he still felt married to his first and only wife, Tory, dead or not.

Then these men had walked into the café. Now he worried what the third bad thing would be and felt sick at the thought as he headed for the men's restroom to wash the blood off his hands, Gene close behind him. All of their lives were in terrible danger. They'd be lucky to live through this, and yet, he couldn't help the pain in his chest at the thought of Bessie. She was his sunshine, his oxygen, his reason for getting out of bed in the morning. He couldn't bear the thought of not seeing her smiling face each morning. He knew that if they survived this, he would shrivel up and die without her in Buckhorn.

Earl Ray stared at the blood whirling down the drain. He'd done his best to wipe off his hands while out in the van. He hadn't wanted to scare the people inside the café any more than they already were.

He took his time washing and avoided looking up in the mirror at Gene. He feared his eyes might give his thoughts away: Gus, the man wounded in the van, was going to die. Not even if Gene raced to the nearest hospital would it do any good at this point. When Gus died, all hell would break loose.

"This is my kid brother," Gene had told him when they'd reached the van. "Don't let him die." The threat was followed by a hard jab of the gun barrel to his back.

The pain had been excruciating, but he wasn't about to let Gene see how much. He'd known when he'd seen the men come in, all armed, and imprinted with a look he recognized, that they were bad. He just hadn't known how bad. Right now, his only thought was saving the people in the café.

That he might not be able to save himself was something he'd accepted. One look at Gus and he'd known the man might have a few hours left in him. Probably less. He could see that Gene knew it as well. But that wouldn't keep him from blaming Earl Ray and maybe all the patrons for it. The man was angry, upset and just looking for someone to take his grief and regret out on.

Earl Ray feared it wouldn't be enough for Gene to simply take it out on him, which meant a lot of people could die today if he didn't find a way to change this situation. But quite frankly, he was at a loss. Gus was going to die. When that happened, Earl Ray had no way to protect anyone. He hadn't come armed for breakfast. It had never crossed his mind that he needed to be. Even if he made some excuse to go to the house for medical supplies, Gene would be right behind him—just as he was now.

"You need to get him to a hospital," Earl Ray had said when they were outside. "There's one in the next town."

Gene had made a disgusted sound. "Patch him up. He'll be fine."

They'd both known that wasn't the case.

He finished washing his hands, rinsed them, turned off the faucet and pulled down several paper towels. Gene had moved to the door, propping it open with his foot, his attention divided between him and what might be going on in the café. Earl Ray realized that Gene didn't trust his two young associates.

"Come on," Gene said anxiously. "How long does it take you to wash your hands, old man?"

Ouch. Earl Ray didn't feel old. Sure, his dark hair was

more salt than pepper now, but he kept in good shape—despite Bessie's baked goods—and he believed he hadn't lost his agility, or at least not much of it. Gene wasn't that many years behind him. Given the man's lifestyle, this man would be lucky to see sixty-five.

He smiled back at him in the mirror. Best to let Gene think he was a doddering old man and not a threat, he thought as he ambled slowly back to his booth and Bessie.

"WHAT THE HELL are you smiling about?" Fred Durham whispered across the table at his son. He was furious with Tyrell after that stunt he'd pulled with not giving up his cell phone—let alone videoing these dangerous men. Why hadn't the fool dialed 9-1-1 instead? If these men realized that he still had his phone…

Tyrell took his time turning to look at him. "Was I smiling? Sorry." He took another bite of his pancake before pushing his plate away. The sullen, angry expression wasn't anything knew. Fred had come to hate it. He wanted to slap it off his son's face. He'd never raised his hand to the boy. Maybe that had been the problem. If his wife Emily were still around, she'd say it was.

Then again, one of the reasons he suspected Emily had bailed on them was that Tyrell had been such a handful from birth. He'd been a colicky baby, a misbehaving and rather cruel boy, a difficult teen and now this sullen, angry, unhappy twenty-four-year-old.

Fred had tried to talk to Tyrell, but his son no longer listened to anything he had to say. Half the time, Tyrell didn't even show up for work. When he did, he'd work on his motorcycle, cussing and throwing things in the garage.

He'd suggested that Tyrell might be happier working for someone else. His son had laughed. They both knew why

Tyrell hadn't left Buckhorn to make a life for himself. His son was lazy. He liked the free rent, the food in the fridge, the garage full of tools and even an occasional paycheck when he stooped to actually do some work.

"Please," Fred said now as he saw his son looking again at the men with the guns. "Please don't."

Tyrell looked over at him and grinned. "Don't what, Dad?"

"Play hero."

His son scoffed. "Who's playing?"

BOBBY WATCHED THE cowboy who'd volunteered to cook look at him a second time as if trying to place him. He was having the same problem. The cowboy looked familiar, too familiar. He didn't look like a cop but… He just couldn't place him. Yet.

He turned away to look out the window. Gene was standing outside the van, glaring into the back. Even from this distance, Bobby could tell that Gene was upset about whatever was going on inside. Which meant the old guy who'd volunteered wasn't going to be able to save Gus. No surprise there, Bobby thought. He and Eric had already figured that out, given Gus had taken the bullet in the stomach. He'd watched enough Westerns on television to know that was bad.

Not that it wasn't Gus's fault. The fool was supposed to have made sure that no one had a weapon while Gene and Eric collected the money. When one of the bank employees pulled a gun, Gus had panicked and started shooting.

Still, it was too bad about the old man trying to save him. Gene would just as soon put a bullet in the man's back as blink. The bank job had been botched. Gene was as much to blame as anyone for bringing his brother into the action.

Bobby had seen how nervous Gus was. His first real job with his older brother. Sad, really, he thought. Gus would pay with his life.

Unfortunately, that was the way it worked. Bobby watched Gene getting more anxious and upset. He had no idea what Gene would do when his kid brother died. Wouldn't matter that Gus had started the gunplay back at the bank that had almost gotten them all killed. Wouldn't matter at all. Gene would lose it and take out his anger on the people closest. Which meant everyone in this café might not see tomorrow if Gene lost it—Bobby and Eric included.

All he could do was hope the old guy out there knew what he was doing. Though at this point, he doubted anyone could save Gus. Gunshots in their line of work were often fatal, since a hospital or a real doctor wasn't an option.

How many more of them would die today? he wondered and turned away to see the cowboy watching him again. Bobby frowned. He knew that guy. Worse, he couldn't shake the feeling that it was important he remember. It would eventually come to him. Hopefully not before it was too late.

CULHANE QUICKLY TURNED his attention back to the grill and the mass of food he had cooking there. When he peered out in the dining section again, he saw that Bobby was watching Gene with definite worry in his expression. He wished he could figure out where he'd seen the man. It was right there, right on the edge of his memory.

He started to turn away when he saw something he'd missed earlier. His heart flopped in his chest. The license plate on the killers' van. The beginning number was six, indicating the county. Gallatin County. The same county where he and Alexis had been detectives with the sheriff's department.

He told himself that the men could have stolen the van. It didn't mean that they were from the Bozeman area where Culhane and Alexis had been deputies and still lived. But he would have laid odds that these men were connected to the area. Which would explain why Bobby looked familiar. What were the chances that they would end up here in Buckhorn—a good hundred miles away?

It could be as simple as Gene had known the cook and had been expecting to pick up another rig here. It didn't mean that Sheriff Willy Garwood was behind it. The crooked sheriff couldn't be behind all the crime in the state, right?

Culhane glanced at the cook lying dead on the floor. The feeling that everything in life was connected sent an electrical current through him. He'd never bought into fate, but here they all were, Alexis included, in this one café. At least he didn't think the killers knew he and Alexis were ex–law enforcement. But he'd seen Bobby eyeing him as if trying to place him. When he did...

Which was why he had to end this before that happened, he thought as he cooked and kept an eye on what was going among the tables. Everyone was getting restless, always a bad sign. One of them was bound to decide to play hero. It was just a matter of time. He just didn't want to be that guy.

BOBBY FELT THE tension building as he looked around the room. What was taking breakfast so long? He was starving. Eric had wandered over to the opening into the kitchen, but he wasn't watching the cowboy cook. Instead, he was giving the woman at the counter the eye. Damn Eric. Bobby hoped Gene didn't catch him.

Gene had dragged the old man back outside again to the van. This time, they'd taken a bunch of towels along. Bobby couldn't imagine how much blood was back there since Gus had been bleeding for a long time.

He let his gaze shift to the two men in the blue overalls sitting at the booth across the room. The name stitched on the pocket of the younger man's overalls read Tyrell. The old man's, Fred. Motor jockeys. Both had grease under their fingernails. He started to shift his gaze to the others when the younger of the two looked at him. Their gazes locked. Bobby saw defiance and bravado in those eyes.

He met the challenge with the slow shake of his head as he raised his gun off his thigh. *Wanna die today, Tyrell? Just say the word.*

He reminded himself that Gene would be pissed off if they killed anyone. But he was getting restless as well. Itchy and twitchy. His nerves felt raw and exposed as if even a stray breeze would set him off. He glanced toward Eric again. "What's keeping breakfast?"

"You ordered a mountain of food. That's what's keeping breakfast," Eric snapped.

They were all hungry and tired and strung out after everything that had happened in the past forty-eight hours. Worse, cops everywhere would be looking for them. Gene had said something about changing vehicles. Is that what the disagreement with the cook had been about?

All Bobby knew was that the longer they stayed here, there was more chance of the law catching up to them. But the real danger was in that van, he thought glancing out there again. He told himself that if he heard gunshots and

Gene came busting in that front door in a blind fury, he'd better be ready.

"Breakfast is served," the cowboy cook announced from the kitchen as the front door of the café opened on a gust of cold air.

CHAPTER SIX

CULHANE FELT THE cold air, felt the tension and turned to see Gene and Earl Ray come through the front door again. Gene locked it behind them, his gun in his hand. He looked sick. Even from where he stood, Culhane could tell that the man was sweating profusely and appeared shaky. He was definitely coming off something.

Gene leaned against the door for a moment, and Culhane hurriedly dished up three to-go boxes wondering why he was wasting his time. They weren't just going to leave. That would be too easy. He filled three containers with eggs, bacon, hash browns. In a fourth box, he piled up pancakes. In a fifth, he scooped up three large cinnamon rolls.

Earlier, Bessie had taken rolls out to everyone but few had touched theirs. His stomach growled, surprising him as the aroma of the food rose up from the boxes before he closed the lids.

Under these circumstances, he would think he couldn't eat a bite. But he'd made cakes and bacon for himself and Alexis. It would give them something to do, a diversion not just for them. He'd seen the way Eric was looking at her.

He took the to-go boxes out and put them on the table next to where Bobby was leaning, cradling his weapon. Without giving Culhane even a glance, the man slid into the booth and, opening the boxes, began digging in.

Earl Ray went straight to the men's restroom. Gene followed him only partway down the hall to make sure that's where he'd actually gone. Back in the kitchen, Culhane loaded two plates much as he had for the gunmen. Taking them out to the counter, he placed one in front of Alexis and sat down in front of the other.

Gene eyed him suspiciously as Culhane slid onto the stool next to Alexis and picked up his fork.

"Hey, I thought we were taking it to go," Eric said behind them, swearing as he slid into the booth across from Bobby. Gene was still standing in the hallway, leaning against the wall, the gun dangling from his hand as he waited for Earl Ray.

Looking over his shoulder, Culhane saw that Bobby was rolling up eggs, bacon and hash browns into one of the large pancakes and stuffing them into his mouth. Eric joined him, both wolfing the food down as if ravenous, their weapons resting on the table within reach.

"You have to be kidding," Alexis whispered as she considered the overflowing plate he'd given her.

"Wasn't sure what you might want for your last meal— other than the pancakes and bacon you ordered."

She gave him a sour look. "I should have listened to you," she whispered. "But under the circumstances, I'm sure you understand why I might not trust you."

"Yeah," he agreed. "It isn't what it seems."

She chuckled as she picked up her fork and cut into her pancake. He'd buttered it and drowned it in syrup in the kitchen—just the way she liked it. "Are you married or not?"

"Not. Well, legally apparently, but married?" He met her gaze. "No. Haven't been for seven years."

Alexis gave him a smile. "Let me guess. It's complicated."

He nodded, grinning. "Boy howdy." He began to eat, even though he'd lost his appetite. But he figured if he and Alexis didn't at least try, it would raise red flags, especially with Gene. Culhane had already seen the distrust in his gaze.

"When the shooting starts, stay down," Culhane whispered between bites.

She shot him a look. "Would be nice if I had some idea before that."

He cut a bite of pancake with his fork. "You'll know when I put my hat on." He winked. "So how's your breakfast?"

"I'm not—"

"Eat, otherwise they'll think something is wrong," he said.

"Something *is* wrong," she whispered back. But she picked up her fork again. "I'd ask if you had a plan, but I know you too well."

He didn't look at her as he took a big bite of his pancake. It could have been sawdust in his mouth.

"You two are pretty cozy," Gene said, suddenly appearing in front of them.

Culhane hadn't heard him move from the hallway. He looked up and grinned. "Just trying to use this time to my benefit, but I don't think the lady is having any of it."

Gene's gaze shifted to Alexis. "That's funny. I got the impression of the two of you knew each other."

Alexis snorted. "My mistake sitting next to a cowboy."

Gene's gaze swung back to him and his Stetson lying on the counter next to him. "Cowboy, huh?"

"This one seems to be all hat and no cattle, though," she said contemptuously. She took a bite of her pancake and mugged a face in his direction.

Culhane laughed. "She's definitely got my number. But I *was* raised on a ranch, if that counts."

Gene smirked. "I grew up on a farm, but it didn't make me a farmer."

Earl Ray came out from the men's room and went to join Bessie in the booth again where she sat with the young waitress.

Gene frowned, his gaze following the man for a moment before he stepped away and raised his voice. "We need medical supplies. I understand someone here has the key to the store?"

No one spoke. Culhane heard a whispered, agitated *"Mother."* He turned to see Earl Ray looking at the older woman sitting in the circular booth along with her daughter, Tina, and the baby and Lars, the man who'd quieted the infant.

"Vi," Earl Ray said quietly. The older woman's face became more pinched, her eyes narrower and colder. "Why don't you give me the key?" Earl Ray suggested. "I can go with them to get what they need." There was no urgency in his tone, but Culhane felt it none the less.

"Give him the key, Mother," her daughter said, a hard edge to her voice.

Vi shook her head and glared at Gene. Clearly she hadn't forgiven him for threatening her grandbaby, let alone pushing her down into the booth. But did she realize just what she was dealing with? Apparently not, Culhane thought.

"Give him the keys," the older man sitting with his wife closest to the door called to her. "For the love of God, Vi, just do it."

She bristled. "Who's paying for these supplies?" she demanded as she looked around the café. "Easy for all of you to say," she said, anger making her words clipped. "It isn't your store. It isn't *your* money."

"Mother, just do as they ask," her daughter Tina pleaded again. Vi slid back in the seat, a stony determination in every line of her body as she glared at Gene again.

Gene was looking at her as if she'd lost her mind. He laughed and, raising his gun, he aimed at her head as he approached the booth.

"Vi," Earl Ray said calmly. "We need to help these men so they can get on their way. Now isn't the time for stubbornness."

Vi pursed her lips and crossed her arms. "If you think I'm going to open up my store for these—"

"I have a key to the store," said the young man who'd settled the baby.

Vi let out a cry. "Lars? You're fired!" she yelled. "I should have known you'd turn on me. Just like you did my daughter. But the joke's on you. You don't have a key to the pharmacy, so there." She gave him a smug smile.

Lars handed the baby to Tina, and the infant began to cry again. "Vi, don't be a fool," he said quietly. "We can break into the pharmacy for what we need. Or you can give us the key. Either way, we're going to get what is needed."

Vi spun on him. "You're the fool, Lars Olson, for sleeping with that…that *woman*." She pointed across the café at the woman sitting alone in the booth. "Shirley Langer is a loser just like you. I'll never forgive you for breaking my daughter's heart and telling people—" the woman's voice broke "—people that this precious baby isn't yours."

"Now isn't the time to talk about that," Lars said, still keeping his voice down.

"Lars is right," Earl Ray agreed as he got to his feet. "He and I will go over to the store and get the medical supplies we need with or without the key to the pharmacy." He stepped between Gene and Vi.

"I'll be going with you," Gene said as if they had forgotten him.

"Of course," Earl Ray said and looked to Lars. The younger man was staring down at the baby in the young redhead's arms. He seemed to shake off whatever thoughts he'd been having and rising, started toward the door.

Vi began to cry, sobbing and beating her fist against the back of the booth seat for a moment before she reached into her purse. Finding the keys, she hurled them at Lars. "You make a mess and you'll clean it up!"

He and the men walked toward the door.

"You know what to do if we don't come back," Gene said over his shoulder to his two men on his way out. "Shoot anyone who moves."

The baby began to cry louder. There was more sniffling in the room as the older woman by the door collapsed again into her husband's arms. The two were glaring at Vi.

"What are you two old fools looking at?" Vi demanded.

"Keep your voice down," Tina cried. "You're upsetting Chloe."

Vi slammed her lips shut but continued to glare around at anyone who looked at her. Bobby and Eric were both shaking their heads. Clearly they knew how close Vi had come to getting shot, Culhane thought.

Fortunately, both men were more interested in the food. They kept eating as if they thought it might be their last meal. It might be, he figured.

He could feel Alexis's gaze on him and knew exactly what she was thinking. That maybe this would be a good time to disarm these two.

"Wait," he said quietly as he turned back to his breakfast. He took another bite before glancing out the side window. The three men were almost to the general store. Once they were inside the store and busy...

CHAPTER SEVEN

ALEXIS FELT HER stomach roil. Morning sickness, *yeah, right*. It could hit her anytime, anywhere. But not here, please not here. She couldn't believe the mess she'd walked into. She would have liked to blame Culhane for all of it.

But she remembered the night in question camped beside the lake, the campfire crackling, the flames dancing against the side of the tent. They hadn't used protection. It was a story as old as time. She'd just never believed it would happen to her.

She took a bite of pancake, hoping it would calm her stomach; otherwise, she was going to have to make a run for the ladies' room under the worst possible circumstances. Taking a few deep breaths, she got past it.

That night at the lake had been glorious. Culhane had gotten up the next morning and made her breakfast over the campfire. The memory hurt at heart level and radiated out all the way to her toes and her fingertips. The next bite was hard to swallow, but she kept eating, knowing she needed the sustenance and hoping she would be able to keep the food down.

"How are things with you?" Culhane whispered.

She didn't look at him. Didn't answer. This didn't seem like the time to get into it, but that didn't stop Culhane.

"I haven't been great," he said.

She shot him a look. That was putting it mildly, given that he was wanted for murder.

"This is hell for me just thinking what could happen to you here," he said.

His words made her heart ache. She swallowed the lump in her throat and took another bite of her breakfast. Her eyes burned. Culhane had always been able to disarm her emotionally with only a few words. Who was she kidding? A look from him was all it took.

Or had taken, she reminded herself. Who knew what other secrets he'd kept from her. Unable to trust the man, she told herself she was no longer under his spell. He could no longer beguile her with one of his lazy grins. Or melt her insides with his sleepy-eyed looks. Or sweet-talk her back into his bed.

"You know how this is going to end if we don't do something," she whispered back.

He nodded and sighed before he turned to look at the two armed men. "How's your breakfast?" he called to them. "Anyone want seconds?"

"Could use some coffee," Eric said. But as Culhane started to rise, Eric stopped him. "I want her to pour it."

Neither of them had to ask who Eric meant.

Culhane glanced at Alexis as he picked up his Stetson and settled it over his unruly blond hair. She saw that it was his lucky hat. She hoped he was wearing his lucky boots as well. "You might want to get that fresh pot from the back," he said to her. "But be careful, it's real hot," he said loud enough for everyone to hear. Then he met her gaze, just long enough.

She nodded and rose slowly, wishing for her gun instead of a coffeepot. Culhane had always been a crack shot, but they'd just both agreed silently that gunfire would get Earl

Ray and Lars killed. Like when they were deputies together, they often could just look at each other and know what the other one wanted to do.

She tried to still her pounding heart as she walked into the kitchen and picked up the hot pot of fresh coffee. If this went sideways, a lot of people could be killed, she and Culhane among them. Culhane would die not even knowing that he was almost a father. A father that if they lived might be headed for jail—or worse—prison.

As she passed the counter, Culhane rose and swore loudly. "Oh, shoot, I left the grill on." He rushed in the kitchen, passing her. The look in his eyes was almost her undoing. It was both a wish of good luck as well as a warning to be careful with something more heart-wrenching tossed in the mix. Goodbye, in case this plan went really bad.

But it was the love she saw there that made her heart skip as she started toward the booth where the two men were waiting, their weapons right there on the table next to them.

LARS BENT DOWN to unlock the door to the general store. Earl Ray couldn't help seeing the way the man's hands shook and sweat beaded on his ruddy face. Lars must have noticed his hands, too, because he fumbled for a moment putting the key into the lock but finally managed.

Pull it together. The door swung open. Earl Ray told himself that of course Lars was nervous. Like him, there were people in that café that Lars cared and worried about. Clearly the man cared more about Tina and the baby that possibly even Shirley had known until today. But Earl Ray suspected that Lars cared about Shirley as well. Also like him, Lars was probably even more worried about what

Vi would do before this was over. He certainly was. The woman didn't have the good sense of a goose.

He watched Gene look around at the vacant main drag before jabbing him in the back with the gun and forcing him inside the store. "Come on. We don't have all day." It was still early. What few people were left in town weren't up and about and probably wouldn't be. Most had gone to the next town for Sunday church services like they usually did when the weather allowed. They wouldn't be back for hours, often making a day of it.

"The pharmacy is back here," Earl Ray said and led the way down the aisle. The Mullen General Store carried everything from muck boots to diapers, canned food to sunscreen, and even rocks for those who wanted to buy a piece of Montana to take home. At the back was a small bank of metal post-office boxes. Vi was the postmistress and also the pharmacist, in that she could hand out medications sent over from one of the large towns. Some drugs were kept on hand for emergencies.

The Mullens owned half the town, including the antique barn just off the main street. Vi's husband Axel had been as close to a mayor as the unincorporated town had ever had. But her husband had left her after what had happened a few months ago. Most people figured she would sell out and leave as well. The rest of them thought she should go to jail longer for what she did.

The law had taken into account her age, that she had a daughter and grandchild, and been lenient. Vi had sworn that all she'd be doing was trying to help her brother. It had been wrong. She could admit that now. But when he'd come to her in tears... How was she to know the depth of his trouble until it was too late?

The whole horrible incident had left Vi even more obstinate and contemptuous and surly. Earl Ray had actually felt sorry for her, given what she'd gone through. He knew her bad behavior was a defense mechanism. But damned if he hadn't wanted to throttle her back there at the cafe.

He moved to the pharmacy part of the store, next to the post office. He knew there was nothing here that could save the man lying in the back of the van. But at least he could make him comfortable until he died. If there had been any way to keep him alive, he would have done it.

Lars handed him the keys, and he opened the drug cabinet, quickly taking out what he needed. He didn't want to be gone from the café long for fear of what would happen in their absence. Nor did he trust those two men Gene had left in charge. The one seemed young and naive, the other was a hothead. Earl Ray had seen him eyeing the woman at the counter. Eric really had no idea what he was getting into if he decided to take it any further with her. Either could make a critical mistake that would end with bloodshed.

He thought of Bessie. She could handle herself. But some of the others? Not so much. At just the thought of Bessie, he thought his heart would break. Why hadn't he told her how he felt about her? Now he might never get the chance.

CULHANE TURNED OFF the grill, made a show of burning his hand and reaching for an oven mitten on the shelf. He knew they had to move fast—and to keep it as quiet as possible. He saw his gun and hesitated before quickly picking it up and stuffing it into the back of his jeans. He covered it with his shirt as he reminded himself that if any of them fired a shot, it would alert Gene, who would probably start by killing both Earl Ray and Lars. Not that he wouldn't anyway before this was over. Unless Culhane could stop it.

Out of the corner of his eye, he saw Alexis heading

slowly toward the table with the two men. Another step and she would block their view of him.

He picked up the heavy metal pan still loaded with cinnamon rolls. As an afterthought, he grabbed up the large spatula he'd been using on the grill. It had to weigh a couple of pounds. He headed into the other room behind Alexis and her full pot of hot coffee.

He was right behind her with the tray of rolls and the massive spatula. Eric's gaze was on Alexis in a way that gave Culhane sick chills. Bobby was still elbow-deep in the food.

They were almost to the table when it seemed something caught Eric's eyes off to his right. Culhane saw the man instinctively reach for his weapon. As Eric did, he jumped up, knocking Alexis back. The coffeepot hit the edge of the table and shattered. Hot coffee splashed everywhere—including onto Bobby. Appearing to have no idea what was happening, the man rocketed to his feet with a curse and, grabbing his gun and Alexis, pointed the barrel at her head.

The sound of a gunshot exploded in the café, followed by screaming.

CHAPTER EIGHT

Down in the general store, Earl Ray started to close the drug cabinet, but Gene stopped him.

"I'll take some of that," the man said, pushing him aside to grab a bottle of amphetamines, then an array of other drugs, stuffing the containers into his pockets.

Closing and locking the cabinet, Earl Ray picked up what medical supplies he could use to at least cover the wound and give Gus some comfort from the pain. It was only a stopgap measure. He had a feeling Gene knew it, too.

Out of the corner of his eye, he watched Gene open one of the bottles of drugs, shake out four tablets and toss them into his mouth dry before pocketing the bottle again.

Earl Ray tried not to shudder at the thought of this dangerous man becoming more unstable as the drugs coursed through his system. Things were bad enough but could definitely get much worse. Earl Ray knew the real problem, though, was in the van. Gus was going to die, and when he did, Gene would probably come unhinged and kill anyone in sight. Earl Ray could only hope that the man would stay alive long enough for these men to leave…

As they headed through the store toward the front door, Gene grabbed handfuls of candy bars, ripping one open and eating it as if starved. Earl Ray was thinking of the two men back at the café and how they had fallen on the food.

The gunshot report echoed down the main drag as they

came out of the store. His heart sank. He thought of the cowboy and armed woman who'd been sitting at the counter. Had they decided to make their move with Gene out of the way? Not a bad idea. But it would have been better if there hadn't been a gunshot.

Gene pulled his gun, shoved Earl Ray and Lars ahead of him, forcing them to hurry toward the café, a gun at their backs. Earl Ray ran as best he could with his hip hurting from banging into the vehicle earlier. His pulse thundered in his ears. Whatever had happened, it wasn't good. He thought about Bessie and felt his chest tighten.

CULHANE HAD NO CHOICE. He carefully put down the pan of cinnamon rolls and the spatula on an empty table as Bobby, using Alexis as a shield, motioned him back toward the counter. The room had erupted in chaos and cries of fear and panic again.

"Tyrell!" the older man was screaming.

"Fred, don't!" Bessie yelled from her booth.

Culhane swore under his breath as he raised his hands and backed up all the way to the counter and sat down. He could see that Bobby was jumpier than hell, as if he'd already been through something like this and was now reliving it. The hand holding the weapon shook with anger and pain. He'd been burned by the hot coffee now staining his blue shirt and was angry enough that he might shoot Alexis without any further provocation.

Meanwhile Fred was trying to wrestle a cell phone away from his son who was shot and bleeding on the floor. The phone, suddenly loose, skittered across the floor, out of Tyrell's reach.

His gun digging into his back, Culhane wanted to pull it

and take his chances. But not with Bobby already on edge with a gun to Alexis's head and Eric—

At the sound of another gunshot, he started. Tyrell let out a scream of pain. Culhane had been hoping he was wrong about the twentysomething from the garage and body shop. But Tyrell had not only done something stupid that had gotten him shot twice, but also he'd completely screwed up Culhane and Alexis's plan. This was why he never planned anything, he thought as he saw that Eric looked ready to fire again. The gunman had moved toward the two wrestling on the floor in their garage-uniform overalls.

Culhane could see that the second bullet had caught Tyrell in the throat. He was now gasping and holding his neck, blood pouring through his fingers. Fred was struggling to get up, to help his son. Eric stalked over to the pair, raised his gun and fired the third shot point-blank into the side of the young man's head.

As Tyrell slumped the rest of the way to the floor, Fred screamed and lunged at Eric, only to be shot. Fred grabbed his chest, stumbling a step before he crumpled to the floor next to his son.

The café erupted in pandemonium. Both Bobby and Eric looked as if they wanted to kill everyone. Bessie hugged the frantic teenage waitress as others in the café began to cry harder—including the baby.

The front door banged open, the tinkle of the bell drowned out by the boom of Gene's voice as he shoved both Lars and Earl Ray into the room. "What the hell is going on?" he demanded, his weapon drawn.

The noise became louder. "Everyone shut up!" He waved his gun around the room. There was a gasp, sobs were choked back and people recoiled.

Bobby gave Alexis a shove away, the weapon still trained on her. She slipped on the spilled coffee on the floor and went down on one knee—just feet from Gene. He aimed his gun at her as she started to get up, but instead of firing the weapon, he shoved her with his foot, sending her sliding across the floor to end up next to the booth with mother and baby.

As if by instinct, she reached for the crying baby in the carrier next to her. "Shh," she whispered as she lifted the baby from the carrier and held the infant to her breast as she got slowly to her feet.

The sight of her holding that baby was almost Culhane's undoing. It looked so natural and so surprising to see this strong, independent, kick-butt former sheriff's detective suddenly so tender as she soothed the infant. He'd known this side of Alexis, this gentle, caring, loving side. Just as he'd known that she wanted marriage and children—something he'd said wasn't in his future. He now regretted ever saying it.

How could he deny her motherhood if she stayed with him? It would have been criminal, seeing that baby in her arms. The baby quieted, and the people in the room began to calm down some as well.

"Go sit down," Gene ordered Alexis, motioning with his gun.

She started to hand the baby to Tina, but Gene stopped her.

"Take the kid," Gene told Lars, who didn't hesitate. Alexis hesitated only a moment before she handed over Chloe and headed for the counter. Culhane watched her approach. He could see the emotion in her face. She was shaken, but hiding it well, not from having a gun pointed at her head but from the contact with the baby and even the thought of what Gene could do to the child, if the infant cried again.

Meanwhile, against Vi's protests, Lars carried the baby over to the booth where he'd been originally sitting with the woman he'd called Shirley. He sat down, cooing at the baby, rocking her. Across the table from him, Culhane saw Shirley watch him as if he were a stranger she'd never seen before.

When he turned back to the killers, he saw Eric pick up Tyrell's cell phone from the floor.

"Did I tell you to shoot someone while I was gone?" Gene demanded, advancing on Eric as the younger man wiped the blood off the phone on his pant leg.

"That one," Eric said, pointing to Tyrell dead on the floor. "He was calling the cops. What was I supposed to do?"

Gene snatched the phone from his hand and quickly checked before letting out a curse that rattled in the rafters. "He didn't call anyone! He was filming the two of you eating like pigs!" Gene shoved the phone at Eric, his disgusted glare shifting across the room in Bobby's direction. "Fortunately, the damned fool didn't have the sense to call the cops. I thought you collected all the phones?"

"He said he didn't have his," Bobby whined, looking terrified. "I *frisked* him. He didn't have it on him, I swear."

Gene was shaking his head, looking as if he wanted to shoot both men. Culhane held his breath, thinking Gene wouldn't stop there if he did. Worse, when Bobby had put the gun to Alexis's head, Culhane had realized where he'd seen him before. He suddenly needed this man alive. Bobby had known Jana, Culhane's so-called wife. That's where he'd seen the man—coming out of her apartment the day she disappeared leaving enough blood on the kitchen floor that the sheriff was convinced Culhane had murdered her.

"You okay?" Culhane whispered as Alexis sat down again next to him at the counter. That had been a close call. He was still shaken. Bobby had come so close to shooting her.

"Fine," she whispered back.

She didn't look fine. She looked pale as if sick to her stomach. He could see that she was also disappointed that their plan hadn't worked. It would have—if not for Tyrell, who now lay dead next to his father. They, unlike father and son, were both still alive. But they'd missed their chance.

Culhane told himself that maybe the three men would leave now—before the baby started crying again or someone else did something stupid—as if anyone in this café could get that lucky today.

EARL RAY SLID into the booth, set down the bag of medical supplies on the table and took Bessie in his arms. "It's all right," he whispered, holding her tight. He said the words, even though nothing was all right. Worse, he couldn't make it all right, and they both knew it.

Soon he would have to go back out to the van with the medical supplies. He prayed he would find Gene's brother Gus still alive. He would do what he could to ease the man's suffering and hope the men would leave before Gus died. Too much was riding on the men leaving. He knew it wouldn't be that easy, and that's what frightened him the most.

Bessie quit crying in his arms and looked up at him. He thumbed away her tears and smiled into her beautiful face. "I love you."

He saw her eyes widen in surprise. He'd never said the words before, but she had to know how he felt, didn't she? "I love you. I have for so long. I'm sorry I haven't said it before."

"I love you," she said, her voice breaking. He'd known that. He just hadn't done anything about it. Hadn't felt he could. He'd thought it would be an insult to his marriage, to his deceased wife, to the man he believed himself to be. He used to wish that he'd died with Tory. For so long, he'd wondered why he was still here without her. But over time, he'd found he could be useful to those who needed his help. And he'd found love again.

But he'd felt guilty for loving Bessie. That's why he'd never said those three consequential words until today. After everything that happened here today, though, he made himself a promise that if they lived through this…

"Come on," Gene ordered, jabbing him in the shoulder with the barrel end of his gun.

Earl Ray let go of Bessie slowly, his gaze holding hers. "I'll be back." She nodded, but he could see the terror in her eyes. She knew that this might be the last time they saw each other, and it was why he'd finally told her how he felt. If he went out to the van and Gus was dead, he likely wouldn't be coming back.

He slid out of the booth, taking the medical supplies with him. The worst part wasn't dying. The worst was that he wouldn't have any chance of protecting Bessie from these men. Since taking the drugs, Gene was even more on a hair trigger. In his life, he'd seen men do horrible things. Gene was the kind who, in his grief and guilt, would be looking for someone to blame for this other than himself. He would kill everyone before leaving here. And he would do it without a shred of regret.

Earl Ray walked out the front door, Gene right behind and prodding him with the gun. He fought the urge to look back, to see Bessie's face one more time. It had taken years to heal after losing his wife. Bessie had helped with her cheerful smiles each morning, her baking and her loyalty and patience with him.

He felt the crack open in his heart and had to steady himself as he neared the van. He'd known he couldn't tell Bessie everything he felt back in the café, but now he wished he'd tried. He knew it would take years to express everything he felt. At least she knew that he loved her. He'd said the words he doubted she had ever expected to hear after all this time. He only wished he'd said them sooner. Not just said them but acted on them. It would be the second-biggest regret of his life.

He stopped at the van, letting Gene open the side-panel door, and climbed inside. With relief, he saw the rise and fall of Gus's chest and quickly went to work bandaging the man and trying to ease his pain.

Outside the van, Gene paced and ate his way through the candy bars, before getting into the pills again. Earl Ray found himself gauging the man's mood. Drugs, like alcohol, affected people differently. With Gene, though, he thought the man would be a mean drunk, which meant one thing.

"I've done all I can do for him," Earl Ray said. "There's a hospital in the next town. The sooner you get him there—"

"I already told you—" Gene jerked him backward out of the van. Off balance, he fell to the ground, pain radiating through his back as he fought to suck air into his lungs. Gene slammed the van door and motioned with his gun for Earl Ray to get up. As he fought to catch his breath, he rolled to his side, got up on his hands and knees and was about to rise when Gene kicked him in the side, then in the stomach. Even in pain, Earl Ray shoved to his feet to avoid his boot again.

He could tell that Gene wanted to kill him. He stared into the dark hole of the gun barrel for a moment before meeting the man's gaze. The anger, the contempt, the hatred and the fear were like a ball of roiling snakes all biting each other. "Move!" Gene ordered, motioning toward the café.

This time he didn't have to pretend to be an old man. He felt it in his body, in his vulnerability, in the fear that had him limping toward the front door. There had been a time that he could have disarmed the man and broken his neck within a matter of seconds.

He could still do it. But he was smart enough to know that Gene was just waiting for some excuse like that. And Earl Ray wasn't as fast or as powerful as he used to be. He wished for even one of the many weapons he kept at the house. Even as he thought it, he knew it would have been too risky with so many people already armed inside.

All he could do was try to keep everyone calm and pray that they got through this.

CULHANE WAS RELIEVED to see Earl Ray come in the door but noticed immediately that the older man was hurting. Something had happened out there. Gene was different as well. There was a distant look in his eyes, one that turned Culhane's blood to ice. The man was on something, high as a kite, and on the edge of something bad.

He watched Earl Ray doing his best not to limp as he approached the table with Bessie and Cheri. But Bessie had noticed. Tears filled her eyes even as Earl Ray waved off her concern, saying he was fine. But Culhane could see that he was in pain as he slipped into the booth.

Gene stood in the doorway, his weapon dangling from his fingertips as he glared at his two men. "Is that my breakfast?" he demanded.

Their table looked as if wild animals had gotten into the food and spread it everywhere. Both men had eaten themselves into semicomas. He figured their reaction times had been compromised while Gene was jittery and waving his gun around.

Culhane couldn't help thinking that if Eric hadn't seen Tyrell videorecording them eating… What-ifs did no good, he reminded himself. He'd done too much of that kind of thinking when it came to Jana and the past.

"We left you some food," Eric said, seeing Gene's expression. "We were hungry."

Gene growled and looked around the room. Culhane held his breath. It was the moment of truth. The men could take the rest of the food, pack up and leave. Or not.

It was the *or not* that worried him. He could see that Gene was trying to decide what to do. What would keep any one of them in this café from tipping off the cops after the four had driven away? Even if they took their cell phones, there was the landline on the wall in the kitchen.

Just then, as if on cue, the landline in the kitchen rang. Culhane's heart dropped. Of course there would be a landline for take-out orders and now Gene knew it. The phone rang again.

He saw Gene's face cloud over before the man stormed into the kitchen and ripped the phone off the wall, jerking the cord free and throwing it across the kitchen. Gene might be high, but he wasn't stupid. He would realize that whoever had been calling would try again. And, failing that, would come down to the café or at least send someone. Time had run out.

His face blazing with the heat of his rage, Gene turned from the kitchen doorway and took in everyone as if making up his mind.

Here we go, Culhane thought, and glanced over at Alexis.

CHAPTER NINE

GENE MARCHED BACK INTO the dining section, his body almost vibrating with his agitation. Culhane felt his skin prickle as he saw the man make up his mind. The moment of truth had come.

"Bring the food," Gene ordered. "If there is anything left after you two devoured it."

"What do we do with all of them?" Eric asked, motioning to the customers as Bobby hurriedly began to close up the to-go containers.

Gene looked around the room. Culhane could feel Alexis tense next to him. Her right hand had moved under her jacket at her side. He took off his hat and set it on the counter again. He could feel her gaze on him, feel the argument in the lines of her body. She wanted to do something because she knew as well as he did that these three weren't just going to walk out of here.

He kept his eyes on Gene, waiting for that moment when he would have to do something even if it was wrong. He could see Gene considering his options. Killing everyone in the café would require a lot of gunfire. It might bring some of the locals to see what was going on even though the earlier three shots hadn't raised a response. Could have been a car backfiring. Could have been a semi shifting down. It didn't feel like there were many people left in this town on a Sunday this time of year. But the gunfire it would take to kill them all would pique attention.

He watched Gene's increasing loss of control. He couldn't hold it together much longer. From the look on the man's face, he wanted to end this in a blaze of gunfire. Culhane could tell that he was itching to kill someone, anyone. But if there were even a little sense left in him that wasn't distorted by drugs, he also wanted to get out of here. Law enforcement in at least four states was on the lookout for him. A cop car could pull up at any moment.

Gene had to decide. He'd been here too long. He would know that. He had to move, and Culhane was pretty sure he knew what was coming—and so did Alexis. The question was what they were going to do when it happened.

Culhane could feel his gun biting into his back, but with Bobby and Eric waving their pistols around and Gene looking like he wanted to kill everyone in the place, he didn't dare pull it. He couldn't risk a shoot-out, knowing Alexis would be right in the middle of it.

"Bobby, bring the food," Gene said. "Eric, grab the basket of cell phones. Let's go." He moved toward the door but hesitated.

Culhane had already considered what he would do when Gene reached this point. So he wasn't surprised when the man hauled Tina out of the booth and put a gun to her head. A roar went up, Tina's mother screaming the loudest.

"Shut up! Shut the hell up!" Gene yelled, putting Tina in a headlock and dragging her toward the front door. "Any of you call the cops or come after us...we kill her!"

Lars had put the baby into her carrier next to the wall in the booth as if trying to keep Chloe as far away from Gene as possible. But the moment Gene grabbed Tina, he was on his feet, rushing the man. Bobby, though, saw him coming and pulled his weapon. As Lars started past him, Bobby swung his gun. Lars caught it in the side of his head and went down hard. He didn't get up.

Gene barely noticed as he dragged Tina toward the door, Bobby with him, their weapons drawn. Only Eric hadn't moved to get the basket of phones.

Culhane saw that Eric's gaze was locked on Alexis like a heat-seeking missile so he wasn't surprised when the man headed for her. Eric wanted Alexis, wanted her for more than a hostage. Only Culhane wasn't going to let that happen.

He watched the man coming toward them, knowing that Alexis already had her hand wrapped around the grip of her gun. Eric wasn't taking her anywhere.

Culhane was considering who to shoot after he killed Eric. He figured Alexis would get at least one of the men by the door. He just hoped he would get a shot off before either of them fired back.

Gene finally noticed what was going on. "Eric, what the hell are you doing?" he bellowed over the pandemonium.

"Getting another hostage," Eric said without looking at him.

Culhane was about to draw his gun and step between Eric and Alexis, when Gene cursed and said, "We aren't taking another hostage. Grab the phones in that basket and then get the hell into the van. *Now*."

For a moment, Eric looked as if he wouldn't comply. But then, as if realizing that Gene might drill a hole in his back if he didn't, he swore and grabbed up the basket of cells.

All Gene's attention had been on Eric. Culhane wondered if Eric knew how close he'd come to dying only a moment ago. "The rest of you?" Gene said. "If anyone leaves this place to call the cops or get help, I'll kill this woman. Do you understand?" He had to raise his voice over the protests.

"My baby," Tina cried as she looked to where Shirley was sitting across the table from the now crying infant in the carrier. Shirley was watching what was happening as if in a daze. She hadn't reached for the baby, didn't even seem to realize Lars had left the infant when he'd gone to defend Tina. "No, I can't leave my baby!"

"You aren't taking her," Vi screamed and threw herself at Gene, who backhanded her. She fell to the floor but continued to grab at Tina's ankles, throwing Gene off balance. Bobby had gathered up the food boxes and had the door open, looking anxious to get out of there.

Culhane would have gone for his gun in the confusion, except that Eric had come back over to the counter after picking up the basket. He held it under one arm, his gun in his other hand. From the look in his eyes, he hadn't given up on taking Alexis. It was as if they were all frozen in place. Gene still had a gun pointed at Tina's head. Bobby stood in the doorway, the boxes of food under his left arm, his gun gripped in his right hand and pointed indiscriminately at the room.

"There is no need to take her with you," Earl Ray said above the roar of noises as he rose from the booth. Bessie, trying to stop him, slid out as well. "Take me," he said as he moved toward Gene and the door. "I can be of help to you. You don't want to separate a mother and child."

"Sit down, old man," Gene said, his voice raised and raspier than before.

"I can give you my word that I will keep everyone in this café for as long as you like," Earl Ray was saying as Gene swung his gun in the direction of the older man. "You don't need to take her." Gene had his other arm locked around

Tina's throat. Culhane could hear her gasping for air. This had to end and soon or...

His curse was drowned out by the sound of the gun's report as Gene shifted Tina off to one side and fired. It happened so fast. Culhane hadn't seen Bessie move until she stepped between Gene and Earl Ray. Apparently Gene and Earl Ray hadn't noticed her, either.

The knife she pulled from her apron pocket caught the light an instant before she buried the blade to the hilt in Gene's stomach.

FOR A MOMENT, Alexis wasn't sure who had been shot, and then to her horror, Bessie slumped to the floor. Loud gasps went out as Earl Ray fell to his knees, cradling Bessie in his arms.

Gene howled as the room erupted in screams and crying. "Shoot them!" he yelled. But Eric hadn't moved, and Bobby, still holding the food and his gun, stood transfixed in the doorway.

She noticed that he was staring at Culhane as if seeing a ghost. She watched Bobby start to raise his gun. Her gaze flew to Culhane, afraid he hadn't noticed. But his gaze was also locked on Bobby. When she looked at Bobby again, she saw that his eyes were wide. A single word left his mouth— "Cop!"—but the sound was lost in the racket.

Shifting from feeling like everyone was moving in slow motion, suddenly everything was happening too fast. She could see Gene struggling as he stumbled backward into Bobby. He had his arm still locked around Tina's throat and his gun in his hand, but his gaze was on the knife protruding from his stomach. She could tell he wanted to pull it out, but that would mean letting go of Tina or his gun.

Had he done either, Alexis would have gone for her weapon—and she knew Culhane would have, too.

"Eric!" Gene yelled, but the man didn't move. He was staring at Alexis as he had been. She'd done her best to ignore him, not wanting to make eye contact. But all the time, she'd had her hand on the grip of her gun.

If he took even one step toward her, she would pull the gun and shoot him.

"Eric!" Gene yelled again, sounding angrier and in even more pain.

Either Eric didn't hear him or he ignored him, because he didn't move nor did he take his eyes off her.

CULHANE WAS TRYING to watch everything that was going on. But he hadn't forgotten Eric. Far from it. Like Alexis, he was waiting for the man to make his move. He'd already decided that he'd take out Eric and then Gene as quickly as he could.

The problem would be the fact that Gene was using Tina like a shield. Then there was Bobby. Culhane needed him alive. When the shooting started, Bobby would drop the food under his arm and fire his weapon. Culhane had no doubt where Bobby would point it. The same place he had it pointed right now—right at Culhane's heart.

It was the kind of crapshoot that Culhane hated. If any of the men got a chance to fire before they died...

Gene pushed through the front door, dragging Tina with him and forcing Bobby out on the sidewalk. Culhane saw that the man's eyes were wild with pain and fury. Dried leaves whirled around them as the wind blew down the main drag. "I'll kill her," Gene was yelling. "Eric! Come on, damn it. Now!"

Culhane saw Bobby rush to put the food onto the floor-

board of the passenger side. "The knife!" Gene was screaming. "Get the knife."

Bobby seemed to grimace as he stepped to Gene and
pulled the knife out of his gut, quickly dropping the blade
on the ground, before running around to climb behind the
wheel. It didn't appear he planned to wait for Eric.

Even from where he stood, Culhane could see that Gene
was bleeding profusely from his wound as he wrestled a
kicking-and-screaming Tina. He opened the van's side door
and shoved her into the back, only to have her lunge at him.
He caught her with a right hook, and she disappeared from
view. The van door closed. Staggering, Gene opened the
passenger-side door as Bobby started the engine. Culhane
could see him wincing in pain, his shirt soaked in blood
as he tried to stop the flow with one hand.

Eric still hadn't moved, even though Gene was screaming obscenities for him to come out. Culhane had known it
was only a matter of time before Eric moved—just not to
leave. The man lunged for Alexis, wanting her more than
he was afraid of Gene.

"Over my dead body," Culhane said under his breath.
Next to him, he knew Alexis wasn't having it, either. Her
hand was under her jacket, making it appear that she was
hugging herself. But he knew her grip was on the gun she
was about to use.

Culhane pulled his weapon and fired it into the side of
Eric's head as he reached for her. The man dropped like a
gunnysack of rocks at Alexis's feet. She had her weapon
out as well.

The two shared a look and, without a word, rushed to
the front door. But the van was already roaring away, Gene
in the passenger seat, Bobby behind the wheel. There was

no sign of Tina in the back. On the ground next to where the van had been lay the bloody knife.

Culhane turned back to the carnage in the café. Earl Ray was on the floor holding Bessie. "You're going to be all right," he was saying as he held his wadded up jacket to her wound. "Lars, get a cell phone!" Lars was sitting up looking dazed, but he struggled to his feet. "Call 9-1-1 for an ambulance."

"What about Tina?" Lars cried. "We have to go after her."

Vi had gathered her wits and rushed across the room to slap Shirley and take her granddaughter. She now wept in the corner of the booth as she rocked the baby.

"I'm going after her," Culhane said from the doorway as he took his phone from the basket Lars held out to him. He saw Alexis's phone and handed it to her.

Earl Ray turned to look at him and nodded. "Thank you, Culhane."

He was only a little surprised that Earl Ray knew who he was. Which meant that the man also knew that the law was already after him. He moved to where Earl Ray was holding Bessie. He saw the worry in the older man's gaze. "How is she?" he asked.

"The bullet appears to have gone all the way through," Earl Ray said. "I don't think it hit any internal organs. An ambulance is on the way. So is the sheriff." With his last words, he met Culhane's gaze. "You need to get out of here. I assume you're going with him?" he said, turning to Alexis.

"I'm Alexis Brand, a former detective, now a bounty hunter."

Earl Ray smiled. "Pleased to meet you. I heard on the scanner earlier, though, that you are also wanted for questioning. Don't worry. I'll deal with law enforcement when they arrive. I was afraid that Gene would go out to the van and find his brother... I thought it was Gene we had to worry about it. I should have known Eric would be the one."

"Culhane and I will find them," Alexis said and gave him a look that brooked no argument. He didn't have time to argue, anyway.

"Let me give you my phone number." Earl Ray reached into his pocket and pulled out a set of keys. "You realize, though, that we can't keep you out of this. I'll try to give you as much time as I can. But since they're already looking for you... I doubt it will help what you did here today, but I'll make sure the authorities know."

"Thank you," he said as Earl Ray put his number into Culhane's phone. He frowned as the man handed him the keys.

"Take my truck. They'll be looking for both of your rigs. It's a dirty-brown color parked two blocks off the main drag up that way." Earl Ray handed the cell back. "I can let you know what's happening here. If you need other help, call me."

"Are you sure about this, Earl Ray? It will get you into a world of trouble."

"Don't worry about me. Go. Gene has a good head start," the older man said. "Good luck to you both." Then he knelt closer to Bessie on the floor, telling her everything was going to be fine.

Culhane looked at Alexis. She didn't hesitate as they rushed to the door and out into the late morning. At her rig, she opened the door and reached inside for her overnight bag before taking off down the street with Culhane to find Earl Ray's pickup.

EVERYTHING HAD HAPPENED SO fast that Shirley hadn't seen Vi headed for her. She'd looked up in surprise to find her standing over her—and the woman's palm headed for her face. She hadn't had enough time to block the assault.

Her cheek stung from the force of the slap. Vi stood over her, rage and anguish and pain in her pinched face. She opened her mouth, but only spittle came out as she tried to speak. Her words seemed to be caught in her throat, choking her.

After a moment, Vi grabbed up the baby crying in her carrier and took her back across the room. Shirley realized with a start that she'd completely forgotten about the baby. When Tina had been taken, Lars had left the baby on the booth seat across from her and rushed to save the woman he'd sworn he no longer loved.

Shirley hadn't moved, hadn't even rubbed her cheek, although it still stung. Everyone was sobbing and moving around the café. Earl Ray had told them they had to stay. That the sheriff's department was on the way as well as an ambulance. Along with the coroner, she thought as she looked over at Fred and Tyrell, both dead on the floor.

The third gunman lay dead by the counter. In the kitchen, she could see the cook also sprawled on the floor, his blood having dried around him.

By the door, Earl Ray was seeing to Bessie. Next to them, she saw that Lars was sitting across from Vi. He had the baby in his arms, and Shirley could tell by the movement of his shoulders that he was crying. Crying for Tina.

She tried to remember waking up that morning to a normal day. There'd been only two guests at the motel the night before. They'd both checked out early. She'd had a whole day of nothing to do ahead of her and was glad of it.

Then Lars had come in her back door. If only she'd turned down his breakfast invitation. She'd been anxious about the two of them going out in public—especially to the café where everyone would see them. But she'd never been able to say no to him, and this morning had been no different.

She could hear the sound of sirens in the distance. Soon the café would be swarming with cops and EMTs. There would be hours of questioning.

Lars lifted his head and looked across the room at her as if he'd completely forgotten her. He wiped his eyes and, getting to his feet, and still holding the baby, walked in her direction. She said nothing as he sat down on the edge of the booth seat across from her. She could see where he'd taken the blow from the gun for Tina. The site was swollen and bruising.

After a moment, he met her gaze looking as if he didn't know what to say so she decided to help him out.

"You belong with Tina." He blinked as if surprised but didn't argue. "She loves you, and you love Chloe. I suspect you love Tina, too. Forgive her, and make the family you deserve. Even Vi will accept you in time."

"What about you?" he asked, his voice sounding hoarse with emotion.

She smiled and looked toward the door. "I'll be leaving Buckhorn. I'm not sure where I'll go. But I've always wanted to see the Pacific Ocean." She nodded as if realizing that was exactly where she was heading. She just hoped she got that far. She turned to meet his gaze, and for a moment, she weakened. Emotion crowded her voice. She cleared it. "Don't worry about me. I'll be fine."

His smile was sad, a smile that told of lost hopes and dreams. But there was relief there, too. Lars would never get out of Buckhorn, and she thought he knew that now. But she could see that, unlike her, he'd never really wanted to. He believed he could fulfill his hopes and dreams here in Buckhorn with Tina and Chloe.

The wail of sirens grew closer. This nightmare was finally over for her, one that had been going on a lot longer than just this morning here in this café.

She couldn't wait, anxious to get on with her life. She'd been stuck here too long. Later she would walk down to the motel, pack up her few belongings and let the owner know she'd quit. She realized as she waited that she'd never seen herself leaving this town with Lars. In her mind, she'd always been alone, driving out of Buckhorn, glancing back only briefly before looking ahead at the horizon.

She felt lighter suddenly. In her mind she could already smell the salty air of the Pacific, hear the waves crashing on the beach, feel the sand between her toes—just like in the movies. She'd always thought everyone should see the ocean before they died. She smiled as in her mind's eye she saw herself driving out of Montana. Only this time, she didn't look back.

CHAPTER TEN

THE TRUCK WAS right where Earl Ray had said it would be. As Culhane slid behind the wheel, Alexis climbed in the passenger side and tossed her bag into the crew cab back.

Culhane hadn't said a word since they'd left the café. She'd seen the look he'd darted at her when she'd said she was going with him. He had to know that he couldn't talk her out of it. But whether or not he had accepted it was yet to be discovered.

That had been so close back there. She was still shaking inside. Not that she would have let Eric take her without a fight, but things could have been so much worse if Gene hadn't been wounded and not in any kind of shape to come back into the café, gun blasting.

Culhane started the engine, and she glanced around the truck, trying to assure herself that they were both fine. "Does this seem too easy to you?" she asked. It was almost too clean. She looked behind the seat and saw neatly stacked blankets and what appeared to be survival gear.

He gunned the engine, backing out and onto the narrow strip of highway, headed east in the direction the van had gone.

Opening the glove box, she blinked. "There's a gun in there and a lot of ammunition. It's as if this truck is equipped for Armageddon." She looked over at Culhane. "Who is this man, anyway, and what is he doing in Buckhorn? As my mother would say, why is he hiding his bushel under a basket?"

Culhane gave her a confused look, shook his head as if to clear it and said, "Ex-military is my guess."

"It doesn't seem odd to you that he helped us like this?"

"Not really. I suspect there is a whole lot more to his story."

"He knew who you were. He knew *I* was wanted by the cops too now."

Culhane rolled his eyes at her. "He probably has a scanner. After all, there isn't even a deputy living in Buckhorn. He probably watches over the town."

She had seen how the locals had seemed to relax a little when Earl Ray had taken charge. She closed the glove box and looked to the two-lane highway ahead. It was empty all the way to the horizon.

"They do have a pretty good head start. You should be able to catch up with that rattletrap van they're driving." She eyed him. "Unless you're just going to run. After all, now there is even more reason for the law to be after you."

He looked shocked and clearly disappointed in her when he turned to look at her. "You know me better than that! I'm going after Tina. Just like I said." He pressed down even harder on the gas. She saw the speedometer jump from eighty to ninety.

"I *thought* I knew you," she said looking away. "Until I woke up this morning to find you gone and wanted for murdering your *wife*."

"There's more to the story."

"I'm sure there is," she said. "I can't wait to hear that story."

The speedometer needle vibrated as it topped one hundred. "Look, you're the one who was determined to come along even if it gets us both killed."

"I'm determined to take you in before some trigger-happy cop shoots you," she snapped. "The BOLO on you says you're armed and dangerous."

He glanced at her. "I thought that's what attracted you to me."

It was so Culhane to try to lighten the mood, especially immediately after being upset with her.

"Being wanted for murder isn't a laughing matter," she said, hating how superior she sounded.

"I don't believe Jana is dead. I think someone put her up to this."

She shook her head. Was this wishful thinking on his part? "But I heard there was so much blood—"

"According to the sheriff."

Alexis stared at him. "You think Garwood is behind this?"

"He told me that if I didn't drop my wrongful-firing lawsuit I would regret it. He doesn't want what I know about the department and him to come out."

"Still, this is even beyond Garwood. Framing you for murder? Once Jana is found alive—"

"That's just it. I don't think he's going to let that happen."

She couldn't help her shock. "I know Garwood is a lousy sheriff, but I don't think he's involved in murdering people."

"It could be out of his hands if he's in as deep as I suspect he is. I don't think he's realized what he's set in motion. I have a feeling this is bigger than Jana, that she's only a pawn in a much larger game. If I'm right, she's become a liability, one Garwood can't afford."

What was all this? Culhane knew the sheriff was dirty. Since the two of them were fired, he'd been trying to get the goods on Garwood. She'd worried because the sheriff had rich, powerful friends. She had been worried about Culhane even before this happened.

As she stared at the strip of black two-lane ahead of them, she felt tears burn her eyes. She had no idea what Culhane had gotten himself involved in, and like he said, she was now along for the ride. They'd somehow survived back at the café, but Culhane was still wanted for murder. Just the thought made her stomach knot inside. The two of them had been in some dangerous situations a few times with their jobs as deputies, but nothing like that circus back there.

And now they were chasing two of them, trying to catch them. This wasn't over, she thought, afraid of what Gene would do with Tina. What he'd already done. She wouldn't let herself think the worst. Instead she concentrated on catching up with the van. After that... Yes, after that, then what?

Her eyes hurt from staring at the road looking for the van. She tried to assure herself that the men inside it wouldn't kill their hostage, but she wasn't convinced. Alexis knew how close she'd come to being one of the hostages if Eric had had his way. She told herself it wouldn't have happened. She and Culhane never would have let Eric take her.

But she knew that had things gone badly, Culhane would be dead now, and she could have been unable to stop Eric. Right now she could be in the back of that van. She'd known he wasn't going to leave without her. She'd seen it in his eyes. She shuddered now at the memory of the darkness she'd seen there, a mixture of hate and lust laced with violence.

Culhane had the gas pedal to the floor, the truck eating up the pavement as it roared east. She could see his big hands gripping the wheel and recalled both the strength and tenderness of those hands. She shoved the memory away, waiting for the back of the van to appear and praying that the woman Gene had thrown in the back was still alive.

She dragged her gaze away from the long stretch of empty highway to look over at Culhane. Now that they were both safe for the moment, she felt her anger return. "Were you ever going to tell me about your *wife*?" she demanded.

"Really? You're determined to get into this *now*?"

She glared over at him, letting her anger force her fears to the back burner for the moment. "We worked together for three years. For another year I shared your bed. At any one point, it seems you might have mentioned that you were *married*."

"I didn't know I was married, that is, yes, I... I knew I'd *been* married, but I thought it had been annulled. I would have eventually told you about Jana."

"Better to wait until she was murdered to mention it," she said. "Especially when it turns out that you're the number-one suspect."

He sighed. "I told you. I don't believe she *was* murdered." The speedometer was hovering at over a hundred, but so far she hadn't seen the van ahead. "I never told anyone about Jana or the marriage, okay? The marriage was a quick trip to a justice of the peace in another state. It didn't even last a month, and it was a long time ago. Seven years."

Alexis frowned, thinking of his friends she'd met, friends he'd known since he was a boy. "Are you saying none of your friends were at the wedding?"

"There was *no* wedding, and no. It was just the two of us. The judge provided the witnesses."

"Not even a friend of Jana's attended?"

He shook his head as he shot a glance in his rearview mirror before focusing on his driving again. The highway was straight and empty. She checked her side mirror, wondering who he thought might be chasing them. The highway behind them was empty as well.

Culhane had cared enough about this woman to marry her. Alexis knew how he felt about marriage and babies, so she had to wonder what about this woman he called Jana had even gotten him to the justice of the peace. "How did you two meet?" she asked, hating the jealousy raising its ugly head.

He groaned. "It was at a party in Big Sky. I just happened to be living with some really obnoxious roommates who talked me into going. I'd just aced a hard test at the academy and was ready to let off some steam. The moment I walked into the party, Jana handed me a drink and one thing led to another." He glanced over at her but quickly went back to his driving. "A month later I got the news about the pregnancy following Jana's and my one night together."

"No one knew about this marriage? I would have thought you'd at least tell your family or a few friends you were married and having a child," she said.

"It wasn't much of a marriage. In truth, I'd forgotten about it."

"Forgotten about Jana and the baby?"

He shook his head. "There was no baby, and Jana wasn't the love of my life or anywhere close. She wasn't even an old girlfriend that I might stop to wonder what happened to her. Once I found out that she'd lied about being pregnant and losing the baby and had taken off with whatever wasn't nailed down in our apartment, I got the marriage annulled as if it never happened. Or at least I thought I had. I was…embarrassed and mad at myself for being so naive."

She stared at him for a moment, seeing how this had shaped the man she now knew. Not that she hadn't known he was gun-shy when it came to relationships. Look how long it had taken him to even ask her out.

So how was it that he was wanted for Jana's murder? The question was on the tip of her tongue when she looked at the highway ahead.

"There it is!" she cried as they topped a hill and she spotted the back of the gray van in the distance.

CHAPTER ELEVEN

SHERIFF WILLY GARWOOD had always been a man who'd taken chances. The deck had been stacked against him from the day he was born. In order to quench his thirst for the finer things in life, he'd had to play a little fast and loose, sometimes risking everything to get where he was.

Hell, he'd been gambling on himself his whole life. Fortunately, he'd won more than he'd lost, and now he'd gambled his way into a pretty sweet deal as sheriff. He would have said that he was on his way to having everything he'd dreamed of.

Until yesterday.

Yesterday his house of cards had threatened to come tumbling down.

He'd made a name for himself playing football as a quarterback at Montana State University. A tall, broad-shouldered, good-looking kid with guts, he'd played as if his life depended on it. It had. *Indomitable*. At least that's what the sports writer had called him in the *Bozeman Daily Chronicle*. He was someone who got the job done.

Now at forty-seven, he still had his looks—and his good luck. His winning seasons on the gridiron had opened doors for him—just as his job now opened even more, he thought as he glanced around his office. Who would have known that being sheriff would turn out to be a gold mine, financially, politically and socially? He was invited to the best parties at the biggest houses by the wealthiest people.

And yet yesterday, it appeared all of that could come to a screeching halt.

It had been like any other day until he'd gotten the call. "Sheriff Garwood," he'd answered like he usually did.

"Is it all right to talk on this line?"

A knot had formed in his chest the moment he'd heard the man's voice. "I'll call you right back." When the other man answered his call back, the sheriff said, "What's wrong?"

"We have a problem. Something else was taken during our recent burglary. Something my wife had left out by accident." He described the necklace. Emeralds and diamonds. A gaudy piece of adornment worth over a half-million dollars.

Willy had sworn under his breath. "I'll take care of it."

"I certainly hope so. I don't have to tell you what will happen if the necklace shows up in a pawnshop or worse."

No, he didn't, the sheriff had thought as he'd hung up. The burglaries up at Big Sky had been one of the top news stories for weeks. He'd known he had to catch the thieves and wrap it all up.

One of the thieves had gotten sloppy and provided him with the perfect way out by leaving behind DNA at one of the houses—and had then been picked up for a separate crime, shoplifting. Garwood had personally interrogated the thief, gotten a confession and the names of two accomplices. He'd played it perfectly.

The reporter at the newspaper had given him credit for solving the crimes, and now the wealthy gated communities at Big Sky were safe once more. Case solved. All he had to do was have his deputies pick up the two accomplices, since he'd made a deal with the one thief who'd turned on them, Jana Redfield Travis.

The problem was that Jana had failed to mention that she'd picked up an emerald and diamond necklace she shouldn't have. He desperately needed that necklace back.

He'd quickly called Deputy Dick Furu. "I need you to go over to Jana's apartment." He'd explained the situation. "Get the necklace. I'll deal with her later." He'd described the piece of jewelry. "If she doesn't hand it over or tell you who has it, convince her otherwise. Tear the place apart if you have to, but find that necklace. Take Cline with you."

Two hours later, his deputies had returned with the bad news.

"What do you mean Jana's gone?"

"When we got there, the place was a mess, there was blood everywhere and she was gone," Deputy Terrance Cline had told him. "It appeared that there'd been a struggle."

He'd looked at Furu who he trusted more than Terrance any day of the week. Terry did what he was told without asking questions, but he wasn't the sharpest knife in the drawer.

"What the hell?" he'd demanded of Furu.

"A neighbor came over and told us that there'd been a man by earlier and a loud argument had ensued," Furu said. "From the description the neighbor gave us, Culhane Travis now knows that his wife is back in town. The neighbor heard breaking glass and screams."

Willy hadn't been able to believe his luck—and it had just dropped into his lap. He could use this apparent altercation to his advantage in a way that he hadn't thought possible. He put a BOLO out on Culhane, saying he was armed and dangerous—both true—and that he was wanted for questioning in the murder of his wife, Jana Redfield Travis.

"And if she's not really dead?" Furu had asked.

Willy had shrugged. "For all we know, she is. Or could be by the time Culhane is caught. You're sure the necklace isn't there?" Furu had nodded. "Okay, we'll get a crime-scene team over there. But just in case Jana staged the whole thing—" he wouldn't have put it past her, now that he knew about the necklace "—find her."

Furu had given him a look he recognized. The deputy would stretch the law to its limits, but murder was one line he wouldn't step over.

"When you find her, don't bring her in. Just call me," Willy had told him. "I'll deal with her."

As the two had left his office, he had realized he would have to be careful. Furu was smart and ambitious. It wouldn't have surprised him if Dick had his eye on the sheriff job. Maybe not this year, but soon.

Willy warned himself not to give Furu too much ammunition to use against him. But he assured himself that a lot could happen before the deputy made a run at him and his position. They were in a dangerous profession. Men in uniforms were killed all the time, often for no apparent reason.

He'd turned his thoughts to Culhane. The deputy had been a thorn in his side from the moment Willy had taken over the sheriff department. It only made it worse that Culhane was good at his job and smart. Plus the former sheriff's deputy had friends in the department. One in particular. Deputy Alexis Brand. Her father had been a sheriff.

Like Culhane, she knew her job and was good at it. He'd had to go out on a limb to get rid of the two of them after a few attempts at sabotage had failed. Now that damned Culhane was suing him and the department for wrongful discharge. At least Alexis had been smart enough to take the severance package he'd offered her without a fight. Last he'd heard, she'd started her own business and was now a bounty hunter.

Culhane hadn't been so easy. Unfortunately, Willy had no idea how much the former deputy actually knew about the way he'd been running the department. But Culhane knew enough to cause him harm, and that was all that mattered. Which was why the man had to be stopped before this ever went before a judge.

The waiting was killing him, though. Since the necklace hadn't been found, it was even more critical that they find Jana Redfield Travis, and quickly. If Culhane should find her first…

Well, Willy couldn't let that happen. He needed that necklace, and now he needed Jana dead. He usually got what he wanted one way or another. He'd gotten this far by playing the odds. Once he had Jana, she would quickly learn what happened to those who turned against him. But he'd never had this much to lose before, and it made him nervous.

He loved his lifestyle, his second home at Big Sky, his rich and powerful friends and all the parties where he actually felt like he belonged. He wouldn't let someone like Culhane Travis take it all away. The former deputy should have been smart enough not to go up against him. Now whatever happened was the man's own fault.

Willy tried to relax. The odds were that everything was going to work out. Once they found Jana—alive or dead— and Culhane was cornered for her murder and brought in, dead preferably, it would be business as usual.

He did love being sheriff of one of the fastest-growing counties in the state—with Big Sky being the sparkling jewel in his kingdom.

BOBBY WIPED ONE clammy hand on his jeans as he drove. He'd been watching Gene out of the corner of his eye. The man was bleeding like a stuck pig. Clearly he was in pain. He kept reaching into his pocket and taking more of the pills. The man was unpredictable enough without the drugs.

"Try to stay on the damned road!" Gene bellowed as Bobby turned back to his driving and swerved hard to avoid the ditch. He heard the woman's body roll over to *thunk* against the side of the van in the back. Or had it been Gus? Was the woman still unconscious back there or already dead?

The smell coming from the back reminded him that Gus was probably gone. Gene hadn't checked on his brother when he'd thrown the woman in. Because he knew Gus was already dead? Or because he'd forgotten about him?

Bobby felt sick to his stomach and wiped his hands on his jeans again. Why had he listened to Eric? Because Eric had made it sound like the bank job was as easy as walking into a McDonald's and walking out with a burger. Also, Bobby had to admit, he'd needed to get out of town fast, and that had played a definite part in it.

When he'd gone by Jana's and witnessed the scene left there... He'd known even before he'd talked to his contact at the jail. Jana had ratted out both him and Leo. Hadn't he known Jana would throw them under the bus?

When she'd called him from jail, she'd sounded scared out of her wits. "They ran my DNA and my fingerprints," she'd said, trying to keep her voice down. She didn't need to spell it out for him. He knew what that meant.

"What did they pick you up for that they ran your DNA and fingerprints?" he'd asked, even though he'd suspected. Still, he groaned when she said it had been for shoplifting. "What the hell were you thinking? *Shoplifting?*"

"You know I can't help it. It's a…disease, like alcoholism."

She'd taken a chance for a tube of lipstick or some cheap piece of jewelry that had caught her eye? How could she do that, knowing what was at stake?

She'd begun to cry. "Can you please just see if you can get me out on bail? You know who to call." He did know.

"Sure. Just don't do anything stupid." But he'd realized that she'd already hung up. He'd called their bail bondsman they kept on speed dial. Thirty minutes later the man had called back to say that when he'd gotten to the jail, Jana had already been released.

Bobby had known then that she'd done something even more stupid than shoplifting. She'd made a deal. Now former deputy Culhane Travis was wanted for her murder.

So he hadn't been surprised when he'd heard about Jana's subsequent disappearance and alleged death. Maybe she'd staged it. Or maybe she really was dead. But the one thing Bobby knew was that Culhane Travis hadn't killed her. Just as he knew that it was no coincidence that the former sheriff's deputy had showed up at the café in Buckhorn.

Culhane was looking for Jana. A man who committed her murder wouldn't be looking for her. But had he thought Leo could help? The cook was as much in the dark as Bobby had been. But now Leo was dead. Bobby didn't think he was far behind even if Gene didn't kill him.

As for Jana… If alive, she would have trouble staying that way because more than the law was looking for her.

He felt his phone vibrate in his pocket. He didn't need to check to see who was calling. His mother had been trying to reach him. Bobby figured the law had come by the house. Maybe with a search warrant. He swore under his breath at the thought of what they would have found—and how his mother was going to take it. She had a weak heart. This time his criminal activity might kill her.

He should have stayed home instead of listening to Eric about the perfect bank to rob. He could have gotten the stuff out of his mother's basement crawl space and faced up to what he'd been doing for money.

But he hadn't been able to face her. Just as he hadn't been able to answer her calls. He was lucky that she didn't know how to text. He felt a wave of guilt at how many times she'd called and he hadn't answered. But by now, it would be no surprise to his mother to realize that her precious baby boy was a coward. A coward in so much trouble that this time, he didn't think there was any way out.

"We have to get off this highway," Gene slurred as he glanced in his side mirror. He sounded stoned out of his mind. Bobby had been waiting for him to pass out. He'd been thinking of ways he could get away. The problem was that he had nowhere to run. Cops everywhere were already looking for him, and after what had happened back at the café…

"Turn at the next road you see," Gene was saying. "That cowboy who probably killed Eric? He'll come after us. I should have taken care of him right away. I could tell he wanted to be some kind of hero." He looked in his side mirror again and grimaced in pain. "Can't you get this van to go any faster?"

Bobby thought about telling Gene who the cowboy was but feared it would only make him more paranoid and unstable. Gene was hovering so close to the edge of sanity he didn't want to push him over for fear of what he might do.

He saw a dirt road ahead and began to slow to make the turn when he heard Gene let loose a string of curses as he watched his mirror. "I was right. They're coming for us. Step on it!"

Bobby glanced in his rearview. There was a vehicle back there, but it didn't look like the one he'd seen Culhane driving the day he'd come by Jana's. He told himself not to let Gene's paranoia get to him as he made the turn and heard another *thunk* in the back of the van. Only this time, it was followed by a moan. The woman wasn't dead. Yet.

RELIEVED, CULHANE HAD been afraid Bobby had turned off the highway much earlier and that they wouldn't find them. Gene, if still alive, would know that someone at the café would have called 9-1-1 and that now the law was on its way. Cops would be all over them unless they found a way to get off this main highway.

He wasn't surprised to see the van's brake lights come on. It turned right onto a secondary road and quickly disappeared in a cloud of dust. After the first snowfall had melted and the weather had turned fairly decent again, everything had dried out. But it would be a short reprieve. Winter was coming with the promise of a whole lot of snow—according to the *Farmers' Almanac*.

Culhane knew he'd let his thoughts take a detour to the weather only because he didn't want to think about what would happen when he caught up with the van. He slowed just enough to make the turn. The van was just ahead. But, now what? he asked himself as he glanced at Alexis and wished like hell that he could have left her in Buckhorn.

Even as he thought it, he knew short of hog-tying her to the cowcatcher on the front of his pickup parked back at the café, there was no leaving her behind. "Can you try to find this road on a map on your phone and let me know where it goes?" he asked, barely getting the sentence out before she was on it.

Alexis already had her phone out and was tapping on the screen. It had always been like that when they'd worked together. They seemed to anticipate the other's needs—in bed as well as on the job. That was a reminder he didn't need right now.

"It isn't on any map I can find, but it heads south so eventually it will hit the Yellowstone River and the interstate. Doesn't look as if there are any towns for miles or other marked roads, for that matter."

Dust billowed up behind the van, making it impossible to see ahead. Culhane didn't want to get too close for fear of coming up on the vehicle without warning and crashing into it. If Tina were still alive, he'd like to keep her that way.

"You think they know we're back here?" Alexis asked.

"Yep. If they can't lose us, they'll set up an ambush." He glanced over at her. "There's a bulletproof vest behind the seat. Put it on."

"Culhane—"

"Please."

With a sigh, she reached behind the seat and pulled out the vest. It was too large for her, but it might help if bullets started flying. He thought about Bessie and how she hadn't hesitated to step between the man she loved and a killer. Culhane knew in his heart that Alexis would take a bullet for him—and vice versa.

Ahead, the dust seemed to dissipate a little, and he saw the blur of brake lights. He slowed as the dust hung in the air ahead of him. The van had turned. Or stopped. The dust began to settle, and he saw the van had turned off and was now heading east on an even-narrower dirt road.

In the passenger seat, Alexis quickly looked at the map

on her phone. "This road has to dead-end." Her gaze went to Culhane. "If I'm right about where we are, the Mussel-shell River is to the east. I really doubt there will be a bridge over it on this road."

"How far before the road dead-ends?" he asked as he turned onto the narrower, less used dirt road the van had taken.

"Half a mile or so... Culhane!" she screamed at the same time there was a break in the cloud of dust—just in time for him to see something lying in the road. He slammed on his brakes making a skidding stop as he realized what it was. A body. He barely got the pickup stopped before Alexis jumped out and ran to the still form.

CHAPTER TWELVE

THE VAN BOUNCED along the rutted dirt road. Gene kept looking back and yelling for him to speed up because they were right behind them.

But when Bobby looked back, all he could see was dust churning up under their tires. He couldn't be sure that his plan had worked.

"Give it some gas!" Gene yelled, waving the gun in his direction again.

Earlier, he'd already been having trouble staying on the road at this speed. He'd had to manhandle the wheel to keep them from going into the ditch. But every time he let up on the gas, Gene threatened to shoot him.

In his rearview mirror, he'd checked behind them again. Nothing but dust. What if they weren't even being chased? There might not be anyone behind them. He wouldn't have been surprised to find out that Gene had imagined seeing someone behind them after they'd turned off the highway. It wasn't like he could trust Gene's judgment. The man was in obvious pain and drugged up to the max.

"Can you see them?" Gene had demanded, twisting in his seat to try to look back before groaning in pain. Blood had soaked through the jacket Gene had wadded up and pressed over the wound. Bobby had wondered how much longer the man could stay conscious with all the blood loss.

"If they're behind us," he'd said, "I can't see them."

"They're there. Take another road. That one!" Gene had said, pointing to a rutted narrow road to his left.

Bobby had taken the turn, even though the road looked as if it hadn't been used in years. Dried weeds stood several feet high in the center of the deep ruts. If they really were being followed, they had to do something besides taking roads to nowhere.

"I know a way to slow them down," Bobby had said, adding silently *if they are back there*. He just hoped Gene would go along with his plan. Otherwise, the man just might shoot him. He'd thought about throwing out Gus's body but had quickly mentally revised his plan. "Tina. Let's dump her out on the road. They'll stop for her and give us time to get away." If they were really back there. Either way, they'd be rid of her. He'd thought she might even survive.

Gene had looked over at him as if he'd lost his mind before he'd let out a curse. "You'd better hope this works. If not, you're a dead man."

Bobby had a bad feeling he was dead either way. The road he'd turned onto was questionable at best. Maybe it didn't matter. There was no way they were going to outrun anyone in this old van. Not that he thought they could stay on the run, anyway. Eventually someone was going to catch up to them: if not Culhane Travis, then the law. Either way, Bobby didn't have much hope. Gene had said he'd die before he'd go back to prison. If it came to a standoff…

Bobby couldn't shake the feeling that his time had run out. If Gene was right and it was Culhane Travis after them, then it would soon be over. Jana had told him about her husband. When he'd recognized the ex-deputy sheriff back at the café, his heart had lodged in his throat. He'd felt fear as cold and deadly as that blade the woman at the café had plunged into Gene. If Culhane was behind them, then they were as good as dead.

LARS OLSON HAD never prayed in his life. Until now. He held the sleeping baby in his arms and prayed for Tina as sirens sounded outside. He'd done her so wrong in so many ways. He looked at Chloe and felt such a well of love that he thought he might drown in it. "I'm so sorry," he whispered to the baby. How had he thought he could walk away from this child? From Tina?

His eyes filled with tears. He'd never been a strong man. That much was clear to him now. He'd told himself that he would only stay with Tina until the baby was born. But months later, he was still there with the two of them— and at the same time still clinging to Shirley. He'd wanted both, to stay with Tina and the baby, and to leave with Shirley. He had to have known that he would have to choose. Wasn't that why he'd insisted on Shirley going with him this morning to have breakfast at the café and force him into a decision?

Looking down at Chloe, who'd fallen into a deep sleep, he whispered, "What is wrong with me?" and he made a swipe at his tears.

"I could tell you," Vi said disagreeably.

"Can you ever forgive me?" he asked her. He must have sounded sincere, because she looked at him, studying him, as if in shock.

"I'm not the one who needs to forgive you," she said after a moment. "Knowing my daughter...she probably already has," Vi added with a sigh. "There's no accounting for taste."

"Tina's going to be all right," he said and looked to her for reassurance as he saw cops surrounding the café. He realized how desperate he was that he thought Vi might offer the encouragement he desperately needed. She didn't, and he went back to praying. He and Chloe needed Tina.

He could see that Vi did, too. They had become a family, and not just the three of them. Vi, alone except for her daughter and granddaughter, needed them as well. In time, maybe she would grow to tolerate him, if not fully accept him as family. Or not, he thought, as Earl Ray rose to open the door for the EMTs and cops.

ALEXIS DROPPED TO the ground next to Tina and placed her fingers against the woman's throat to search for a pulse. Culhane followed, fearing Tina was already dead, had been dead before she'd been thrown from the van.

But as he reached the two women, he heard Tina let out a moan of pain as she opened her eyes. She instantly recoiled, first from Alexis and then from him before she seemed to recognize them. As Tina tried to sit up, she groaned in pain and fell back. He could see that she was skinned up from being thrown out of the moving van onto the dirt road. But her injuries appeared to be minor, given what she'd been through.

"Don't try to get up," Alexis said next to her. "Can you tell me where it hurts?"

"It's my arm," Tina cried. "I think it's broken, and I… can't…breathe. I think my ribs are…broken, too."

Culhane looked over at Alexis. "We need to get her to the hospital to make sure she doesn't have any internal injuries." He met her gaze and held it. "You need to take her to the next town."

"What are you trying to pull?" she whispered from between gritted teeth.

"Let's get her into the pickup," he said, and she helped him help Tina to her feet and into the passenger seat.

Closing the door, he turned to Alexis and talked fast. "Tina needs medical attention. I have to talk to Bobby. I recognized him as the man I saw leaving Jana's the night she was allegedly murdered. I have to find out what he knows. He's the one person who can prove that I didn't kill her."

"Other than Jana herself," Alexis snapped. "I knew you'd pull something like this," she said with a curse.

He shook his head. "I swear that's not what this is about. You need to get Tina to a hospital. Beyond her arm and her ribs, she might have injuries that will kill her otherwise. Either way, she needs medical attention." He could see that her big heart wouldn't let her leave a woman in pain. "It's not that far to the next town to the east. Then come back for me. I promise I'll be here at the end of this road waiting for you."

When she shook her head angrily, he took her chin in his palm and lifted it up until their eyes met. "I promise." He felt her weaken. "Go, and hurry back."

"So help me, Culhane, if you—"

He kissed her, pulling her into him and kissing her as if he might never see her again. There was a good chance he wouldn't. Not that it was what he was thinking about as he'd kissed her with the passion that only this woman evoked in him. The thought of losing her made it hard for him to catch his next breath.

THE KISS TOOK Alexis completely by surprise. There was an intensity to it that frightened her. Was he saying good-bye because he thought he might die? Or because he had no plans to see her again? During the kiss, it hadn't mattered. She'd melted into him, caught up in her unrelenting desire for him, in the hard lines of his body, in the warmth of his arms around her. She never wanted the kiss to end.

But, of course, it had.

"Go," he said again. For just an instant, their gazes locked, and she thought he was going to say the words she'd yearned to hear. But then he turned and took off up the road at a run.

Alexis sighed and turned back to the pickup. Her legs felt weak under her, the kiss still churning in her system, making her soft inside and more vulnerable than she wanted to feel. The man could get to her with just one kiss. At the thought that she might not see him alive again, she felt sick to her stomach and had to throw up in the ditch before taking off the too-large vest and climbing behind the wheel.

She looked over at Tina and felt badly that she'd been here in pain even for the length of a kiss. "Hang on," she told her. "It's not that far to the hospital." The woman was covered in dirt and dust, her face streaked with tracks of dried tears, but she looked strong, sitting there holding her arm and taking shallow breaths. She'd faced death and had lived through it. Something like that either made a person stronger or left them frightened and weak.

Alexis started the pickup. She could barely make out Culhane's dark figure on the horizon. According to the map, he wouldn't have to go far before the road dead-ended at the river.

Tina also looked down the road after Culhane. She was shaking from fear or relief, Alexis thought maybe both. "You two know each other."

It wasn't a question since Tina had probably seen the kiss, but Alexis answered it, anyway. "We both worked for the sheriff's department as deputies. That's how we met."

"You don't anymore?"

"No." She sighed as she turned around and headed back up the road. "The new sheriff… It's a long story. I became a bounty hunter. Culhane…well, he's still figuring out some things." She wondered how much Tina knew and realized there was no reason to hold anything back. In fact, telling a stranger felt freeing. Maybe if she said it out loud, then what was happening wouldn't be so bad.

The rough road was jarring. She saw Tina wince in pain and tried to drive as carefully as possible to avoid the bumps. "His…wife—another long story—was recently murdered. Culhane is the sheriff's number-one suspect."

"Sounds complicated."

Alexis chuckled as she reached the smoother dirt road. "You could say that."

"You trust him?"

The question caught her flat-footed. She gripped the wheel, biting back her instant smart-ass response of *Not a chance*. She thought about it for a few moments. "I do." Glancing over at Tina, she said, "Your life a little complicated, too?"

Tina let out a humorless laugh but quickly stifled it as she grimaced in pain.

They drove in silence for a few minutes before Tina said, "I did something unforgivable, I'm afraid. Lars—"

"The baby whisperer?"

Tina nodded. "I love him, but a year ago I left him because he wouldn't commit, even though we'd been living together for several years. In a weak moment, I met a man at the hotel bar and…" She sighed. "I realized my mistake at once and returned home. Not long after that, I discovered my one-night stand had resulted in pregnancy."

She took a few shallow breaths. Alexis could hear the woman fighting tears. "Lars knew at once the baby wasn't his, but he agreed to stay with me until the baby was born. But unfortunately, my one-night stand and pregnancy made him turn to another woman for those months." More breaths, more tears. "The two of them had an affair that the whole town knew about. I thought he would leave the minute Chloe was born, but…" Her voice broke, and she began to sob quietly. "My precious baby. Lars…"

"I'm sure Chloe is fine," Alexis said hastily. "Lars is fine, too. She's with him."

Tina nodded and tried to pull herself together. "Lars is wonderful with her." Alexis nodded. She'd seen the two of them together. She'd held the baby in her arms. The thought made her reach down and put her hand protectively over her stomach for a moment.

"Today was the first time Lars and Shirley had come out in public as a couple," Tina said.

She heard the woman's pain. She wanted to say something to make it better but knew there were no words. She'd seen Lars with that other woman, Shirley. "You still love him."

"With all my heart. My mother…" She cleared her throat and let go of her broken arm for a moment to wipe at her tears. "She keeps saying I need to—" she made air quotes with one hand "—kick him to the curb. I guess there is nothing keeping him from taking off with Shirley now— once I come back for my baby."

"I doubt things are that clear-cut," Alexis said. "I saw the way he was with Chloe and the way he came to your defense. I think he cares more than you think."

"He really was all right when you left?" she asked. Alexis nodded. "And my mother?" She nodded again. "What about Bessie?"

"Earl Ray was taking care of her. An ambulance had been called."

Tina seemed to relax. Ahead, Alexis saw a town appear on the horizon, this one larger than Buckhorn. She thought about Culhane and worried what would happen when he found the van. *Please don't get yourself killed.* Would he be there when she returned? Or would he be long gone? She thought about the promise he'd made her and the look in his eyes. The tip of her tongue touched her upper lip as she thought about that kiss.

From the moment she'd met him, she'd known she could trust him with her life—just not her heart, but damned if he hadn't stolen it, anyway.

AS THE VAN came up over the rise, Bobby had only a few moments to take in the scene in front of him. A river with rushing water and large boulders. A few dilapidated buildings off to one side. And what had once been a narrow wooden bridge spanning the deep, fast water.

End of the road, he thought. In more ways than one. In that instant, he felt a wave of relief as he slammed on the brakes. It was over.

"Get your foot off that brake, you son of a—" Gene screamed.

"It's a dead end," he yelled back.

"Take the bridge."

Bobby shot him a look. The van was still moving too fast. If he didn't get it under control soon… But it was what he heard in the hard gravel of Gene's voice—and the sight of the gun pointed at him that made the decision for him.

Take the bridge.

Or take a bullet.

It wasn't over. But it would be soon.

He let up off the brake, knowing that, either way, he was going to die, and tromped on the gas. The van jumped forward even as fast as he was already going. Hadn't his mother warned him how it would end if he didn't change his ways?

"Sorry, Mom," he whispered under his breath as the van roared toward the bridge and the two wooden signs that someone had crudely painted with the words *Danger* and *Bridge Closed.*

The front of the van hit the first sign, sending it cartwheeling off to the side as the second sign crashed into the windshield before being flung off. And suddenly they were up on the wooden planks that had once spanned the river.

That's when Bobby saw how many of the boards had rotted away. He hesitated, and Gene saw him. The bullet tore into his side, burning through his stomach and lodging in the door panel. He hadn't had to look at Gene to know he would shoot again. He stomped down on the gas harder. He could feel the boards breaking under the tires, under the weight of the van. He could see the rushing water and boulders below them, feel the bridge groan and shudder under them.

As the searing heat of the bullet doubled him over the steering wheel, all he could do was keep his foot pressed to the gas pedal. It no longer mattered. And yet, a part of him was determined to see if he could reach the other side of the river before he died.

CHAPTER THIRTEEN

CULHANE SLOWED TO a walk at a rise in the road. He could smell the water and the scent of decomposing leaves in the air. He could see the willows and cottonwoods growing along the edge of the water and hear the wind blowing through their bare branches. He stopped to listen, but all he could hear was the wind rustling the dry leaves at his feet.

Dropping down into the barrow pit next to the road, he edged his way to the top of the rise until he heard a sound that made him stop—the roar of an engine and then the sound of a crash, the kind that twisted metal and broke glass.

He topped the rise, his weapon drawn, to see a cluster of old, dilapidated buildings squatting next to the river. The water looked deep and dark, as it rushed over large boulders in the middle of the stream. That's when he saw the bridge. Or what was left of it. Surely they hadn't tried to cross it. Even from where he stood he could tell that most of the bridge had rotted away.

He knew before he dropped down the slope to the water. The sound he'd heard had been the jarring sudden impact of a vehicle crashing into something solid. Beyond the old structures, he looked across the river and saw steam rising from the van's engine that was now wedged into the far bank on the other side of the river.

The fools had tried to cross the bridge—and they'd almost made it. Following the fresh tracks the van tires had left, he ran to the edge of the river—and the tumbledown bridge over the water. Off to one side a weathered warning sign lay in the dirt. At the edge of the water lay another sign of caution. This one had been split in two after apparently being hit by the force of the van.

The vehicle had to have been moving at a high speed when it hit the signs blocking entry. Bobby, if he were still driving, would have had to be out of his mind to try to cross what was obviously an abandoned bridge. He could see where the missing boards had rotted away and plunged into the river. More of them were broken and hanging loose.

Culhane quickly climbed up onto the bridge and looked across to the other side. The wind tore at his clothing and kicked up dust along the shore. He squinted, thinking he saw movement next to the van. Bobby had almost made it all the way across before going off and driving into the embankment on the other side with obvious force. The back of the van lay in the river, water rushing around it.

The driver's door stood open, and so did the passenger door. Culhane couldn't tell if there was anyone still inside or not. He couldn't imagine how anyone had survived the crash. But with the doors open, it was possible they had gotten out. So where were they?

Gene was badly injured from the knife wound. He couldn't have gotten far. If Bobby had survived the crash, he could be anywhere. The man in the back, Gus, had to be dead. Culhane had known that the man's gunshot wound was serious when he'd seen Earl Ray's grim expression when he'd returned to the café to wash the blood off his hands the first time. They'd thrown out Tina to give them time to escape. But faced with the river and no way out but the bridge, they'd taken a gamble that he doubted had paid off.

But there was only one way to know if anyone was still alive. Culhane told himself that crossing over the bridge—especially after the damage the van had caused—was a fool's errand. They were probably all dead. Or someone could be lying in wait inside the vehicle.

Either way, Culhane had to find out. He could only hope that Bobby was alive. Bobby could clear him of the murder charges. Or at least tell him if Jana was still alive and where he might find her. His future depended on it.

He considered the deep, swift current of the river with its large boulders just below the surface. Swimming it wasn't an option. The bridge was even more dangerous. A gust of wind sent the dry leaves whirling past. Somewhere close by, a hawk cried out before the scene took on an eerie wind-scoured quiet for a moment.

Cautiously, Culhane began to pick his way along the rotted boards.

ALEXIS DROPPED TINA off at the hospital's emergency entrance after calling her mother to let Vi know she was all right. Tina also got to speak to Lars. Chloe was fine. The police were there. Bessie was on her way to the hospital by ambulance but expected to survive.

Alexis didn't hang around long enough at the hospital to get involved in the police investigation. "You understand why I can't stay with you," she'd said to Tina after they'd made the call.

"It's all right. You're worried about him."

She'd nodded, afraid of what she would find when she returned. "I hate just leaving you, though."

"I'll be fine," Tina had assured her as they'd neared the

entrance. "Does he know?" At Alexis's confused look, she added, "About the baby?"

She felt a moment of surprise, then shook her head as she pulled into the emergency lane and helped Tina to the door. As she pushed the button, she could see a nurse heading in their direction with a wheelchair.

"He'll do the right thing," Tina said.

Alexis felt tears burn her eyes. "That's what I'm afraid of."

The emergency-room door opened, and Alexis hurried back to the truck. Starting it up, she headed west again as fast as she could go without getting pulled over for speeding.

She kept checking her rearview mirror as she left town. Once on the highway, she began to relax a little. She knew Tina was right. Culhane would do the right thing. He'd marry her. Just as he had Jana.

Once she'd heard about his first marriage, she'd known she couldn't tell him about the baby she was carrying. She didn't want that kind of marriage. She wanted Culhane to love her so much that he couldn't live without her. She wouldn't trap him with a baby as Jana had done.

She knew why he'd never told her about Jana. She suspected there was more he'd been keeping from her. In the almost four years that she'd known him, he'd never told her much about his family or obviously any other part of his life before they'd met, when she'd gone to work as a deputy at the sheriff's department and they'd been thrown together.

All she knew was that he and his father didn't get along. She'd never met the man before attending his funeral a few months ago. Culhane had been dry-eyed at the viewing, which was well attended. It surprised her that he hadn't seemed to know almost all of the people who'd come to pay their respects, except for his friends that were there.

"My father had a life completely separate from mine after my mother died when I was twelve," he'd told her.

She'd wondered how that was even possible and said as much.

"Right after her funeral he sent me to boarding school. I went to friends' homes during holidays and summer break." When she'd tried to question him further, he'd shut down. She'd been horrified that a father would do that to his own flesh and blood. But between his father and Jana, she figured she now understood why he'd said marriage and kids weren't for him.

Alexis was watching for the turnoff when she caught the flashing lights in her rearview mirror. Her heart dropped as she slowed down and started to pull over. At least she was driving Earl Ray's pickup. But by now the law might already know that.

She rode the shoulder as the sound of the siren came closer and closer. She thought she might be sick. She had to get back to where she'd left Culhane. She couldn't help being worried about him. Maybe if she told the patrol officer what was going on...

The cruiser streaked past her, siren blaring, lights flashing in a blur. Alexis stared after it and tried to breathe. Her heart was a thudding drum in her chest. She willed her stomach to settle down, and hastily she wiped at her tears.

The patrol hadn't paid her—or the pickup—any mind at all. Instead, he was probably looking for a gray van with bank-robber killers inside. Lucky for her. Lucky for Culhane, she thought as she got the truck going again.

But as she did, she wondered if she should have waved down the officer. After all, she knew where the gray van and the men were. She also knew where Culhane might be found. What she wouldn't know was what had happened since she'd been gone, and that's what assured her that she'd made the right decision. At least she hoped in her heart of hearts that she had.

She drove, watching for the road where she had to turn, unable to shake the feeling that if Culhane needed her, she was going to be too late to help him.

A BOARD CRACKED under his boot and fell away, throwing Culhane off balance for a moment. His pulse thundered in his ears as he looked down at the long drop to the water and the large boulders just below the surface. He had to stop for a moment to get his balance, to get his breathing under control.

He tried not to look in the direction of the van and instead concentrated on his footing. If he was walking into a trap, he was giving them plenty of time to take him out. The wind whipped around him, kicking up dust and dried feathers along the shore. The air held the promise of a new season, one that would bring cold and ice and snow, even as the sun beat down on him.

Just a few more steps, and he would be at the spot where the van had gone off the bridge. That Bobby had almost made it all the way across was nothing short of a miracle. He must have just floored it. He had to have known he wouldn't make it. Otherwise, the van would be fully in the river, the current rushing through it.

Stepping around the gaping, massive hole in the bridge, Culhane found a little better footing on the opposite side. Just a few more yards, he thought, picking his way carefully. He would hate to make it this far and then have the rest of the bridge collapse, dropping him to the rocks and rushing water below.

A board snapped under his left foot; he quickly shifted his weight to his right and then froze there for a moment, the wind buffeting him. As he'd seen from across the river, the driver's-side door was hanging open. The passenger's-side door though was only partially open. Something appeared to be lodged in the door, keeping it from closing. The wind whistled through the open doors. Were the men still inside?

Culhane took another step, then another. He had to watch where he stepped and yet, at the same time, he was trying to keep one eye on the van. He was close enough now that even a bullet from a handgun could find its mark.

Almost to the other side, he caught sight of what was stuck in the door. A leg. The pants were covered in blood. He took a misstep at the sight of the mangled limb and almost fell through a yawning hole in the bridge floor. He swallowed back the bile that rose up his throat and froze, not even breathing until he got his balance again.

As he stood, he listened for any sound coming from the van, but all he could hear was the wail of the wind as it rushed downriver. Nothing moved in the vehicle. He took another step, then another until he reached the other side of the river and bounded off the bridge.

Weapon drawn, he approached the wrecked vehicle. He had no idea how much time had passed since Alexis had left to take Tina to the hospital. She would come right back, he had no doubt about that. The next town wasn't that far away. He hoped he hadn't made a mistake by sending her. If she came across the law... Then she might not be back at all with both of them wanted for questioning in the café shooting.

The van had gone off the left side of the bridge. As he moved along the edge of the embankment, Culhane could see Gene slouched in the passenger seat. It appeared that he'd tried to get out before the crash—his leg getting wedged in the door. Was it possible he was still alive?

As Culhane neared, he realized there was no need to check for a pulse. The front of the man's face was caved in much like the windshield that now butted up against the facade of the riverbank.

Of course Gene would have unfastened his seat belt to try to jump out before the crash. Had the embankment not been there, Gene would have been thrown from the van— that's if his leg hadn't been caught in the door. As it was, he'd gone face-first into the windshield and the rock and dirt. The impact had probably broken his neck.

Whose idea had it been to try to cross the bridge? he wondered. Back at the café, right before Gene and Bobby had left with Tina, Culhane had seen the moment when Bobby had remembered where he'd seen him.

He doubted, though, that Bobby had shared that information with Gene. Bobby would have known that Culhane would come after him and why. He'd know that Culhane was desperate. Was that why Bobby had tried to cross?

So whose idea had it been to throw Tina out to slow him down? Maybe Gene was hoping anyone after them just wanted the woman.

He edged closer, gun trained on the van and caught the coppery smell of blood as he approached the van and what was decaying inside it. Something creaked inside.

Culhane froze.

His gaze shot to the bloody leg trapped in the door. Had it twitched? Or had he imagined it? He knew he was going to have to look inside. Making his way down to the water's edge, he waded in and approached the side of the van. He could feel the current trying to pull him down and sweep him under the van and away. Another creak as if someone was in there moving around. Or was it the river slowly pushing the van out deeper?

Avoiding looking at Gene's destroyed face or breathing in the smell of death, he leaned out and grabbed the van's side-door handle with his free left hand and jerked it open. As the door slid back and water began to pour inside, Culhane pointed the barrel of his gun into the darkness inside.

Nothing inside the van moved. From the looks of the man lying there, Gus had been dead for some time. The van creaked again as the river swept in and the back of it groaned against the pressure.

The report of the gunshot was almost lost in the wind howling through the van. The bullet shattered the driver's-side window and lodged in the side of the van only inches from Culhane's head. From the trajectory of the shot, he now knew exactly where Bobby was. He stepped back, making himself less of a target and flattening himself against the side of the vehicle as he edged toward the front again. In order to get to Bobby, he could either swim around the back end or climb up over the embankment. It was an easy choice. He started to backtrack to the bridge, when a bullet whizzed past so close it felt as if it had brushed his cheek.

"Bobby, I just want to talk!" he called across the wrecked van before he ran back to the bridge and up the slope of the road until he was on top of the riverbank. Crouching down, he moved as swiftly as he could to the spot where he thought he'd find Bobby. That was, if he hadn't moved.

Bobby had to be hurt. Otherwise he would have taken

off or found better cover, Culhane told himself. But how badly hurt?

He slowed and peered over. He could see a spot where fishermen had made a path down to the water yards down from the crash site. He hurried to it, staying low, and dropped down to the water's edge. He couldn't see the van because of a bend in the river. Working his way along the rocky edge, he finally reached a spot where he could see the rear bumper.

Between gusts, he thought he heard a moaning sound. Cautiously, he edged closer and could see where Bobby had crawled up onto a stretch of shoreline out of the wind. He sat with his back against the earth. His gun lay in his lap, his hands and body covered with blood.

"Bobby, I just want to talk." No answer, but from here, he could see that Bobby hadn't moved to pick up the gun. "Bobby?" Nothing. Maybe he had died from his injuries. First Leo. Now Bobby? Another dead end when it came to clearing himself?

Then he heard another moan and carefully approached the man. When he was close enough, he reached over and picked up the gun lying in Bobby's lap. He saw why the man hadn't bothered to try to shoot him. He was out of ammunition.

He squatted next to him. Blood still oozed from a bullet hole in the man's side. Who'd shot him? Had to have been Gene. Bobby was struggling to breathe.

"I need to know about Jana."

Bobby raised his gaze but seemed to be having a hard time staying focused. "I know you were there that night. I saw you coming out of her house after she was allegedly murdered. You saw me, too."

There was a moment of recognition. When Bobby spoke, his words came out as gasps. "I don't want to die."

He wished he could give the man hope, but he figured Bobby knew that even if Culhane called for an ambulance, it would never get here in time. "Do you know where Jana is hiding?"

Bobby swallowed and shook his head, his gaze starting to slide away.

"Bobby, please. Is Jana dead, or did she fake her death?" Another shake of his head. "If she's alive, who is she running from?" He could see the young man's lips moving and leaned closer.

He coughed. "Water—"

"I'll get you some water. Tell me why she would fake her death. It has to be more than a shoplifting arrest."

Bobby began to wheeze. "Wat—"

Culhane heard the sound of the pickup engine. *Earl Ray's* pickup engine. Alexis would reach the other side of the river any moment.

Bobby heard it, too, and for a moment he seemed to brighten. Then his head slumped to the side, his eyes going blank as his face relaxed, the pain gone as he took whatever he knew about Jana with him.

Culhane swore as he saw his chance to clear his name die with the man. He swallowed before gently closing Bobby's eyes. As he pushed to his feet, he pulled out his phone and called 9-1-1 to tell them where they could find the gray van. Then he turned off his phone again and turned to see Alexis come flying over the rise.

She hit the brakes before coming to a dust-boiling stop on the other side of the river. He couldn't see her behind the wheel for the sun glinting off the windshield.

Climbing up the embankment, he walked back to the

bridge. He suspected she was surprised to see him still there. That made his heart hurt. He'd broken trust with her. He wondered how long it would take to rebuild it and if he had the time.

He could only hope as he headed back across the bridge toward the pickup—and Alexis.

CHAPTER FOURTEEN

BY THE TIME Culhane reached her, Alexis was standing on the bank staring across the river at the wrecked van. He took her in his arms and held her close for a few moments. They couldn't stay here. He wasn't sure where to go next. Both Leo and Bobby were dead. For all he knew, so was Jana.

"Are they…"

"Dead," he said as he released her. "We have to go."

"You didn't get to talk to Bobby?" she asked as she followed him to the pickup.

"He was still alive," Culhane said as he climbed behind the wheel and Alexis slid into the passenger seat and buckled up. "But all he kept asking before he died was for water, even though he was lying by a river full of it," he said and shook his head.

"I'm sorry."

He started the engine and turned around to head down the road. "I called 9-1-1 so it shouldn't be long before the cops arrive." She nodded as if there was little else to say. They couldn't be here when the law enforcement arrived— just like back in Buckhorn. He hated being on the run but had been since he'd left Alexis's warm bed last night.

Time was running out. If he didn't find evidence to clear himself soon… The part he hated most was involving Alexis. He turned onto the two-lane highway and headed west until he could find a road that headed north. They couldn't go back to Buckhorn. Not yet.

"I'm worried about what happened back at the café," she said as if she too had been thinking about it.

He pulled out his phone. Earl Ray's number came right up. "It's Culhane. Can you talk?" He turned to her. "He's at the hospital now with Bessie."

"Ask him how she is," Alexis said.

He put the phone on speaker. "How's Bessie?"

Earl Ray said "She's doing great. She's strong. The doctor said she has the constitution of a mule." They could hear Bessie say something in the background, then Earl Ray laugh.

"Sounds like she's holding her own."

"Always. I'll let you know how it goes," Earl Ray said. "Also, I still have a few contacts so if you need help, just call me."

"Thanks." As he hung up, he felt Alexis's gaze on him.

"You get the feeling Earl Ray is more than he lets on?"

Culhane chuckled as he pocketed his phone. He drove for a few miles before he said "You understand why I can't let you turn me over to the cops. If I'm right and Jana is alive, she's fighting to stay that way. I don't know what all she's involved in—just that if she's alive, it's dangerous enough to make her do something as drastic as faking her own death. I need you to get out in the next town and walk away from this, from me, until I find out what's going on. So far you're not so deeply involved. But if you stay—"

"I'm staying." He swore under his breath. "You need me."

"Alex—" The word was a plea and a curse.

"Culhane, originally, yes, it was all about taking you to the cops, collecting my fee and letting you rot in jail," she said. "Well, maybe not rot in jail, but you have to admit, you probably deserve to be behind bars for a while for not being honest with me." He started to speak, but she waved him off. "But you need me now to help you find Jana. We have to find out who is trying to frame you for murder before the cops catch up to you and shoot without even bothering to ask questions."

He knew she was right, which was another reason he didn't want her in the crosshairs. Just being with him put her in danger in so many ways.

"I can help you. But from this point on, you can't keep anything from me. We're in this together. If I suspect you're not telling me everything, then all bets are off. Deal?"

He glanced over at her as she held out her hand. Seriously? She wanted to shake on it? With a sigh, he took her hand, thinking there was still so much he'd kept from her. So much he wanted to tell her. But now wasn't the time. He couldn't make any promises because right now, he wasn't sure of his future or if he would even have one.

ALEXIS PULLED HER hand away. "You're going to try to ditch me at the first opportunity, aren't you?"

He shook his head, even though that was exactly what he wanted to do. "If I did, it would only be to protect you."

"I can protect myself."

"I'd be doing you a favor," he said, not looking at her.

"You want to do me a favor, then stay alive."

He glanced over at her. "When you look at me with those big brown doe eyes…" He shook his head. "Damn it, I'm worried about how bad things are going to get before this is over. I don't want anything to happen to you. I never wanted you involved."

She gave him a pointed look. "I'm already involved. I've

been involved for the past year. Want to tell me what last night was about?"

He sighed. "I came over to your apartment to tell you everything, to warn you, to try to convince you to stay out of it." He met her gaze for a moment. "Then I saw you, and I just wanted to hold you and kiss you and—"

"Yes, I remember."

Their gazes locked for a few seconds, and the chemistry in the cab of the pickup sparked and popped like lightning. She felt the heat rush to her center and thought she might burst with her desire for this man.

"You should have at least said goodbye," she finally said, remembering what it had been like waking up alone in that big bed, his side cold, and wondering if she would ever see him again.

"I didn't want it to be goodbye," Culhane said, his voice sounding husky with emotion.

But it had felt like goodbye when she'd realized he'd left without waking her. Then this morning, finding out that there was a BOLO out on Culhane for *murder*! The murder of his *wife*!

"Imagine how I felt like when I got the news about the murder and the BOLO out on you," she said, realizing that she was still angry with him and yet wishing he could pull over and take her in his arms again and explain all of this away.

But she knew it wouldn't be that easy. Nor would it be enough. It would never be enough. Her love for this man made her weak with need and stole her good sense.

"I know I hurt you." He sounded as if he did. "I'm sorry. If I had stayed, maybe I could have talked you out of coming after me."

She laughed and shook her head. "I think you know better than that."

His smile was sad. "Alex, I could have gotten you killed back there at the café. I still might." He shook his head. "I can't bear the thought of what I'm dragging you into."

Alexis swallowed the lump that had risen in her throat. "You aren't dragging me into anything. I'm here because there is no place else I want to be. They're saying you're armed and dangerous. The first law you run across might just shoot you. If there is any way I can prevent that—"

"You can't."

"Well, I'm going to try."

CULHANE STARTED TO answer when he caught movement out of the corner of his eye. His gaze shot to the rearview mirror an instant before he heard the siren.

"Cops," he said as the flashing lights of the patrol car raced closer.

"What are you going to do?"

"The only thing I can." He slowed and began to pull over.

He hadn't realized that he'd been holding his breath until the patrol car sped past, the officer behind the wheel not even looking in their direction. The sound of the siren was a wail dying in the distance.

Culhane looked over at Alexis and saw her relief as well. She was right about one thing. He did need her. He hadn't realized how much. After Jana's murder and everything that had happened today, he'd been reminded of how short life could be.

The other night he'd gone to Alexis, knowing it was the last thing he should do. He had known that someone from the sheriff's department would let her know about the BOLO. While the new sheriff wasn't a fan of either of them, they still had friends in the department.

He'd known that once she heard about the BOLO out on him, she would come after him—especially if he made love to her and then sneaked away. But he'd had to see her. He'd had to be with her. He couldn't bear not seeing her one more time in case it was his last.

Now he had to decide if keeping her close was safer for her than trying to ditch her. He knew this woman. No one was more headstrong or determined. She'd be even more dogged now about finding him and taking him in if he ditched her.

"Okay, total transparency," he said. She was right. He did need her in so many ways. He turned north to go around Buckhorn, staying right at the speed limit. With the shoot-out at the café and now the robbers dead at the river, there would be even more law enforcement out looking for them.

Which meant he had to fight the urge not to tromp on the gas pedal and put as many miles as possible between them and the crime scenes they'd left behind. There would be hell to pay when this was over—and not just for him but for Alexis as well.

He felt as if their trouble had only just begun. He'd already had all of law enforcement looking for him. After the shootings back at the café, Alexis was now an accomplice. For better or worse. He wondered if she knew what she'd signed up for with him. He just hoped she'd never regret it.

ALEXIS THOUGHT ABOUT everything that had happened since she'd opened her eyes this morning. She'd hoped that Bobby would have been able to tell Culhane something about Jana—a woman she hadn't even known had existed until this morning.

"Maybe you should start by telling me about the last time you saw Jana," she suggested as Culhane drove. "You said you hadn't seen her for years? Thought the two of you were no longer married? Must have been a surprise when you heard from her." She hoped she didn't sound as jealous as she felt, no matter how he'd played down the marriage.

He drove for a few moments before he answered. "She apparently got my cell number from my dad's lawyer. I hadn't seen or heard from her in seven years. When she told me that we were still married, I was more than shocked."

"Let me guess. She wanted something."

Culhane nodded. "She said she needed fifty thousand dollars to get out of town."

That made Alexis's eyes widen. "Did you tell her what sheriff's deputies make a year in Montana—when they have jobs?" Alexis caught his hesitation and groaned. "Not another secret."

"She knew I could get the money."

Knowing how he lived, his answer caught her by surprise. "What are you telling me? That you moonlight as the head of a drug cartel in your spare time?" She tried to joke away the hurt. How was it that Jana, who hadn't been around in years, knew he could get that much money but Alexis didn't? Especially if this woman really had been out of his life all these years.

He sighed. "I might have left out a few particulars about my life."

"A *few* particulars?" She scoffed and tried to control her hurt and anger. She had believed that the two of them were as close as any two lovers could be. What a laugh. He hadn't trusted her with anything real about his life at all. Angry, she said as much.

"That's not true. I didn't tell you some things, because they didn't matter."

Was he serious? She could barely speak. "Apparently they do matter. At least the money part and the marriage to Jana."

CULHANE KNEW WHY he'd never told Alexis about his family. Her parents were like something out of an old family sitcom. A stable, loving couple who lived in a nice home.

Alexis had come from such a low-key background that he hadn't wanted her to know how screwed up his upbringing had been. He didn't want to admit that after his mother died, his father couldn't stand the sight of him.

"You know I don't like talking about it," he said but knew from her expression that he couldn't leave it at that. "I told you I grew up on a ranch. That was partly true. My father was a businessman who bought a hobby ranch for my mother. So I grew up there until I was twelve and my mother died. Apparently she was the glue that held our family together. The day after my father buried her, he sent me to boarding school, sold the ranch both she and I had loved and moved into a condo in Bozeman. A *one-bedroom* condo."

"I'm sorry."

He couldn't look at her. He didn't want to see the pity in her eyes. "I told you that I spent holidays and summers with friends. My father and I rarely spoke. When we did…" He shook his head. "The point is my mother's family had money and my father made a lot of money, and I am his only heir."

"Jana knew about your family wealth."

Culhane wished he'd told her before Jana came back into the picture. Now it was so much worse. "My father, while he hadn't wanted anything to do with me, had people keeping a close eye on me. He found out that Jana was pregnant and that's why we were getting married. I would imagine her father called mine. Anyway, my father insisted on a prenup, threatening to disinherit me if she didn't sign it. Jana was so upset. I was worried about the baby. My father had paid for my education, but I'd always made my own money. I knew I could support us."

"Knowing you, you got disinherited."

HE LAUGHED. ALEXIS loved that laugh under other circumstances. Just as she loved the way he smiled at her, the smile lighting up his blue eyes like liquid silver on water. "Once Jana found out that I'd been disowned, suddenly she lost the baby and took off."

Alexis realized that he had never wanted proof of the pregnancy. Oh, Culhane, you sweet, naive man. "But then she came back seven years later wanting fifty thousand dollars."

He nodded. "Before my father died…"

"He put you back in his will." She realized this could explain why Culhane had been so upset at the funeral. She knew that he and his father hadn't been close, but she'd assumed he'd been grieving not just the loss of his father but the loss of a chance to ever have a relationship with him.

"His lawyer's been calling me about the will. I didn't want his money. I'm happy the way things are."

She heard the words, words he'd said before when it came to the two of them. When he'd mentioned that he didn't do marriage or kids.

"How about dogs?" she'd asked.

He'd grinned and said, "I have nothing against dogs."

"I saw all of it as an unnecessary burden since both my

parents came from old money. Jana coming back wanting money says it all."

She stared at him. Old money. "You didn't tell me because of the money." He looked shamefaced, and she knew it was true.

"I would have eventually told you. Truthfully, I'd hoped it wouldn't matter to you."

"It doesn't. You keeping so much from me, well, that's another matter. So did you give Jana the money?"

"No. She made all kinds of threats, cried, said she was in trouble with some bad people and that if she didn't get the money they would kill her."

"You thought it was another con," Alexis said, seeing how guilty he looked.

Culhane glanced away, pain in his expression. "I did. We argued, the neighbors heard. Jana was throwing things and screaming. The neighbors called the law."

"Which only made you look more guilty when it appeared that she'd been murdered." She understood now why the sheriff had been so quick to put out a BOLO on Culhane. Garwood might actually believe he really was guilty. "How was it you were at the scene of the crime?"

"Jana had left an urgent message. Feeling bad about the way I'd left things, I called her. She said she couldn't talk. I heard a man's angry, threatening voice in the background. When I tried to call her back, it went straight to voice mail. Worried, I went over there and played right into her hands. Or whoever is behind this. I saw the blood and the broken glass. I realized it was a setup the instant I heard the sirens. I barely escaped, making me look all the more guilty."

And he'd come straight to her, Alexis thought. "Any more secrets you want to reveal? Or would you rather wait and surprise me?"

He glanced over and shook his head. "I probably should have told you I'd been married and maybe a little about my family."

She nodded. "There are worse things than being left a whole lot of money."

"Yeah," he said and swore under his breath before glancing at her again. "I don't even want to know what he left me. You're sure it isn't important to you?"

"Actually, I think I liked you better when I thought you were poor."

He grinned, but it never reached his eyes. "I told his lawyer to give it all to charity and was told I can't. I have to hang on to it for future generations."

"Future generations you aren't interested in having," she said, hoping her words didn't sound as bitter as they felt.

"You can understand now why I told you up front that I wasn't interested in marriage and babies."

"Right." She had to look away. "I remember. It was the one thing you told me about yourself."

CHAPTER FIFTEEN

CULHANE STARTED TO tell her that he hadn't meant it. That his attitude had changed in the year they'd been together. He could now see himself married to her with babies.

He reached over to touch her, but she pulled away. She had every right to be angry. If he were Alexis, he wouldn't want anything to do with him, either. His relationship with her was the longest he'd ever had. He'd quit other relationships when they'd started to get serious.

But it had been different with Alex. He'd been drawn to her the moment they'd met. She radiated strength, determination and independence. He thought of her as an equal. She challenged him, didn't play games, told it to him straight. He admired the hell out of her.

At first, he'd tried to keep his distance from her, knowing how screwed up he was when it came to opening up to anyone. But he couldn't stay away from her. The deeper he got into the relationship, the more he found himself wanting more—something new for him.

He should have told her a lot of things, given how he had begun to feel about her. But he'd loved the way things were between them and had wanted them to stay that way. He'd wanted her to love him in spite of his first marriage, in spite of the money and what came with it, in spite of the baggage he carried from the loss of both his mother and father at the age of twelve. He'd wanted a clean slate with Alexis as if he'd only been born yesterday.

"Enough confessions for one day?" he asked hopefully, telling himself that when this was over, he'd tell her everything, especially the one thing he'd needed to tell her for months.

"Sure," she said in a clipped, all-business tone. He saw her glance in her side mirror. He checked the rearview. Nothing. But he could feel the clock ticking. "Where are we going?"

"Into the grizzly's den. Back to the Gallatin Valley. Did you happen to notice the plates on the van? They had the number six, signifying the van was licensed in Gallatin County."

She turned to him, looking as if their problems were quickly forgotten as she got down to business. "That's odd since they robbed a bank in Idaho, right?"

So she'd heard the news on the café radio before he'd turned it off. "I suspect Bobby is from there, and he was the getaway driver."

"His van?"

Culhane shook his head. "Probably stolen." He felt her gaze on him.

"I'd ask if you have a plan…"

He chuckled. She knew him so well. "Actually, I do. The first thing we need is a different means of transportation since this pickup has been seen now by at least two highway patrols, right? I know where we can get a loaner—at one of the places I used to spend holidays and summers. The Cardwell Ranch in the Gallatin Canyon. I think I introduced you to Ford Cardwell once."

She nodded. "But is that wise? Wasn't his uncle a marshal, and isn't his wife the state medical examiner?"

Culhane nodded. "Don't worry. He's a good friend, and I trust him. I can't say that about a lot of people. His wife Hitch is on a case up north, and his uncle is retired. We're just popping in and out fast before Dana Cardwell Savage insists we stay for a meal. Which is a shame since she's a great cook."

"I love it when you smile like that," she said, a catch in her throat.

He glanced over at her, seeing that if she hadn't forgiven him, she would soon. That was another thing about Alexis: she'd enfolded him in that big heart of hers. It was the reason he had to do everything he could to keep the two of them alive—and make it up for hurting her. The last thing he wanted to do was break that heart.

Sheriff Willy Garwood was just finishing his lunch when he got the call.

"Guess where Culhane turned up?" Deputy Dick Furu said.

He was in no guessing mood, especially when it came to Culhane Travis. He let out a growl in answer.

"Buckhorn, Montana."

"What the hell was he doing there?"

"Apparently having breakfast in the café there. But those three who robbed the bank in Idaho? They showed up, and there was a shoot-out. Culhane apparently shot one of them and chased after them when they took a local woman as hostage."

Garwood couldn't believe what he was hearing. It was certainly not what he'd been hoping to hear. "You're telling me he's not in custody?"

"Afraid not. He left before the law arrived. Last he was seen, he was chasing after the bank robbers. The local

Buckhorn woman who was taken hostage turned up at the hospital in the next town."

"That sounds like something Culhane would do. So where the hell was law enforcement?"

"Everyone was headed for Buckhorn, I would imagine. But it wasn't Culhane who dropped off the hostage. It was a woman with short dark curly hair."

"Alexis Brand," Garwood said and cursed under this breath. "So the two are together?"

"They weren't when Tina Mullen was dropped off at the hospital. Hold on, something else is coming through." Garwood could hear chatter in the background but couldn't make out the conversation. Furu came back on. "They just found the bank robbers that got away from the café shooting. All three are deceased. No more information than that."

"Culhane." Garwood shook his head. That man had been a burr under his saddle from the day Willy took the sheriff job. "Find him. Bring in his girlfriend as well. Clearly she is aiding and abetting." He hesitated, not sure Furu was in a place where he couldn't be overhead. "What about that other matter?"

"No luck yet."

So they hadn't found Jana Redfield Travis yet, either. And Culhane Travis was still on the loose with the help of his girlfriend.

"You know we have to find her before they do," the sheriff said of Jana.

"We're on it."

He disconnected, his lunch sitting uneasy now in his stomach, making him feel sick. He had a BOLO out on Culhane. Someone was bound to pick him up. Or, with luck, shoot him on sight. But with Alexis Brand tagging along, it would be harder to kill him without killing her, too. But that was an option.

As for Jana, the woman had pulled a fast one on him. For that she would pay. He wanted to take care of her personally.

ALEXIS HADN'T BEEN paying any attention as to where Culhane was driving. Her mind had been on all the revelations he'd dropped on her, along with the horror that had played out earlier and the fact that now they were probably both wanted by the law.

But hearing him talk about his friend Ford and seeing him smile like that, she was looking forward to meeting the man. It reassured her that she hadn't made a mistake about Culhane. But in spite of his loss, he'd managed to make the best of it by finding good friends. Except for Jana. That experience had left scars. Scars she'd known nothing about until all this had happened.

"So this is Cardwell Ranch?" she said as he turned off the highway. The ranch sat in the picturesque canyon with its dark pines and towering granite cliffs. The Gallatin River carved a winding path through all of it as puffy clouds floated above in a sky of blue. Snowcapped mountains surrounded them, making the whole scene remind her that Christmas was coming. She'd tried to imagine having Christmas on a ranch like this.

As they crossed a bridge over the cool green of the river, a barn loomed up in the distance and then a large ranch house against a pine-tree-covered mountain as background.

"It's beautiful," she said, noticing the small creek that tumbled out of the mountains to join the river.

The dark-haired cowboy who came out of the barn had clearly been expecting them.

Culhane parked and got out to shake the rancher's hand. Ford pulled his friend into a hug. "Ford, don't mean to put you on the spot."

"You know better than that. I've got a ranch pickup all gassed up and ready to go. I'll put the one you're driving in the barn."

"I owe you." His voice broke.

Alexis could see that Culhane wanted to say more. But she suspected he didn't need to tell Ford that he hadn't killed anyone. His friend trusted him as well.

She'd gotten out to stretch her legs, but Culhane called her over. "Ford, this is—"

"Alexis Brand," Ford said, smiling as he drew her into a hug. "I've been wondering when I was going to get to see you again. Culhane talks about you all the time." He grinned at his friend as he gave him a ribbing. She knew Culhane must be squirming in his boots. But she liked hearing that he'd told his good friend about her. "I hear you're a bounty hunter now."

"I'm planning on taking Culhane in, once we have proof of his innocence," she said.

Ford laughed. "I'm betting she can do it, too." Ford looked to him, eyebrow raised, and laughed. "You picked a good one."

"It's a long story, but now we have even more cops after us," he said.

"Then, you best get going." Ford tossed him the keys to a nondescript older-model brown pickup. "Good luck."

"We're going to need it," he said. "Thanks again. Hope this won't get you into hot water with Hitch."

"I can handle Hitch," Ford said, jokingly. "She loves me."

"Who wouldn't?" Culhane said. "Remember, if things go sideways, I stole the truck."

As HE DROVE AWAY, Culhane lost himself in the beauty of the Gallatin Canyon. Some of the trees along the river still had a few golden leaves on them in stark contrast to the dark green of the pines and the snowcapped peaks. He loved fall in Montana, the scents that carried on the cooler breezes, the promise of winter as snow powdered the peaks.

"I like your friend," Alexis said as he reached Highway 191 and turned toward Bozeman.

"Wait until you meet his wife, Hitch." He shot her a look. "She's a lot like you. I think you two will hit it off." He just hoped they got the chance to meet. He saw her look in her side mirror, saw the worry on her face.

"Once we find Jana, then the sheriff will have to resend the BOLO."

When he said nothing, she looked over at him in surprise. "You can't think that he would leave it on you. I know Garwood can be vindictive, but you can't believe..." Alexis said as he drove down the canyon headed north.

"That this is about my wrongful-discharge lawsuit? That he'll do anything to stop me, including using Jana to do it? Alexis, I'm being framed for murder. It's no coincidence that Jana called me, knowing I would come to her if I really thought she was in trouble."

"Maybe she was. Maybe she was killed right before you got there."

He shook his head. "I saw Bobby leaving. I don't believe he killed her. There wasn't enough time for him to get rid of the body from when I called her. She's still alive."

"So Jana set it all up to make it look like you'd killed her?"

"Not without help," Culhane said. "The woman is deceitful, but she couldn't have come up with this plan alone."

"The sheriff? Or someone else?" she asked. "This is extremely risky for Garwood, and it's an election year. He's not stupid." But the sheriff was worried about what Culhane knew about the way he'd been running his department. She said as much.

"Exactly. I think what I found out is only the tip of the iceberg, and that is why he's panicking," Culhane said.

"Let's say you're right," she conceded. "How do we prove it?"

"By finding Jana. If I'd had a chance to talk to the cook in Buckhorn... Or Bobby..." He shook his head. "So far I'm not having much luck. Gene shot Leo before I could talk to him. He also shot Bobby."

"You're telling me you think Gene purposely killed them to keep them quiet?"

He shrugged. "I don't know. Gene had a temper, and both Leo and Bobby were involved in a violent profession. But it seems as if when I get close, a witness dies."

"If you're right, and she's still alive—"

"She's a liability to whoever is behind this."

"So how do we find her?"

Culhane drove in silence for a minute. "I've been thinking about that. It's a long shot, but she might have been so desperate that she'd go to her father. Jack 'Red' Redfield owns a bar between here and Butte."

Alexis seemed to settle in as they turned onto Interstate 90 and headed west.

Culhane reached over and took her hand. This time, she didn't pull away. He squeezed gently, and she smiled at him, squeezing back. He felt his heart lift. They would get through this. He'd die trying to make that happen. He wanted a future with this woman more than he wanted his next breath.

A few minutes later, he looked over, and Alexis was

asleep. He hoped going to Jana's father's bar wasn't a wild-goose chase. But right now, that's all he had for a lead.

In truth, Culhane had no idea what Jana would do or where she would go. He hardly knew the woman before that night at Big Sky. He hadn't seen her in seven years. He hadn't even known that she was back in the area.

But now he couldn't help the guilt he felt for not believing her when she'd told him she was desperate and in danger—not until he'd seen what appeared to be a struggle at her apartment and the blood. Too much blood.

What if he were wrong? What if he were looking for a dead woman?

He thought about the last time he'd seen Jana. She'd sounded desperate enough, but she'd played him before. He'd had no doubt that she would do it again. He liked to think that he wasn't that gullible twentysomething anymore.

"If you don't help me, they'll kill me," she'd cried.

"They?" She'd shaken her head stubbornly in answer. "Stop!" he'd snapped. "Do you ever tell the truth? Would you even recognize it if it bit you in the—"

"I loved you. When we were married. That's why I left. At first, it was the money, I'll admit that bit. But you were so nice, I fell in love with you. I didn't want to hurt you."

He'd laughed. "You lied to get me to marry you for *money*. Do you really think there is anything you can say that I would believe?" She'd looked away, unable to meet his gaze. But he'd seen the answer in those eyes. It still hurt that he'd fallen for her act. Worse, that he'd bought into the whole package. The marriage. The baby. A family to replace the one he'd lost. For a moment he'd let himself believe he could have that with her. He'd wanted to be a father, believing he could be a better one than his own.

"Tell me the truth, Jana. Who have you gotten involved with? Who are you still involved with who's put you up to this? I don't believe you came up with it on your own."

"Because I'm not smart enough?" She'd glared at him, her jaw tightening. "That's what you always think, isn't it? That someone is manipulating me. If it's not my father, then it must be some other man."

He hadn't been able to argue differently. "History says you're in trouble because you've ripped off some man and he isn't taking it as well as I did. You promised me that you signed the annulment papers. That, too, was obviously a lie."

"I thought I did. I swear it. Maybe I forgot to mail them back in."

He'd shaken his head, studying her, seeing the lies on her lips before she even formed the words. "Don't drag me into whatever it is this time. You hear me, Jana? I'll get the marriage annulled without your help. As far as I'm concerned, we never were married." He'd started for the door when she'd called after him.

"You're in love with her, aren't you? Alexis Brand."

He'd been so surprised that he'd stopped to look back at her. "How did you know about—"

"You didn't think I knew?" Jana laughed, enjoying not just his surprise but his concern. He'd never wanted Alexis to know about Jana, about any of it. "Oh, I know all about the two of you."

"Jana—"

"Don't worry. I'm not going to make any trouble for you." Anger reddened her cheeks and fired her eyes to flames. "Does she know about me?" Before he could answer she'd said, "I didn't think so. Shame on you. I would imagine she'll be surprised that she's been dating a married man. Dating is what the two of you have been doing, isn't it?"

He'd taken a step toward her. "If you had signed the annulment papers like you'd promised…" He'd raised both hands in surrender. "I didn't come here to argue. I'll have my lawyer take care of it."

"I'll get a lawyer. I'll sue you."

He'd had his back to her as he'd laughed and slowly turned around. "When you married me, I had nothing. No judge is going to give you access to my family's money, given our marriage was a sham."

"Culhane." Her voice had broken, tears filling her eyes. "Can't you see that I'm desperate? What's fifty thousand dollars to you? I promise not to fight the annulment. You'll never have to see me again. Please."

"Sorry, Jana. I don't believe anything that comes out of your mouth. I suspect fifty thousand with you won't last longer than a snowball in hell. Then you're back at my door threatening me with something else. Like making it look like I'd tried to buy you off with the money. After lying to me about the baby, do you really have the gall to come to me for money?"

She'd wiped at her tears, eyes narrowing as she straightened to her full height. "You'll be sorry if you don't give it to me."

He'd stared at her. "Another threat?"

"I'm trying to protect you, you damned fool."

Culhane had let out a howl. "Do. Not. Involve. Me. Whatever it is, do not drag me into it. I'll get my lawyer to handle this. We're done, Jana. I won't be extorted, and I'm through being used."

"You'll regret this," she'd screamed after him as he'd stormed out. He could hear her shouting at the top of her lungs and breaking things inside the house. As he'd started to get into his pickup, she'd come running out, yelling obscenities.

He'd stopped, surprised to see that her hair was wild, her T-shirt ripped and hanging off one shoulder. Blood dripped down her face from what appeared to be a cut on her forehead. What the hell? Several neighbors had come out. One was making a call on her cell phone, no doubt to the cops. The other was videoing both of them.

Culhane had seen at once what Jana was up to. She was setting him up. But for what? He'd shaken his head as he'd climbed into his pickup and driven off, knowing he'd be getting a visit from the law—and probably a lawyer. This wouldn't be the last of it. Jana was going to make him pay, one way or the other.

It was the last time he saw her. Maybe the last time he would ever see her.

CHAPTER SIXTEEN

VI MULLEN SAT in the back of a squad car in a daze—and it wasn't the first time. She'd lost so much this year. Uniformed men and women scurried about in a flurry of activity. In and out of the café where crime-scene tape fluttered in the wind and blood stained the floor.

She'd finally quit crying and screaming for someone to find her daughter. The female deputy who'd been questioning her had informed her that Tina had been rescued, was in the hospital in the next town with minor injuries, but would soon be released and returned to Buckhorn.

Vi finished answering the deputy's questions feeling empty inside. Tina was going to be fine. Chloe was fine, although with Lars. What had happened here today was over. It would dominate the news for a day or two, and everyone would forget. Hardly anyone even knew where Buckhorn, Montana, was—or cared.

"That will be all for now," the deputy said. "You're free to go home."

Home? The deputy had gotten out to help her from the back of the squad car, making her feel old and weak.

She pulled free of the woman's steadying hands, straightened her back, lifted her chin and reminded herself who she was. Vivian Mullen. She practically owned this town. Buckhorn needed her. She was just fine.

But she wasn't. Even after she got the call from Tina. Her

daughter was alive and well and getting her broken arm in a cast at the hospital. She hadn't felt anything—it was as if the past year had left her unable to feel any emotions at all, except for anger.

"Vi? Are you all right?" Lars asked as he appeared next to her. "If you want, I could walk you home."

She glanced at him and the baby. Not his baby. That much she knew now to be true. Yet seeing him standing there holding her granddaughter, Vi knew she was never going to be able to get rid of Lars Olson. Her daughter had forgiven him for his so-called indiscretions with that slut, Shirley Langer. The two had been humping like rabbits for months, and yet Tina had taken the man back.

Vi thought of her own husband who'd jumped ship the moment he'd found out about her own indiscretions. She hadn't strayed with anyone. She'd only lied to help someone she loved, and Axel couldn't get away from her quick enough.

She sighed. "Did you hear me, Vi?" Lars asked again.

"I heard you. Tina's fine. I'm fine. We're all fine." She stood to her full height and took a deep breath of the warm fall air. Hadn't she heard that the weather was supposed to change? Winter was coming, long months of darkness and cold. The thought made her shudder. "I should get down to the store and see how much of a mess you made down there."

"Vi, you should come home with me and Chloe," Lars said. "I'll make us something to eat."

With a huff, she told Lars what he could do with his suggestion.

"Well, I'm going, and I'm taking Chloe with me." He held the baby closer as if worried that she would try to rip the infant from his arms. Not likely, Vi thought.

"Go, get out of my way. I have work to do." She started down the street.

"Is there anything you want me to tell Tina when I go to pick her up?" he called after her, but Vi didn't bother to answer. As she walked, she looked down the main drag of Buckhorn. The two-lane blacktop cut right through the heart of town.

As she walked toward the center of town and her store, she could smell the promise of snow on the afternoon air. Winter would come swiftly. A few clouds already huddled on the mountaintops to the west.

On the other end of town in front of the motel, Shirley Langer was loading her car as if leaving for good. Maybe something good had come out of this after all, Vi thought and was surprised that she didn't really care anymore.

She surveyed her hometown. Some of the businesses were already boarded up. Most of the snowbirds had left. Soon only the heartiest and most determined of residents would be left in Buckhorn. She worried that Buckhorn would die. Her husband used to joke that they'd be the last ones left and would have to lock up before they, too, departed.

But Vi knew there would be only one way she would leave Buckhorn. It would be in a coffin. The thought actually cheered her. She would die here. The thought didn't bother her in the least. She had to die somewhere. Why not here?

Before she left though, she would make her mark on this town whether people liked it or not.

ALEXIS WOKE AS the pickup tires kicked up gravel. She sat up, surprised that she'd fallen asleep. But then again, she hadn't had much sleep the night before. Culhane's late-night visit seemed like days ago. Now it was late afternoon, the day already feeling incredibly long. Night came quickly this time of year in Montana, and so did the cold.

Culhane drove through the gravel parking lot and pulled into a spot in front of Red's Bar between a motorcycle and a truck with a four-wheeler and a blue heeler in the back. The dog growled at them as they climbed out and walked toward the front door. Alexis stepped over some smashed beer cans dumped on the sidewalk and shot him a look.

"Red's is an acquired taste, I'm told. So is its owner, Jack Redfield. I should probably warn you about him," he said, but she shook her head.

"Don't worry about me." She could see that Culhane was anxious. "When was the last time you were here?"

"Jana and I stopped by to tell her father that we were getting married. He bought us a beer and wished us luck. She asked him if he wanted to pay for a wedding. He laughed."

"I see," she said, and he opened the door for her to step inside.

As Culhane pushed open the door, a large redheaded man looked up from where he was wiping down the bar. He froze for a moment before he went back to what he was doing as they approached.

Jack stood well over six feet with a barrel-shaped body and large hairy arms. He wore a filthy tank undershirt exposing his numerous tattoos. Both hands, Alexis saw, were badly scarred. That and the odd angle of his nose told her he was a brawler. No doubt some of the fights had taken place right here in this very bar.

"Remember me?" Culhane asked, even though Alexis had already seen the recognition in the man's eyes before the shutters had come down.

"You look vaguely familiar," Jack said with a sneer. "Aren't you wanted for the murder of my daughter?"

"Who says she's dead?"

The man laughed. "The cops."

"You've never believed anything they had to say. Why start now?"

Jack leaned his elbows on the bar. "You come here to give me shit? Because I only take that from paying customers."

Culhane reached into his pocket and tossed a twenty on the bar. The bill disappeared like magic under Jack's big hand. "Two beers?" Culhane looked at her when he asked, and she nodded.

"Bud Light?" Jack inquired in a mocking tone.

"I'll take a Moose Drool," Alexis said as she climbed up onto a stool.

The man's gaze swung to her as if he hadn't noticed her before. His eyes narrowed as his lips turned up in what could have been a snarl or a smile.

"I'll take the same," Culhane said and joined her on an adjacent stool. Neither spoke as they watched Jack pull two bottles of Moose Drool from the cooler, uncap them and place the bottles on napkins in front of them formally as if he were serving royalty. "You don't seem very concerned about your daughter."

Jack shrugged. "I'm concerned about all three of my daughters."

"Are the other two also missing and believed murdered?" Alexis asked, and this time Jack's lip curl was most definitely a snarl.

"Not that I know of," he said before shifting his gaze back to Culhane. "Jana's thirty years old. I no longer change her diapers or get her out of jail. She's on her own."

Culhane nodded. "Which tells me you suspect the same thing I do."

"And what is that?"

"That she faked her death to either get out of the trouble she's in or to frame me. Maybe both."

Jack lifted one bushy red brow. "Sounds like you're screwed either way. Otherwise, you wouldn't be here."

"Where is she?"

Jack crossed his bulky arms to meet Culhane's gaze. "What makes you think I've seen her?"

"Because she's your blood. She's in big trouble. She needs money. She came to me. She'd come to you next—if she hadn't already. Did you give her money?"

Jack laughed and wagged his big head. "Like I said, she's not my responsibility anymore. If she came by here...well, I would have told her to ask her husband. Aren't you still married to my daughter?"

"Funny you should ask. She promised to mail in the annulment papers after she signed them. But the fact that you know she didn't means she's been here. She mention why she's on the run? I'm pretty sure she isn't just running from snitching on her partners in crime. I think there's someone in law enforcement who doesn't want her to ever surface. If I'm right, she's involved with even worse people than she was before. I think she's realized that and is hiding out. If you know where she is—"

"I don't. But then again, I wouldn't tell you if I did."

Culhane swore under his breath and looked away.

"Even to save her life?" Alexis demanded.

"I'm sorry, who are you?" Jack snapped, swinging his gaze to her.

"Alexis Brand. I'm a former sheriff's deputy—"

"Turned bounty hunter," Jack finished for her.

"Only recently. Jana tell you that, too?" Culhane asked. Jack grunted again.

"So Jana fakes her death. Maybe her idea, maybe someone else's. But the problem is the sheriff missed his chance to arrest me last night. Now he knows that I'm looking for Jana to prove I didn't kill her. He has to find her first and make sure she stays dead."

"What did you do to piss off the sheriff?" Jack asked.

"I filed a wrongful-discharge suit against him and the department. He doesn't want what I know about him and his department coming out."

Jack rubbed a ham-sized hand over his face for a moment. "Jana's smart. She can take care of herself."

"Not this time, Jack. I suspect this time, she's in over her head."

Jack scoffed. "Won't be the first time. Or the last. That one attracts trouble. Drink your beer and get on with your business, or I'll call the cops." He moved to busy himself partway down the bar, his back to them.

ALEXIS MET CULHANE'S gaze for a moment, then excused herself. Sliding off the stool, she called down the bar "Restrooms down this way?"

"That big sign over the opening to the hallway wasn't plain enough for you?" Jack asked, not bothering to look at her.

As she started down the hall, she listened to make sure she hadn't been followed. Culhane struck up an argument with Jack as she slipped into the open doorway of what she saw was the bar's office.

She hurried to the desk, having no idea what she was looking for or how much time she would have to search. The top of the desk was a half-foot deep in bills, junk mail and liquor-order receipts. She quickly sifted through the pile, pretty sure Jack wouldn't remember exactly where each item lay.

Seeing nothing of interest, she tried the drawers. Most held the usual office-desk items. It wasn't until she tried the bottom drawer that she found it locked.

Culhane was still arguing with Jack. She just hoped that the bar owner didn't suddenly realize how long she'd been gone and come looking for her.

Grabbing a paperclip she began to pick the lock. It took her longer than she'd hoped, but she finally picked it. Opening the drawer, she saw it held a series of file folders. Most had to do with the bar business.

Disappointed and about to give up, she spotted a folder at the back titled Letters. She pulled it out quickly, opened the folder and felt her pulse leap as she saw the top letter was from Jana to her father from seven years ago. Quickly, she opened the envelope to find a letter written on Lost Sunset Ranch stationery. She quickly pulled out her phone and took a photo before looking for more letters from Jana. She found none, but she did discover some receipts for payments to Lost Sunset Ranch. Hurriedly photographing them, she quickly put everything back in the folder.

Jack's voice boomed down the hallway. Hurriedly, she pocketed her phone and stuffed the folder in the back before closing the drawer. She could hear Jack approaching with heavy, angry footfalls. There wasn't time to exit the office and get to the ladies' room. She had only one choice since either way she would probably get caught.

She ducked down into the space under the desk as she heard him stop in the office doorway. He stood there so long she feared he knew where she was hiding and was just waiting for her to come out. She hadn't realized that she was holding her breath until she heard him let out a curse and stomp on down the hall, headed for the ladies' restroom.

At the sound of the bathroom door banging open and the boom of his voice as he called "You in there?" she slipped out from under the desk and hurried to the door. She heard him step in to check the stalls and made her move, rushing back to the bar. Instead of going to her stool, she went to the jukebox in the dark corner near the small dance floor. She was looking through the songs when she heard him come storming back into the room.

"What the hell?" he demanded. "Where have you been?"

Alexis turned, giving him her most innocent look. "I went to the bathroom and didn't want to interrupt the two of you, so I was looking to see what songs you had on your jukebox."

Jack frowned, his naturally red face growing redder. "I didn't see you come out of the bathroom."

"Sorry," she said. "Culhane, I found a song I like, but I don't have any change."

"I'm afraid we don't have time to hear it," he said as he grabbed up a pen and cocktail napkin lying on the bar. "Here's my cell-phone number, Jack. Have Jana call me. It could save her life." He shoved it in the man's direction, but the bar owner didn't move.

"If you care anything about your daughter…" Alexis said as she joined Culhane at the bar.

Jack looked at her, his gaze hard as a slap. "This from the woman who's sleeping with my daughter's…husband?"

"Jack." From Culhane the warning in his voice was more than a threat. "We came here because we're worried about Jana. You should be worried as well. Alexis and I can help her."

The bar owner scoffed at that, picked up the napkin and crushed it in his big palm. "Get out. Don't come back."

"You'll only have yourself to blame when she's dead," Culhane said, and the two of them walked out.

It wasn't until they were in the pickup and had driven away that he asked, "Find anything of interest?"

She thought about the papers she'd photographed. "Have you ever heard of Lost Sunset Ranch?"

He frowned. "It's some offbeat, pseudoreligious group that says it's a safe haven for troubled young women. I've had to go out there a couple of times when I was a deputy in that county to do welfare checks on the women."

"Did you know Jana went there seven years ago?"

Culhane stared at her a few moments too long. A horn honked, and he jerked the wheel, sending the pickup careening back into the right lane. "That's where she went?"

Alexis could tell that he was shocked by this news.

"Why would she go there?"

"I don't know, but it cost Jack a pretty penny. She stayed for seven months."

CULHANE FELT AS if he'd been hit upside the head with a baseball bat. He shook his head, trying to clear his whirling thoughts. Jana spent seven months at the ranch with a cult out there? It made no sense.

But then, knowing Jana, nothing she did should surprise him. She'd thought by marrying him she would have money. Once she realized that wasn't going to happen, she'd pretended she'd lost the baby and left. But why would she go to a place like Lost Sunset Ranch?

"You might want to see this," Alexis said. "But I suggest you pull over first." He did and she handed him her phone.

He read the letter from Jana to her father, recognizing her handwriting.

"I'm fine. I know what I'm doing. Don't worry about me and don't tell anyone where I am—especially Culhane."

He shook his head as he handed back the phone and pulled back onto the highway. "This makes no sense."

"She was apparently troubled," Alexis said. "Do you think she'd go back there?"

Culhane didn't know what to think. He couldn't see Jana at the ranch unless she was involved in some kind of scam. But there was only one way to find out.

The driver behind them laid on his horn as Culhane swung into the passing lane. He ignored the driver as he turned left at the light and headed toward the Lost Sunset Ranch.

THE SHERIFF WAS in his office when his deputy Furu came in and closed the door. Willy swore, seeing the deputy's expression. "What now?"

"Leo Vernon. The parolee who worked as a cook in Buckhorn, Montana? He's dead in that café shoot-out."

He'd thought it was going to be bad news. "That saves me having him arrested."

"Same for Bobby Braden. Also deceased."

"Sounds like my lucky day." He was growing impatient. "I already heard about all of this. The bank robbery in Idaho, the disturbance at the café and the men being found dead down the road."

Furu waited. "Why was Culhane there in the first place? Coincidence that he just happened to be in the café where Leo worked and then Bobby ends up there, too?"

"How should I know? So somehow Culhane knew that

Leo and Bobby were involved with Jana." Willy couldn't believe that Jana would have told him.

"What if Culhane knows now? He could have spoken with either Leo or Bobby before they died. Culhane and Alexis left both scenes before law enforcement arrived."

The sheriff felt as if his head might explode. "We have to assume that Culhane knows that Jana is alive. He's probably looking for her. We have any idea where he is?"

Furu shook his head.

"I can't believe someone hasn't picked him up," the sheriff said as he swore and rubbed the back of his neck. Culhane was determined to bring him down. If he found Jana… "You know what has to be done." He looked up to meet Furu's gaze. He could see that it was a line the deputy wasn't comfortable stepping over. "First, Jana. Find her, and have Cline keep her on ice until I get there."

"She hasn't been easy to find. She's streetwise and running scared."

"You sure she isn't already dead?" the sheriff asked. "I saw the report that just came across my desk. Sounds like there was a lot of blood. Maybe Culhane killed her." He wanted Furu to agree with him, but the man shook his head.

"She wants us to believe she's dead," Furu said. "She's out there, and if anyone can find her, it's Culhane."

"I don't want to hear that," the sheriff said, shooting to his feet and sending his chair flying. "You're better than Culhane. Find that bitch. And then get me Culhane, dead or alive. Preferably dead. Same with his new girlfriend." When Furu raised a brow, he added, "She should be more careful of the company she keeps."

CHAPTER SEVENTEEN

DARK SHADOWS HUNKERED under the pines as they neared
Lost Sunset Ranch. Culhane felt the temperature outside
the pickup dropping as nightfall came on quickly. He still
couldn't believe Jana had spent seven months at this place.
Maybe she'd only told her father that she was staying here
and taken the money.

"Is that a guard booth?" Alexis asked as they neared the
gate. "This place has better security than the White House."

The closer they got, Culhane could see why she was surprised and suspicious. Two armed men stepped from the
booth and blocked the already-gated entry into the com-
pound.

"They need this kind of security?" she asked.

"My thought exactly, the first time I came out here.
There is definitely something off about this whole place."
The times he'd come out to do sheriff's department welfare checks at Lost Sunset Ranch with its cultlike following of young women had creeped him out. Something was
off about all of it.

The general feeling was that the Reverend Jerome Franklin was either a saint to help these young women or a dirty
old man. Culhane hadn't seen anything illegal going on during his previous visits. He and another deputy had found
the young women in question, talked to them, asked them
to call home and left. Because the women were over eigh-

teen, there wasn't anything they could do. With churches, even ones as sketchy as this one, the law tended to keep hands-off.

But Culhane had picked up on something at the ranch that left him feeling uneasy and concerned about the young women he'd seen living out there. Hearing that Jana had come here made him all the more suspicious.

He pulled up to the guards, both holding assault rifles.

He whirred down his window. "I'm here to see Jerome."

"Do you have an appointment with the Reverend Franklin?" the guard asked, bristling at his use of the man's first name.

"Tell him it's about Jana Redfield Travis. I'm her husband, and I'm not leaving until I see him." He didn't add that he was going in there one way or the other.

One of the guards remained in front of the pickup while the other went inside the booth.

"If Jana is here," Alexis said, "at least she's safe, right?"

Culhane said nothing as he watched the man in the booth turn his back to them to pick up the phone. A few minutes later, the man hung up, stepped out and signaled the other guard to let them pass, and the gate opened.

As they drove, dense pines lined the narrow paved road. Several more guards appeared from out of the trees. Ahead he could see women and children, all wearing bonnets and long full dresses as if this were the 1800s.

But it was the way the women and children looked at them as they drove in, the suspicion and fear as they hurried away, that raised red flags.

"I have goose bumps," Alexis said. "Who are these people, and what is going on out here?"

Culhane shook his head. "I would imagine the young women are lost souls. I suspect Jerome preys on them in

some way. Maybe just financially. You said it was costly
to stay here?"

"Very. Especially for seven months."

"From what I understand, they're also required to work."
As they came around a curve in the road and the pines
opened, the massive rock-and-log structures that made up
the ranch complex appeared. "But someone's picking up
the bill for this place. Jerome was a former hippie with no
visible means of support before he found his *calling.*"

Having been here before, Culhane wasn't surprised by
the staff that came out to escort them to Jerome. They all
wore one-piece tan jumpsuits and slack expressions.

"We'll take you to the Reverend Franklin," one of the
staff said in a monotone.

"Don't bother. I know where to find him," Culhane said,
striding off in the direction of the man's office.

"They're like zombies," Alexis whispered, forced to trot
alongside him to keep up as he left the staff behind. She
hugged herself, feeling an uneasy chill.

Culhane stormed into the reverend's office, Alexis at
his heels. He told himself not to lose his temper, but everything about this place, this man and this situation had him
fuming. As he looked at the man behind the huge desk, he
wanted to grab him by his throat and shake the information he needed out of him. As if sensing his growing anger
and frustration, Alexis laid a hand on his arm.

ALEXIS HADN'T KNOWN what to expect—but certainly not the
man in front of her. The Reverend Jerome Franklin had a
shock of white hair that stood on end as if he'd been rak-
ing his fingers through it.

As they burst in, he looked up with mild amusement
rather than concern. Which seemed strange, given all the

security she'd seen. He settled his startling blue eyes on the two of them and smiled.

"Hello." As he rose to his feet, he looked younger than his white hair suggested. "Welcome to Lost Sunset Ranch. I'm sorry you had trouble at the gate. We have to be careful who we allow in for the protection of the young women here." The man's voice was calming, almost hypnotic, but it didn't seem to be having a soothing effect on Culhane.

"Right," Culhane said. "A *sanctuary* for young women."

"Would you like to sit down? I could have my assistant bring you a cup of coffee, tea or—"

"We won't be staying that long," Culhane interrupted. "We want to see Jana Redfield Travis."

Alexis suspected it wasn't going to be that easy, even though the reverend didn't seem in the least ruffled.

"The name doesn't ring a bell," the man said as he lowered himself back into his chair behind his desk. "But I'll check to see if she's with us." He picked up his phone and asked his assistant to check to see if they had a follower by that name. "It should take just a moment," he told Culhane as he hung up the phone and gave them his disarming smile.

Culhane refused to sit and began to pace as they waited. Jerome turned the full force of his attention on Alexis, making her feel as if she were in a bright warm spotlight. His blue-eyed gaze was so intense it was almost spellbinding.

"I know the former sheriff's deputy, but I don't believe we've met," he said.

"Alexis Brand, also former sheriff's deputy, now bounty hunter."

Jerome clasped his hands together as if in prayer and smiled broadly. "Bounty hunter, how wonderful! What an interesting profession."

His phone rang. He excused himself and picked up. "Yes, thank you so much." He hung up and said, "I'm sorry, but Jana isn't staying with us at the moment."

"But she was here seven years ago," Culhane said.

"I'm afraid that isn't public information, but I will tell you that she has been a guest of ours."

"*Guest*. Her father paid you for her to stay here seven months."

"Possibly. I would have to look at her file, but that sounds about right."

"What was she doing here?" Culhane demanded.

"What most of the women do who come here," Jerome said. "They rest, they rejuvenate, they contemplate their lives and heal." He turned those eyes on Alexis again. "I wish we had more time. I'd love to hear about this bounty-hunter business you've just started. Can I assume you're taking in Mr. Travis here? I understand he's wanted for questioning in Jana's murder. But then, I believe you, too, Ms. Brand, are now wanted for questioning as well, in another incident. Such exciting lives you two lead."

Culhane advanced on the desk like a mountain lion about to disassemble its prey. "You didn't call for her file, did you?" He swore. She could see that he was estimating how long it would take the law to get here. He swung away from the desk. "Come on," he said, and they headed for the door.

"We can't get out of here," she said as they jumped into the pickup and he started the engine. "You know those guards have been told to detain you."

"We're not going out the front." He revved the engine and backed up, heading in the opposite direction they'd come in. He took what looked like a service road, tires

squealing on the pavement before the road turned to dirt
and wound through the pines.

Alexis had to hang on as he took one curve after another. Ahead in the pickup's headlights, she could see an
electronic gate blocking the road. It wasn't as fortified as
the front gate, but still…

Culhane tromped on the gas. "Hang on," he said. "I'm
going to have to buy Ford a new pickup."

But right before they reached the gate, it slid open. They
raced through and up onto a two-lane highway. As he made
the turn, a piece of paper fluttered to the passenger-side
floorboard. Alexis reached for it, just as she heard Culhane curse.

Sitting up she followed his gaze and saw the flashing
lights before she heard the siren.

"They're looking for a man and a woman," Culhane said
as he pulled off his Stetson. "Get down."

She quickly lay over in the seat and, taking his hat and
holding it close, held her breath. The hat smelled like Culhane. She breathed it in and closed her eyes. This might be
the end. No way could they outrun a cruiser in this pickup.
The sound of the siren was deafening as the cab filled with
the glow of the patrol's headlight. She could imagine the
officer behind the wheel studying the back of Culhane's
head. Then the siren screamed on past.

She stayed down, waiting until the wail was lost in the
darkness of evening. It wasn't be the first cruiser they'd
seen nor the last, she thought. They were both wanted by
the law now. She'd left the scene of a crime and was on
the run, aiding and abetting a suspected killer. Her parents would be so proud, she thought grimly and wondered
how long before they heard that their daughter was now a
wanted woman.

Alexis leaned over to pick up the scrap of paper that had fluttered to the floor. As she unfolded it, she read what had been hurriedly scrawled on it. She showed it to Culhane. "Appears you have a friend at Lost Sunset Ranch."

CULHANE READ THE short note. *I can help you. April.* Followed by a phone number. He looked over at Alexis. "April was one of the young women we checked on one of the other times I went to the ranch. I wondered at the time why someone who seemed to have it all together like she did was living there."

"You think she's working undercover?" she asked.

He feared that might be the case. She hadn't seemed like the others he'd come across out there. She hadn't seemed lost. She'd seemed smart, observant, capable. He just hoped she knew what she was doing.

After putting some distance between them and the ranch, Culhane took a back road south, then pulled onto the shoulder and made the call.

"You're looking for Jana, right?" April asked on the fifth ring. He got the impression that she hadn't picked up until she was in a safe place away from the others. He was surprised that she had a cell phone. He thought that was something they weren't allowed to have.

"Yes. Is she staying there again?"

"No. But I'll call you back. It might be late."

"That's fine." He disconnected. "April's checking her file. In the meantime, I'm beat. Let's get a motel for the night." He could see he wasn't going to get an argument out of Alexis. Even with her earlier nap, she looked as tired as he felt.

"I can't believe Jerome called the cops on you even as he gave us that smile and offered us coffee and made small talk," Alexis said. He could hear her getting madder by the moment.

"He got to you, didn't he?" he asked with a laugh. His own temper had cooled. He'd expected as much from Jerome. Also, not much surprised him anymore since he'd become so cynical.

Like Alexis, he'd gone into law enforcement because he believed in justice, and look how that had turned out. He'd found himself working for a crooked sheriff and a couple of dirty deputies.

"Jerome with his smooth talk had you believing that he's this caring, loving father figure to those people at the ranch. Maybe he's for real and was just doing his duty back there. Or maybe he's a fraud."

"Do not give me your life-isn't-fair look," she snapped. "I'd just like to see more justice meted out on earth, thank you."

He smiled. "Which is how you ended up in law enforcement."

"What's your excuse?" she demanded, but he could see that she was starting to calm down.

"I guess you and I have that in common," he said and grinned over at her. "Among other things."

She shook her head at him even as she felt her cheeks heat. The look in his eyes was a tantalizing reminder of his touch on her naked skin. She swallowed and said, "I think we need to establish some ground rules. For the next forty-eight hours, I try to help you clear your name. That's it."

"Why forty-eight hours?" he asked, even though he could guess.

"I figure if we get lucky, we have forty-eight hours before some trigger-happy lawman finds us. I plan to take you in before you get us both killed."

"I'm glad you brought that up," he said. "How about this? I drop you off in Bozeman. You tell the sheriff I held you at gunpoint and made you leave Buckhorn with me." He hurried on before she could object. "I promise to turn myself in forty-eight hours from now."

"Not a chance."

"Alex—"

"You also don't get to call me Alex."

He looked over at her as he pulled back onto the highway and headed toward Bozeman. His grin was all sexy-cowboy Culhane—just like the look in his eyes.

"And you don't get to look at me like that. This is a business arrangement. Nothing more, since you're a married man."

He scoffed at that. "If that's the way you want it." He drove for a few moments before he said, "By the way, you've been amazing. I'm still surprised we got out of the café alive."

She didn't look at him, couldn't right then. She'd been terrified that Gene was going to kill him. All the hours she'd spent denying her feelings for this cowboy had gone up in a puff of smoke. The thought of him dying...

"You were pretty amazing yourself." She looked out the side window, knowing that one look at him and she'd be melting into his arms. They weren't out of the woods. Far from it. Every lawman in the state would be looking for them. Forty-eight hours. She had little hope they could find Jana in that amount of time, but she was willing to risk her life trying.

She was also no fool, she thought as she glanced over at him. He'd try to ditch her the first chance he got. She would have to keep on her toes. But the real danger was letting that grin of his get to her. He knew exactly how to charm her. If she made the mistake of letting him into her bed again…

"We've got a tail," Culhane said and hit the gas.

CHAPTER EIGHTEEN

THE DARK-COLORED SUV had appeared out of nowhere. Now it sped up, just as Culhane had done. He considered leading the SUV into the foothills and trapping the driver in a spot where they could have a conversation but discarded the idea immediately. He couldn't take the chance that a confrontation could turn violent since he had no idea who was tailing them.

Right now it could be anyone from dirty deputies or Jack's friends to guards from the ranch or even friends of Jana's. Everyone was looking for them—just as they were looking for Jana and the truth. Culhane wondered how many were set on keeping them from finding both.

"Hang on."

He knew this road. Not far down it, the Jefferson, Madison and Gallatin Rivers came together to make the mighty Missouri. Dust rose behind them even as clouds gathered on the horizon with the promise of a snowstorm. Winter was coming late this year.

He came around a corner and hit his brakes hard. The pickup fishtailed as he took a narrow dirt road that left the river and climbed up into the foothills. Fifty yards later, he took another one, this one doubling back toward the valley and Bozeman.

A few more back roads and even one section that was more of a trail than a road, and they dropped down through the Horseshoe Hills. Lights winked on across the Gallatin Valley as a cloak of darkness fell around them.

When he looked back again, there was no one following them. Alexis hadn't said a word the whole time. He glanced over at her now and felt that tug at his heartstrings like he had from the first time he saw her. There was something so calm, so confident, so solid in her.

He figured it was the way she was raised. Her parents had encouraged her to be anything she wanted to be, even though they'd worried about her being a sheriff's deputy and now a bounty hunter. However, they'd never stood in her way. That's probably why he'd fallen in love with her parents the first time he'd met them—and was in awe of what a normal family looked like.

He'd taken a long time before he'd even asked Alexis out. Even after that he'd been hesitant, fearing the woman had no idea what she was getting herself into. He carried the scars of his childhood. She knew that, but he doubted she knew how deep they ran.

Culhane drove a few minutes, feeling the weight of the silence between them. "You haven't asked me if I did it."

Alexis frowned over at him. "Did what?"

He mugged a face at her. "Killed Jana."

Her eyes widened. "You didn't."

"What makes you so sure?"

"Are we really having this conversation?" She looked away. "Because I know you."

"Do you?"

She let out a sigh and turned back to him. "You're a good man, Culhane."

He chuckled at that, but it held no humor. "I hope you always feel that way." He saw that his words unsettled her. "I have a lot more baggage than I let on."

"Clearly," she agreed. "Is there something else I should know?"

He studied her, not sure what he wanted to say or if he even did want to talk about it. His cell phone rang, saving him. They were on the outskirts of Bozeman. He saw it was his father's attorney and declined the call.

As he rubbed the back of his neck, he realized how tired he was. Talk about a long day. "Let's just find a place for the night." When she didn't comment, he looked over at her. She seemed to be lost in thought. "Are you all right?"

She shook herself out of her thoughts and smiled. "I'm fine. But you're right, it's getting late. I'm tired and hungry. Maybe we could use a drive-through?"

"Sounds good," he said and looked for a motel off the beaten path.

THEY'D NEVER BEEN to a motel together before. Most of the time they'd known each other, they'd been working a variety of shifts. When they were able to get the same shifts in summer, they went camping and slept in a tent.

It seemed strange and almost unseemly for them to be getting a motel room together. Culhane had been married only on paper, but according to the law…

"I can get the rooms," Alexis said as he pulled up to the office.

"Rooms?"

She shot him a look. "Aren't you still married?"

He rolled his eyes. "I don't feel like I've ever been married. Jana and I…" He shook his head. "She was pretending to have morning sickness the few weeks we were together. Basically, the marriage—if you want to call it that—was never consummated."

"Are you telling me that you only slept with her the one time?"

He looked embarrassed. "See why I don't tell anyone about it? You must think me a fool."

She shook her head. "I think you're a nice guy who was trying to do the right thing."

"Yeah, and look where it got me. It would appear that Jana is in on setting me up for murder. Not to mention this latest with whatever she was doing at that ranch."

"We'll get it sorted out," Alexis assured him. "I'll be right back."

A few minutes later she walked by the front of the pickup holding up a single key. Getting two rooms felt silly given that she was already pregnant. Also, she wanted to keep Culhane close for a number of reasons. She didn't want to be alone tonight, either. She heard him open the pickup door and come after her.

"I need a hot shower," she said as she opened the door to the room and stepped inside. She saw that he'd brought the overnight bag she'd grabbed from her vehicle before they left Buckhorn. She met his gaze as she took it. "Are you going to be here when I come back out?"

"I promise I'll be here. You're right, I need you." He smiled, those blue eyes warming like a tropical sea washing over her. "There is no doubt about that."

His words sent a frisson of pleasure to her center. Last night on the run, look where he'd gone. Straight to her. How could she think that she didn't know this man? Because sometimes even lovers kept secrets from each other. She thought of her own secret and had to look away. Culhane was no fool. If they ended up making love in that queen-size bed, he'd know. He knew every inch of her body. He would notice that her breasts were bigger. He would see the changes in her hips, in the soft roundness of her belly. He would see it in her eyes. She couldn't hide the truth much longer—if he hadn't already noticed last night even in the darkness.

In the intimacy of the motel room, she thought about telling him. But she reminded herself that it would change everything. He'd be distracted and even more worried about her. If he knew about the baby, he'd want to protect her even more than he did now.

"If you need company in the shower…" His grin widened.

She shook her head and, entering the bathroom, closed the door behind her. For a moment she stood, trying to catch her breath. Being here with him made her heart race. So much had happened. So much more could. It left her even more off balance than she'd been lately.

"You all right in there?" Culhane called.

"Fine," she called back and turned on the shower before beginning to strip down. Having shed her clothing, she stood in front of the full-length mirror. Her body was changing, there was no denying that. Her breasts were tender and larger. She placed her hand on her usually flat stomach and felt the slight bump. It wouldn't be long and she would be showing.

She thought about what Jana had done to Culhane. She never wanted to put him or herself in that position. Last night when he'd used his key to let himself into her apartment and climbed into her bed, he apparently hadn't noticed the changes to her body. Or at least he hadn't said anything. But how long could she keep this from him? How long did she want to?

Stepping into the shower, she let the water run over her. Alexis knew exactly when she'd gotten pregnant. The one time they hadn't used contraception. They'd gotten carried away, and at the time it had seemed so natural that neither of them had stopped to consider the chance they were taking.

She heard the bathroom door open and close, and a moment later, the shower curtain was drawn aside.

"Say the word, and I'll go back to the ballgame on TV in the other room."

She looked over her shoulder at him, saying nothing, yearning for his arms around her. He stripped and stepped in. Pressing his naked body into the back of hers, he held her as if needing this as much as she did.

They stood like that under the spray for a long time, the warm water showering over them as they were locked together against the coming storm.

"I love you," he whispered next to her ear. He gently pushed aside a lock of her wet hair from her ear and repeated, "I love you."

She squeezed her eyes shut, surprised by the burn of tears beneath her lids. She had longed to hear those words. "I love you, too." The words came out in a hoarse whisper while her brain cried, *Why now? Why say them now?* Because he thought one or both of them was going to die?

He turned her to face him and kissed her. It felt like kissing in the rain. She pressed her body against his, feeling his desire, feeling her own, as the warm water cascaded over them.

The water suddenly turned cold. Culhane quickly turned it off and hurried to get them towels. The bathroom at the motel was so small that there really wasn't room for both of them, so he stepped out into the bedroom to finish drying off.

She was glad of that as she let the door close. Her nausea was more intermittent through the day than just in the morning. She quickly locked the door and turned on the faucet at the sink as if brushing her teeth before heaving into the toilet and hoping he wouldn't hear. After she'd emptied her stomach, she brushed her teeth before wrapping a towel around her, unlocking the door and stepping out.

Culhane was waiting for her, looking worried. He'd wrapped his towel around his waist, his broad muscled chest still glistening with water. "Alex." She stepped past him to reach for her bag with a change of clothes in it.

He came up behind her, put his big hands on her shoulders and slowly turned her to face him. She couldn't look this beautiful caring man in the eye, knowing what she was keeping from him. He lifted her chin with a finger until their gazes met. "Anything you want to tell me?" His gaze pierced her straight to her heart.

She brushed her wet hair back, straightening her shoulders. He had every right to know. She ached to tell him. But that was before she'd found out about Jana and how she'd trapped him into marriage.

Culhane would do the right thing. He'd proven that. But she wanted more for herself and her child. "Just an upset stomach, that's all. I think it was that fast food we got on the way here." She held his gaze, hating herself for lying to him.

CULHANE'S PHONE RANG. He glanced at Alexis, then at his phone. He didn't want to leave things where they were. It rang again.

"It's probably April," she said and turned away to dig in her overnight bag.

He sighed, not wanting to end the conversation with her, but anxious in case it was April calling back. It was. He quickly picked up. "Hello."

"I have the information on Jana Redfield Travis. She was

here just short of seven years ago. She stayed in the maternity wing. Until the baby was born and adopted."

"*Baby?* No, she wasn't—" He caught his breath. "She was pregnant? You're sure?"

"She had a son."

The words ricocheted off him like rubber bullets, leaving only the pain. "She had a son?" His thoughts swirled around in his head. He could have a six-year-old son. A son he never knew about.

Jana had lied to him on so many levels, and yet he'd never hated her. Until now. If she really had his son and gave him up for adoption… A son he hadn't gotten to see grow up? A son who didn't know he was alive? He swallowed the lump in this throat.

He told himself there had to be a mistake. Not even Jana was that cruel. Nor did it make any sense. Why lie about losing the baby? Why take off to go to the ranch rather than stay with him? She had to have known he would have welcomed the baby. A son. Jana could have used the baby as leverage to get anything she wanted. His father would have probably even come around—after a simple paternity test proved the boy was Culhane's.

So why had she left? Why had she lied? He tried to imagine Jana as a mother. It was a frightening thought, since she'd been raised by Jack who hadn't shown any sign of being a role model.

"The baby was born full-term and healthy on March 9. The adoption records are sealed and not kept here on the ranch so I can't help you with that."

"Thank you," he said as he did the math in his head. "Please be careful." He hung up and felt his heart drop. *The baby couldn't have been his.* That's why Jana hadn't stayed. She'd known he would count the months and know the truth.

For just a few minutes, he'd had a son.

"Culhane? Are you all right?" Alexis asked and got to her feet to come to him.

"Jana was at the ranch to have a baby and give it up for adoption." He shook his head and quickly added, "It wasn't mine."

He slowly pocketed the phone, still in shock. He'd done the math again in his head. There was no mistake. "Jana had the baby on March 9." A wave of conflicting emotions rolled through him. "He couldn't have been mine." He found himself battling both disappointment and relief. Relief because he hadn't missed more than six years of his child's life. Disappointment because no child of his had existed.

Alexis quickly stepped to him, putting her arms around him. She pulled him close, and he closed his eyes, feeling an ache in his chest. For a few moments, he'd had a son. He hadn't realized how much he'd wanted it to be true.

"Let's go to bed," she said. Crawling into bed in the nightshirt she'd brought with her, she picked up the remote and began to flip through the stations. The game he'd been watching was over, not that he would have been able to concentrate on the score now, anyway.

"My favorite Christmas movie is starting," she said, looking over at him as he pulled on a pair of briefs and climbed in beside her, sex no longer at the forefront of his thoughts.

"*It's a Wonderful Life?*" he said. "I don't think I've ever seen it."

"*Seriously?*" She was looking at him as if he'd grown

three heads. "How is that possible? Didn't you ever watch Christmas movies over the holidays? I would think your mother—"

THE MINUTE THE words were out of her mouth, she realized her mistake. "I'm sorry. I just thought—"

"That I would have seen it with my mother?" He shook his head. "We spent more time in the kitchen around Christmas. My mother loved to bake and decorate holiday cakes and cookies. We often had a lot of friends over during the holidays. It was always busy at the ranch."

She couldn't imagine what it must have been like for him to lose his mother and then the ranch and his father, too. The movie began. Culhane put an arm around her, and they snuggled together. She had seen the movie dozens of times but never tired of it.

Except her mind kept wandering back to waking to the bad news, Buckhorn, the café, the brush with death and the news about Jana and the baby. Mostly she kept coming back to Culhane's reaction to Jana's baby not being his. He'd looked more than disappointed; he'd looked heartbroken. She told herself that she'd misunderstood since he'd been clear about not wanting children.

She was completely distracted by her thoughts and not paying attention to the movie at all. What if they didn't find Jana? What if the law caught up to them? Christmas was nearing. Her mother had left a message asking about their plans. It would be her first Christmas with Culhane. They'd planned to spend at least part of it with her parents. She needed to call them. By now they would have heard the news about Alexis being wanted by the law. She doubted she would be able to sleep a wink.

CULHANE WATCHED THE movie credits roll. Alexis was right. It was a great movie. He felt a little choked up, not that he would admit it. He glanced over to find her sound asleep. When had she drifted off?

He smiled to himself. He'd been so content with her head resting against his shoulder, his arm around her, he hadn't noticed that she hadn't been watching the movie with him.

Carefully, he turned off the television and the lamp beside the bed, not wanting to disturb her. He loved watching her sleep. She looked so peaceful. So beautiful. Like someone without a care in the world.

Maybe before she'd gotten involved with him that was true. But not anymore. He'd pulled her into his orbit and his mess. She sighed in her sleep and turned to spoon against him. He thought about how her body had changed. He hadn't seen that with Jana because she hadn't let him get close to her.

But with Alexis, he knew that body better than his own. He'd warned her when they'd first started dating that he didn't do marriage or babies. It had been a stupid thing to tell her, but the memory of being burned by Jana had left scars. That and his upbringing after twelve.

What a fool he was, he thought now. He thought about earlier when there'd been a chance that he had a son. It had made him realize the truth. He did want children with Alexis. With her, he could let himself believe in the fairy tale of happily-ever-after. Just the thought of her as his wife and of a house and the patter of little feet made him ache for just that. After what had happened when his mother died, the way his father had dealt with it and then Jana and their so-called marriage, he really had thought it wasn't for him.

But then along came Alexis. He brushed a lock of her hair back from her forehead. She smiled in her sleep, her lips turning up at the corners. She snuggled into him and fell back into a deep sleep. She'd changed his life. He thought about the engagement ring he'd purchased over a month ago. He'd planned to pop the question at Christmas.

What he hadn't planned on was his past coming back to haunt him. Now he was wanted for murder, and if he couldn't find Jana… He might not get the chance to ask Alexis to marry him.

He reached under the covers to place a warm hand on her slightly rounded stomach. He closed his eyes, imagining a future with this woman and the child she was carrying. He held that image as he welcomed sleep, even with its demons that he would have to battle.

CHAPTER NINETEEN

CULHANE WAS AWAKENED from a troubled sleep by the phone. He fumbled for it, his eyes still closed. Alexis stirred, still curled next to him. He found his phone. He didn't expect another call from April. But maybe Jack had given the number to Jana. "Hello?"

"Sorry to wake you but I've some news you'll want to hear."

"Al." It came out on a sigh. He hadn't talked to his deputy friend since early yesterday morning when he'd asked him for help.

Alexis sat up at the name and blinked, quickly wide-eyed.

"Any chance we could meet?" Al was asking. "I'll bring the coffee and doughnuts."

Ten minutes later, Al tapped at the motel-room door. He was a wiry man, standing about five ten, but Culhane had seen him take down men twice his size. His fresh-faced, average-guy appearance made his adversaries often underestimate him. He just didn't look like someone who would kick your butt with the least amount of provocation.

"I don't know what's going on," Al said after he brought in three coffees and a bag of doughnuts and the three of them had sat down. "But something's fishy. Jana Redfield is picked up for shoplifting, but when she's fingerprinted, her prints and DNA come up in the ongoing criminal investigation involving break-ins up at Big Sky. Then the sheriff lets her go. We've been trying to solve that case for months, and he just releases her."

"You think she and Garwood made a deal," Culhane said, thinking it was just like the Jana he'd known. "Which means she ratted out her cohorts. Makes perfect sense. If one of her partners in crime found out that she'd snitched on them, it could explain why she was now missing and presumed dead."

"Bingo," Al said. "Right after that, Garwood ran two names through the system. Leo Vernon, a parolee working as a cook at a café in Buckhorn, and Bobby Braden, a nineteen-year-old local handyman. Both had records. But he didn't put out BOLOs on them. I think he was waiting for you to be picked up first."

"You'd already tied Leo to Jana when you gave me his whereabouts yesterday morning," Culhane said, feeling himself wake up as the pieces began to fall into place. "I wonder if Garwood heard that I ended up meeting both of them?"

Al laughed. "I think he heard. He was in the worst mood yesterday."

"There's no way he can track that information back to you, right?"

"Don't worry," Al said. "I'm being careful. The sheriff treats me as if I'm not all that bright, and I let him believe it." He smiled and took another doughnut.

Culhane hated that both Leo and Bobby had been unable to tell him anything. But the sheriff didn't know that. He couldn't shake the feeling that Jana hadn't just thrown the two men to the wolves. What if she'd lied and neither had been involved in the robberies? What if she was protecting someone else she was much more afraid of?

But he reminded himself that he'd seen Bobby coming out of her apartment. Bobby had known her. But neither Bobby nor Leo could have killed her because Leo was in Buckhorn at the café grill and Culhane had seen Bobby coming out of her apartment not long after he'd talked to her.

"What bothers me is that I can't see Jana being the mastermind of the burglary operation," he told Al. "Nor Leo or Bobby."

Al nodded. "Whoever is robbing these expensive homes has inside information, knows exactly what to take and doesn't seem to be worried about getting caught," he said. "These break-ins are often in broad daylight. They all involve jewelry. Jewelry that is insured to the max."

"Jewelry the owner just happened to leave lying around after a cocktail party or late-night dinner with friends instead of putting it in the safe, right?" Culhane said. "We aren't talking crooks who blow safes, right?" Al nodded. "Have any of them been caught?"

"Not that I've heard."

"These rich folks who are robbed, they're the same people the sheriff parties with, right?"

Al smiled. "You're thinking what I am. Insurance fraud."

"Sure sounds like it to me. The jewelry owner collects the insurance. Later he secretly gets the item back, and the thieves get paid. If we're right, then the sheriff has to be involved."

Al took a sip of his coffee. "So yesterday, Garwood sends Furu and Cline over to Jana's. Apparently they tore the place apart. I don't believe they were looking for evidence. The crime-scene techs had already been there. Whatever they were looking for, they didn't find it."

"You think it's something Jana stole during one of the

burglaries at Big Sky?" Alexis asked. She'd been sitting quietly, drinking her coffee and listening.

"Something she shouldn't have taken," Culhane agreed. "How did you come up with that?" he asked her curious.

"Shoplifting," Alexis said. "She probably has a problem with sticky fingers."

Culhane laughed. "You nailed it. Jana's kleptomania was a problem even seven years ago. I'm betting you're right and that she has taken something that the sheriff needs back pronto."

"Which would explain why she faked her death and disappeared," Alexis said.

"She could be using whatever she took as leverage," Al said.

"More like blackmail," Culhane said. "She could have already stolen it before. Any idea how long she's been back in the area?"

"I could check her employment records," Al said. "You didn't know she was back?"

He shook his head. "Who does Garwood have on the burglaries? Furu and Cline?"

"You guessed it."

"Al, I think you need to be really careful. If Garwood suspects you're looking into this…"

"I'm not worried about losing my job."

"I'm talking about losing your life," Culhane said.

The deputy chuckled. "Garwood is corrupt but—"

"He's dangerous, maybe more so now. If I'm right, he is trying to frame me for murder. He doesn't know how much I know about his illegal activities, but I think he's afraid of what will come out in my wrongful-firing lawsuit against him."

Al seemed to think about that for a moment. "If you're

right, then he must have something pretty big that he fears will surface."

"He's always hung out with some of the rich and connected in Big Sky, so there's that," Culhane said. "I think you're right about insurance fraud. He's in the perfect position to cash in on this—and help his rich friends as well."

"Because of that, he'll do whatever it takes to protect himself," Alexis said. "Culhane and I getting fired was nothing compared to what he might do to you."

Al looked at her. "I'm curious. Why didn't you sue for wrongful discharge, too?"

She shook her head. "I'd had enough. I prefer to be my own boss." She looked over at Culhane. "I tried to talk him out of it as well."

"It's not that I want the job back. It's that someone has to stop Garwood," he said.

Al nodded. "That's why I'm willing to stick my neck out." He reached into his jacket pocket. "I got a copy of the names of the Big Sky residents who have been burglarized over the past two years and a list of what they say was taken. It seemed safer to copy them from Garwood's computer last night than photograph or scan them on my phone." He grinned. "I just happened to get the sheriff's password one day when I was in his office." He shrugged and got to his feet. "When I applied for the detective position, the sheriff said I wasn't ready." He handed the papers to Culhane who handed them over to Alexis. "I'd better get back. I know that no one from the sheriff's department followed me here, but I have had a tail lately, usually by Cline when he's off duty. I doubt it was his idea to trail me."

"But that means you're on Garwood's radar," Culhane said as he rose to see Al out. "Please be careful. Just meeting us could get you thrown into jail for aiding and abetting a criminal—if you're lucky."

Al smiled. "Don't worry. I'll keep my head down. I bought a disposable phone to call you."

"You're worried about him," Alexis said after Al left.

"He doesn't believe Garwood would go so far as to have someone killed."

"But you do."

His expression confirmed it. "See anything in the names that jumps out at you?"

"Not yet."

"Jana's partial to emeralds," Culhane said. "She used to talk about what she would buy if she were rich. Emeralds were at the top of the list."

"That might explain why Garwood sent Furu and Cline over to search her apartment," Alexis said, studying the list.

"Jana is neck-deep in all this," he said. "If we're right, she has something that Garwood desperately needs. And if he wants the murder rap to stick, then Jana has to be found dead. She's running scared because she made a deal with the devil. Now the devil is after her. Garwood must be shaking in his boots. This could bring the whole scam down and him with it."

"But only if Jana—and whatever she might have stolen—is found," Alexis said and noticed Culhane move to the window to peer out.

CULHANE FELT THE hair rise on the back of his neck. He got up to move to the window and, parting the curtains, looked out. He had a feeling. He searched the almost-empty parking lot. Nothing looked amiss, and yet he couldn't shake the feeling that they were no longer alone.

As he was rubbing his neck, he spotted her. Jana. She

stood across the street next to a large pine tree. Clearly, she was watching their room. How had she known they were there? Al. He'd been followed. Just not by any law enforcement. Or maybe she'd followed them from the ranch last night. He'd been looking for large black SUVs and cop cars—not whatever transportation Jana had now.

Quickly turning from the window, he grabbed his jacket. "Jana's out there. I'm going after her on foot." His gaze met Alexis's. All the worry he had about her—and his suspicion that she was carrying his baby filled him. "Please. Stay here. Stay safe."

With that he turned and raced out the door. Jana saw him and took off at a run as well. He streaked across the busy street, nearly getting run down, but didn't hesitate. His legs were longer. He could outrun her.

He just hoped that Alexis did what he'd asked her as Jana turned down an alley ahead as if doubling back toward the motel. He'd never been able to understand the woman, and now was no exception. Why had she been watching the motel?

Around another corner, down an alley, and he saw her ahead. But it was what he heard that had him concerned. Tires spinning out on pavement. Someone was chasing them in a vehicle. Jana hadn't come alone, apparently.

ALEXIS SAW CULHANE nearly get run down on the busy street and knew she had to do something. She quickly threw her things into her bag, grabbed the truck keys Culhane had left on the small table and headed for the pickup.

As she climbed behind the wheel, she could see the course the two seemed to be taking. That wasn't all she saw. A large black SUV was also chasing them, trying to second-guess where they were headed. She saw the vehicle race up the street and come to a screeching halt. Both doors flew open, and Furu and Cline jumped out and took off down an alley.

Shifting the pickup into gear, Alexis drove quickly to the abandoned SUV: the engine was still running. Pulling up behind it, she grabbed the Swiss Army knife her father had given her for Christmas when she was ten from her bag and jumped out.

"What you are doing is highly illegal," she said as she opened the knife and jabbed the blade into one tire, then another, before getting back into the pickup.

She'd seen the direction Culhane had been headed. Now she drove in a wide circle around the blocks as she tried to catch sight of Jana. She had her window down, thinking she might hear something as she passed one alleyway after another. The sound of a gunshot startled her because it was so close by.

Another shot rang out. Alexis stopped short and jumped out, this time with her weapon, although she knew that if she used it against either deputy she'd be more than breaking the law. It didn't matter that they were dirty. Or that they were trying to kill Jana and Culhane as well.

But it wasn't the deputies who came flying out of the alley. It was Jana. She ran to a small vehicle parked at the curb and jumped into the passenger seat as it sped away. Alexis got the license-plate number but little else before Culhane came limping out of the alley not a minute behind her.

"How badly are you hit?" she cried as she rushed to him.

"It's not from a bullet," he said, sounding as if in pain, as she helped him into the passenger side of the pickup and quickly jumped behind the wheel and took off. "It was a splinter from a wooden door frame. Cline always was a lousy shot. But he's death on door frames."

In her rearview mirror she saw the two deputies come out of the alley and onto the main street—and notice their flat tires.

Fortunately, she and Culhane were too far away for them to shoot.

It wasn't until she'd put distance between them and the deputies that she looked over at Culhane. He was pulling up his jeans and wriggling out of his boot.

For a moment all she saw was blood. She must have made a sound because he said, "It's just a flesh wound. I thought I told you to stay in the room?"

"You're welcome," she replied.

"Thanks." He smiled and reached over to place a hand on her thigh for a moment before looking in his side mirror.

"They won't be coming after us for a while," she said. "I slashed a couple of their tires." Out of the corner of her eye, she saw him grin.

"What would I do without you?"

She hoped he never had to find out as she felt a flutter in her stomach and kept driving.

"You had them both?" Sheriff Garwood demanded of the two deputies standing in front of his desk. He'd seen the way they'd come into his office and closed the door and known that they'd blown it. "Obviously not."

"We were so close," Cline said. "We followed Jana to this motel."

"Why didn't you bust her there?" Garwood demanded.

"She wasn't staying there," Furu said. "She was across the street watching it."

"Because Culhane was staying there," Cline said excitedly. "When he saw her and started chasing her, we thought we'd bag them both. I wounded him." The deputy sounded proud of himself. "I could have finished him off, but Alexis showed up, and he got away. But we were that close."

The man actually thought he got points for getting close. "This isn't horseshoes, Terry," he said with a curse and looked at Furu. "Now what?"

The deputy seemed to consider that. "The way I see it, we have several problems. I don't know if you've been following the news out of Buckhorn, but some law enforcement has been questioning why a man wanted for murder would stick around to save a hostage."

Willy groaned. "That damned Culhane. It's like he's taunting us."

"I think you might have missed the point," Furu said. "Without a body, we have no murder case."

"I think you're the one who's missed the point. Get me the body."

Furu sighed. "The second problem is that they may be connecting the dots. I got a call from Jerome at the ranch."

Garwood felt his stomach knot. Jerome had called Furu instead of him? True, he'd had Furu handle things out there as needed, but Jerome had to know who was in charge. "They know about the baby?"

"Jerome isn't sure. But even if they did, they don't know who the father is or who adopted the boy. Those records are conveniently not available. Jerome assured me they have no way of learning the truth. Not even Jana knows."

Garwood tried to still the sick feeling inside him. "With everyone looking for him, why hasn't Culhane been picked up by now?"

Furu shook his head. "Is there any way to reach out to Jana?"

The sheriff studied the deputy for a moment, again aware of the intellect behind those dark eyes of his. Furu was too good at his job. Once this was over, Furu was going to have to go. No firing this time. That was the mistake he'd made with Culhane.

"Are you suggesting we try to make a deal with her after the last deal I made with her went so well?" Garwood asked.

ALEXIS STOPPED AT a pharmacy and went in for what was needed to patch Culhane up. When she'd come back out, he'd insisted on taking care of it himself. He was right. The wooden sliver had only sliced through the flesh of his calf. He'd been lucky.

She tried not to think how close he'd come to getting killed. Wasn't this what she'd feared? They weren't planning to take him in alive. If the deputy had been a better shot...

"Do you have that list handy that Al gave you?" Culhane asked.

She knew what he was trying to do. Keep his mind off his injury. She pulled the sheets of paper from her bag. "What am I looking for?"

"I'm not sure," he said. "Emeralds."

"Emeralds."

She began to go down the list, fighting to concentrate. He acted like this was just another job like so many other deputy jobs they'd worked on together. But it was hard to focus.

"The jewelry taken was expensive," she said. "It would have taken a trained eye to know what to take. Or a list from the owner. Definitely an inside job." Didn't she remember another case a few years ago like this one?

Her head hurt, and her eyes blurred. She could tell Culhane was in pain as he disinfected the wound and began to bandage it. She could have done it so much more quickly and probably more neatly if he had let her.

Sighing, she looked at the list again. Sometimes they felt like an old married couple. Except for the passion that arced between them, making the air around them hum. She could feel it in the close confines of the pickup cab and knew he did, too.

The list. The words jumped out at her. "Here we go. An emerald-and-diamond necklace worth half a million was stolen almost two years ago." She felt her heart bump in her chest. "Oh," she said as realization hit her when she saw which house had been burglarized. "What if Bobby wasn't saying *water*?"

"He was saying *water*," Culhane said without looking at her.

"Or was he saying *Atwater*?" She saw him raise his head and shift his gaze to her. She had his full attention now. "Gilbert Atwater of Atwater Construction, Big Sky, Montana, was burglarized almost two years ago and again recently." Even Alexis knew that the man was a powerful, wealthy builder who was active in politics. "Isn't he one of Sheriff Garwood's friends?"

She handed Culhane the list and heard him swear. "Atwater."

"According to the list, the emerald-and-diamond necklace stolen the first time was never recovered," she said. "Estimated value? A half mil. If they collected the insurance on it, it might be embarrassing if the thief stole it again."

He shook his head. "It had to be insured for at least that. But we can't prove any of this without the necklace. If Jana took it…"

"She probably wishes she hadn't, if she did. Maybe that's why she was at the motel this morning," Alexis said. "You're thinking she followed Al, huh?" He smiled. Like him, she loved it when they were on the same page. "So were Furu and Cline following Al or Jana?"

"Good question. But you're right about Jana. She has to regret taking that necklace. It isn't like she planned to pawn or sell it. She'd know that would be impossible and get her arrested—if not killed. But it wouldn't surprise me if she thought she could use it to make a better deal with the sheriff."

"Blackmail?" Alexis asked.

Culhane nodded. "If he agrees to it, she'll be walking into a trap."

His cell phone rang. He glanced at Alexis and then picked up.

CHAPTER TWENTY

THE MOMENT HE heard crying on the other end of the phone connection, he knew. "Jana."

"I thought they killed you," she said through her sobs.

"I'm fine. Let me help you. Trust me, you need my help."

More tears, more sobs. "No one can help me. It's too late."

"No, it's not." She'd followed Al to the motel because she'd wanted Culhane's help. Or she'd been put up to it. He hated that, with her, he had no idea what was the truth. But she was more than his proof that he wasn't a murderer. He didn't want to see her dead. "Wherever you are, I'll come there. I'll get you out of all of this."

Her strangled laugh sounded more pained than her tears. "I never wanted to involve you. I swear. That's why I lied about the baby. I know you went out to the ranch. You know, don't you?"

He wanted to ask about the father of her baby but told himself it no longer mattered. "Tell me where you are."

Another sob. "They'll follow you."

"No. I've lost them. You know you can trust me."

Silence, then finally, "It's a small old cabin all by itself at the foot of the mountain." She gave him the directions. "Promise me that you'll come alone."

He didn't promise, but he wished he could come alone. "I'm on my way. Stay there." He disconnected and looked at Alexis. His love for her, coupled with the fact that he was sure she was carrying their child, made him want to lock her away for safekeeping. Not that she would hear of it.

"I don't think we should both go. It could be a trap. Furu and Cline followed her to the motel. Maybe Jana had tracked Al there, but if not…"

"I was thinking the same thing," Alexis said and smiled. "I heard enough of the conversation to agree. It is probably a trap."

For just a split second, he thought she would take his advice and stay safe.

"But you aren't going alone. I have a plan."

He shook his head, seeing that there would be no talking her out of it. "I do love a woman with a plan. But we're going to need a few more supplies first."

ALEXIS COULD SEE how hard it was for him to agree to her plan. She thought about last night in the shower with Culhane and later curled up in bed. He knew. He hadn't said anything, but there was no doubt that he knew about the pregnancy. Now he wasn't just scared for her. Just as she'd feared, he would be more protective. He needed to take care of himself and let her do what she knew how to do. But he was Culhane Travis. He always did the right thing, the good thing. Just like now.

"I know where this cabin is," she said as he gave her the directions Jana had given him. "I'll get out some distance from the cabin and circle around back. You take your time and go to the front." She could see he wanted to argue, but she wasn't having it. "I'll fire a shot if it looks like a trap. You do the same. Otherwise, text me when you get in and the coast is clear. Unless you think she's more apt to tell you what you need to know without me there."

He shook his head. "She knows about you. Whether she likes it or not, we're a team." His words sent a waterfall of pleasure rushing over her—just as did the look in his eyes. "We do this together."

She swallowed, feeling as if he was talking about more than this trip to meet Jana. There was worry in his tone but also resignation. He couldn't change her nature any more than she could his. She looked away as he drove. She couldn't think about the future, unsure if they would survive the next thirty minutes.

Would Jana set a trap for Culhane to walk into? Alexis had no doubt that the woman would. But would she involve Furu and Cline? Only if she'd already made another deal with the sheriff.

As deceptive as the woman was, Jana could have lied about where she was or could even take off before they got there. Or she could just simply set him up. No wonder Culhane had trust issues, she thought.

Clouds hung low over the mountains as he turned down the road. Snow. She could feel the temperature dropping. It had been an especially dry fall, but this coming storm could change that. Once the ground was covered with snow, it would probably stay until spring. The weatherman was predicting a white Christmas.

"We'll go with your plan," Culhane said. "If it's a trap, we get the hell out of there." He glanced over at her. "No taking any chances, agreed?" She nodded.

The road narrowed as it wound back into the deep pines at the base of the steep mountains. Alexis put down her window and breathed in the cold, fresh air. The clouds seemed to drop around them making it hard to see. Through the fog, she could barely make out a small cabin ahead.

Smoke curled up from the chimney, and one light shone inside.

"Stop here," she said and checked the clip in her weapon before she dug another from her purse, making Culhane groan. Hopefully she wouldn't need anywhere near that much firepower, but it was nice to know she had it just in case.

She looked over at him. There was so much she wanted to say. He leaned over and gave her a quick kiss. She felt him reach for her as if to pull her to him, to keep her from going. "Good luck," she said as she bailed out too quickly, before either of them changed their minds.

In an instant, she had disappeared into the trees and fog as snowflakes began to fall.

CULHANE SAT FOR a moment listening to the sound of the pickup's engine as snowflakes whirled around him, making him feel as if he were caught in a snow globe. He felt a chill, even though the inside of the pickup cab was still warm, still carried Alexis's scent.

He didn't want to do this. He didn't want Alexis doing this. The two of them had faced other challenges together. But now the cost was so much higher. They both had too much to lose. Not that it would stop them. The only way they would be free of this was by making sure that nothing happened to Jana.

Culhane checked his weapon to make sure it was loaded and then turned around. He found a side road and a place to hide the pickup in the pines. Getting out, he took the backpack he'd bought along with the supplies they'd picked up. Then he sprinted in the direction of the cabin. As per Alexis's plan, they should both arrive at the cabin about the same time.

Culhane didn't see Alexis, but he knew she would be close by, if not already at the back door of the structure. He'd gone along with her plan because he thought she would be safer bringing up the rear. As the cabin came into view, he hoped he was right. He headed for the front door, weapon drawn.

ALEXIS WORKED HER way through the pines. She could see the cabin ahead. She felt a quickening in her belly and slowed. Now wasn't the time to think about how badly things could go wrong or to chastise herself for taking chances with not just her life but that of her baby. If she felt this way, she could just imagine how Culhane did.

She reminded herself that she was good at her job. She wasn't taking unnecessary risks. She doubted, though, that Culhane would see it that way. As she moved quietly through the thick pines and falling snow, she could smell the smoke rising from the cabin's chimney.

There was no movement around the building. No vehicles that she could see, as Culhane had hidden the pickup in a spot back down the mountain. They were to meet there, should they become separated. Or worse. As the snow began to fall harder, she wondered if she would be able to see him.

Alexis dropped down the mountainside to the back of the cabin. She was anxious to meet this woman who'd conned Culhane Travis and ruined him on marriage and children.

As she approached the small weathered dwelling, she pulled her weapon. Nothing around her moved. The snow was falling harder now, silencing an already-quiet world. She felt a chill. Maybe it was the quiet. Or the snow. Or knowing that they were meeting a woman they couldn't trust, but she felt as if they weren't alone on this mountainside.

She tapped at the cabin door lightly. No answer. She knocked harder and heard movement inside. She knocked again and heard the door being unlocked. Had whoever opened the door already let Culhane in?

The knob in her hand, she moved quickly the moment the door was unlocked, shoving the door inward with her weight behind it, and heard someone stumble and fall. She quickly forced her way in, her gun drawn, not sure of who or what she would be facing.

An attractive blonde woman lay sprawled on the floor. Jana? Seeing Alexis, the woman began to crabwalk backward. "Where's Culhane?"

"I'm right here," he said as he crashed through the front door.

Jana swung around at the sound of his voice and clamored to her feet to back up against the wall. "You were supposed to come alone. I can't believe you brought...*her*."

"Don't act like the jealous wife, Jana. Tell me what's going on. Did you set me up for murder?"

Alexis sheathed her weapon and quickly locked the back door before moving through the small space to the front window. Something about this felt wrong. She couldn't shake the feeling she'd had earlier. She peeled the curtain back just enough to look out, but she didn't see anyone. Then again, with the snow it was impossible to see in the distance.

"How can you even ask if I set you up?" she cried. "I just had to disappear. I had no idea you'd be blamed for my murder."

"Tell me about the necklace."

Jana frowned. "I don't know anything about—"

"The emerald-and-diamond necklace you stole."

"I don't—"

"Jana, I'm trying to help you," Culhane said, pleading in his voice. "Tell me what's going on."

Alexis turned away from the window for a moment. She could see that Culhane didn't believe Jana. She knew the feeling.

"After you were picked up for shoplifting, you made a deal with the sheriff. Don't deny it," he said.

For a moment the woman looked as if she would keep lying, then she broke down. "That's why I had to disappear."

"Where is the necklace?" Culhane demanded. "I know you stole it from Atwater's house at Big Sky. Come on, you can't sell or pawn it. All it will do is get you killed. Hand it over, and I might be able to save your life."

She made a pouty face but then dug the necklace out of her jacket pocket and dropped it into his hand. "The jewels aren't real, anyway," she said.

Alexis blinked. They jewels weren't real? The Atwater necklace that had gone missing months earlier had to have been real jewels. The necklace would have had a certified gemological appraisal to confirm its value. "You took it to a jeweler?"

Jana scoffed. "What? You think I'm stupid? I took it to a fence I know. They told me the jewels weren't real. It's worthless."

Culhane stared at the jewelry in his hand. "What did you hope to do with this when you stole it?"

"I don't know. I saw it. I liked it. It's a sickness," she whined. "I didn't know it was *fake*. So why is it such a big deal that the sheriff wants to kill me?"

"I don't have time to explain it to you," Culhane said and glanced at Alexis.

She turned her attention back to the road outside. Through the crack in the curtain and the falling snow, she saw movement. Two figures dressed in dark clothing were headed their way. Sheriff's deputies.

"We have to get out of here. Now," she said as she hustled away from the window. "Out the back. Just as we thought. It's a trap."

CULHANE SWORE. ONE look at Jana, and he knew it was true. She'd set them up, letting them walk into a trap. "Jana—"

"I told you they would follow you," she cried.

He shook his head as he pushed her toward the back door. But at least he had the necklace. "You fool. I don't know what kind of deal they offered you, but they have no intention of keeping it. Jana, they plan to kill us both."

She began to cry. "I was scared. They said they would let me go free if I did this one last thing."

The three of them scrambled out the back door into the falling snow. Jana went first with Culhane right behind her. He had hold of her coat sleeve, but when he turned back to check on Alexis, Jana pulled free and took off at a run down the mountainside.

"Get her!" Alexis cried, coming out of the cabin right behind him. "They'll kill her!" And frame Culhane.

He could see that Jana was headed for the road—the same road the two deputies were coming up. If they saw her and killed her... But he didn't want to leave Alexis.

"Go!" she cried again. "I'll double back to the truck."

That was enough to get him moving. He raced after Jana down the mountain, hoping he could reach her before the deputies saw her. Maybe with the snow falling so hard—

He hadn't gone fifty feet when he heard the gunshot. His heart dropped as he slid to a stop. He blinked in the falling snow, unable to tell where the shot had come from.

His heart pleaded with him to turn back, to find Alexis. He stumbled forward, knowing that Alexis was trained for this. She was armed. Jana was completely ill-equipped for any of this. If they killed her, he knew they would plant evidence that would send him to prison—if he was lucky.

He'd taken only a few steps when he saw her. Jana. She stood below him on the mountainside, a gun pointed at his heart.

At least now he knew where the gunshot had come from. So would the deputies if he didn't move fast.

"Give me the necklace, Culhane," she said, the gun wavering in her hands. Fortunately the woman was a bad shot, or he'd be dead. "I need it to buy my freedom."

He nodded. Arguing with her right now seemed like a bad idea. "Fine." He reached into his pocket and pulled out the necklace. Even with the fake jewels it was heavy, unless that, too, had been a lie. Then he took a step toward her.

ALEXIS HEARD SOMEONE go charging into the cabin's front door as she took off out the back. Huge snowflakes fell in a wall of white in front of her. She started through the pines the way she'd come when she heard a gunshot. Her pulse jumped. Culhane?

Jana had set them up. She'd seen at least two deputies earlier. What if there were more? The pickup was parked down the road in the pines. For a moment, she didn't know where to go or what to do. She didn't know who'd been shot.

She stopped to look back, feeling disoriented and scared that the deputies had shot Culhane. Or shot Jana to put the nail into Culhane's coffin for her murder.

She had to go back. She couldn't leave Culhane.

Alexis started to turn when she heard a sound off to her right. A twig broke under a boot heel. She couldn't see anything for the snow and the dense pines around her. But she knew she was no longer alone.

Move! Another twig broke off to her left. She started to turn, her weapon ready, when the gun was wrenched from her hand. She heard heavy breathing and was grabbed from behind. Something dark and scratchy was dropped over her, her arms quickly pinned to her sides as straps bound her. She struggled only to find herself being bound even more tightly. She tried to breathe, but the smell of the thick blanket made her gag.

"Calm down. We aren't going to hurt you." Alexis recognized his voice and heard the lie. Deputy Terry Cline was one of the sheriff's thugs who did his dirty work.

But he was right. She needed to calm down. She was panicking, her heart pounding so hard it made her chest ache as she gasped for each breath. Taking shallower breaths, she tried to compose herself and think. Panic did her no good. She had to keep her head. If they were arresting her, they would have cuffed her and taken her down to a patrol car. Instead...

It was the *instead* that made her heart hammer even harder. She felt herself being lifted roughly and thrown over a shoulder like a sack of potatoes as she was carried down the hill. She could hear Cline breathing hard. There was another man, the one who'd taken her gun. He was busting through the woods behind them. Both men appeared to be in a hurry, making her wonder about the other two men she'd seen. Deputies who weren't taking questionable orders from Sheriff Garwood?

As Cline came to a stop, she heard a vehicle door being

opened, then a sliding door like on an SUV or a van. He dumped her unceremoniously into the back and slid the door closed. She wriggled around trying to free herself until she was breathing hard again and stopped herself. She could hear the two of them climb into the front. The engine started, and the vehicle began to move.

Where were they taking her? What about Culhane? Jana? She listened, but she couldn't hear anyone else in the back with her.

Bound, wrapped tight and sheathed in darkness under the heavy fabric, she closed her eyes and concentrated on her breathing. If they were going to kill her, they would have already. Instead they were taking her somewhere. To keep her out of the way? Or were they taking her to someone?

She tried to get a hand free, but she was bound too tightly. At least she had to try to push the fabric away from her face. She had about the same amount of luck. What if she could bite a hole in it? She leaned back, trying to stretch the fabric out some. Finally she was able to get some between her teeth. She began to work at it, all the time not letting herself believe that the worst had happened to Culhane. If he were dead, she assured herself, she would feel it. Her heart would know. It would break. He had to be alive. But for how long?

The vehicle bumped down the road and finally onto the interstate. She tried to keep track of the length of time it took before they slowed and turned off, even though she felt sick to her stomach. A turn to the left, then another to the left, then one to the right and another to the left.

She had managed to get a small hole into the heavy fabric as the vehicle came to a stop. The engine shut down. Both men climbed out, and an instant later, the side door slid open and she felt hands grab her and lift her out. They carried her into a building and down some steps.

As she was dropped on what felt like a mattress, she caught the smell of fresh paint and sawdust. She lay perfectly still, listening. One of them was still in the room with her. She didn't dare breathe for fear of what might happen next. She'd never felt more vulnerable, bound the way she was.

She felt a hand on her shoulder and jerked away.

"We aren't going to hurt you," Cline said again, making it sound even more like the lie that it was.

She said nothing, knowing that asking about Culhane would be a waste of her time. Just as would asking what they planned to do with her. She didn't want to believe that Garwood had gone from insurance fraud to kidnapping. Murder wasn't that far off, she feared. But knowing what he had to lose if the truth came out, she hoped he hadn't reached that point yet.

"Leave her be," said a male voice from another room. Deputy Dick Furu, of course.

She said nothing as she listened to Cline's retreating footfalls. She heard him close and lock the door. She waited until she heard him move away from the door before she began struggling with renewed effort to get free of her restraints.

CULHANE HELD THE necklace out as he took another step down the mountainside, then another. The falling snow and the deepening shadows of the late afternoon made it hard to read Jana's expression. She was having a hard time holding the gun in her hand steady.

He dropped the necklace into the snow at his feet. Jana's gaze followed it to the ground—just as he'd hoped.

He moved swiftly, wrenching the gun from her hand and grabbing her around the back, before picking up the necklace from the ground and pocketing it again.

She started to scream, but he quickly covered her mouth. The deputies would be following the sound of the gunshot. They could be on them at any moment. He had to get her out of here, but going anywhere near the cabin would only get them caught. He had to keep Jana quiet. She really thought these men were here to save her.

He stuffed a glove into her mouth and held her down until he could get the supplies he brought from the backpack. As a deputy, he had experience with cuffing squirming perps. Within seconds, he had plastic cuffs binding her wrists behind her. He put duct tape over the glove already in her mouth and jerked her to her feet. Her eyes were wild with fear and anger, but damned if he was going to let her be killed.

Spotting an animal trail below them, he quickly took it and headed higher up into the mountains. Jana fought him, refusing to move, so he flung her over his shoulder and headed up the trail. He could see a rock cliff ahead with an overhang where they could get out of the snow. With luck they would have a view of the cabin below.

He climbed quickly even with the weight of his ex-wife on his shoulder. Below he thought he heard a door slam and movement at the cabin. As he reached the cliff and the rock overhang, he stopped and set her down.

Through the pines, he caught sight of two sheriff's deputies far below them. They'd come out of the cabin and were looking around. One of them was on his phone. He could hear their voices but not what they were saying. He'd expected this trap would involve only Deputies Cline and Furu. But he didn't recognize these two deputies.

With luck, Alexis had gotten away, he thought as he forced Jana to sit in a spot where she couldn't run from him. He had no idea what he was going to do with her. Just keep her alive was his only plan right now, while they waited out the deputies on the mountain below them.

He'd been sitting under the rock ledge high on the mountain for some time when his cell phone vibrated in his pocket. He quickly checked it, hoping it would be Alexis.

With a groan, he saw it was Sheriff Willy Garwood.

He stared at it, debating whether or not to take it. The fact that Garwood was calling wasn't good news. He felt his stomach roil, fearing what this was about. Garwood wouldn't be calling unless they had Alexis.

He hit Accept and took a calming breath. Saying nothing, he waited.

"Culhane? You there?"

He didn't answer.

Garwood didn't need him to, apparently. "I think we should meet and talk."

"Talk?" he scoffed. "I'll do my talking before a court of law, thanks."

"I think that might be a mistake on your part. Your ass is in a sling, son. I'm just trying to help you."

"I don't need your kind of help."

"I guess it depends on how much you care about your girlfriend. Not to be confused with your wife."

The words hit him like fists, one after the other. The man had Alexis—just as he suspected. But he had Jana. Garwood had apparently thought that Jana had gotten away. He looked over at his former wife. Didn't she realize her days were numbered if she kept making deals with this man? Apparently not.

But Alexis...

"Listen, Garwood—"

"It's Sheriff Garwood to you."

"I'm betting that Alexis isn't in your nice, warm jail right now. I'm betting that you've crossed yet another line and stooped to *kidnapping*."

"For a man about to be arrested for murder, I wouldn't throw stones, if I were you."

Culhane gritted his teeth until his jaw hurt. Garwood thought he had him boxed in, but below him on the mountainside he could see the deputies packing it in. Which explained why he was calling. The sheriff wanted to know where he was and why he hadn't been caught in the net.

But Alexis hadn't been so lucky.

He held the phone in a death grip and said nothing because he didn't want Garwood to know that he was shaking in his boots. If the sheriff hurt a hair on her head, he'd kill him with his bare hands.

But he held his tongue. The last thing he needed to give Garwood was affirmation of his feelings for Alexis.

"I just thought you might want to know how she is. Things are going so badly for you, I'd hate to see anything else happen."

It would be dark soon. The only thing that kept the sky light was the white of the falling snow. "What do you want?"

Silence. Then slowly, "Jana Redfield Travis is wanted as a material witness. I guess I was wrong about you killing her before, but now…"

"You know damned well I didn't kill her."

"Really? I'm not sure anyone will believe that if she's found dead. With this storm moving in, I hope she's somewhere safe."

He thought about telling him but changed his mind. All

it would take was one phone call to the deputies that were leaving and they'd be back searching not just for him—but also for Jana. Garwood was hoping she had gotten away and would freeze to death up here in the mountains. She might have if he hadn't hogtied her and brought her with him. "I asked what you want."

"I want the necklace."

Of course he did. Apparently that was the deal he'd made with Jana. She was to give the necklace to him. "What necklace would that be?"

"Stop playing games. Are you telling me that you didn't get it from Jana?" He wasn't telling him anything, he thought. He said nothing as he waited.

"Neither of us have the time to debate this. Also, I'm not sure whoever took your girlfriend will be able to keep her alive that long. So if you don't have the necklace, then I guess we don't have anything to trade. What a shame for your girlfriend, though."

Culhane swore silently, the threat making him ache inside. He had never felt this kind of fury. This man had Alex. This man had the woman he loved. The woman who was now carrying his child.

"I have the necklace," he said through gritted teeth and hated the relief he heard in the sheriff's voice.

"Well, then, I could put a couple of my boys on it to see if they could find Alexis before it's too late," the sheriff offered.

"You mean your deputies or your *boys*?"

"Listen, Culhane, you aren't in a position of strength here. I'd watch your mouth if I were you. Isn't that why I fired you?"

"No, you fired me because you're a crooked cop, and I caught you at it." Silence. He thought for a moment that he'd gone too far. But Garwood was wrong about one thing. He was in a position of power. The sheriff needed Jana. He needed the necklace. Just not as badly as Culhane needed Alexis, but he was hoping Garwood didn't know that.

"As I was saying," the sheriff began again, "I might be able to find her, and maybe we could make a trade. But part of the deal is that you drop the lawsuit. I want to see it in tomorrow's newspaper."

Culhane said nothing even as his heart pleaded for him to speak. The deputy vehicles were all gone.

Make the deal. Get Alexis back before they hurt her. Just the thought had him shaking inside. But he knew that even if he agreed to the deal, he couldn't depend on Garwood to uphold his end. He made an oath. He would bring Garwood down or die trying.

But right now, he had to get Alexis back.

"Why would I make a deal like that?" he asked finally. "So you can kill Alexis and continue framing me? I don't think so."

"You don't care about your girlfriend."

Alexis was all he cared about. Which made him vulnerable. Garwood had to suspect that.

"I should have told you. I am recording this conversation. I think the judge will find it interesting, don't you, Garwood? Especially if anything happens to Alexis. Do you know what happens to cops who end up in prison? Best make sure your boys don't hurt her. Otherwise, you're screwed." He laughed and disconnected.

For a moment, he couldn't catch his breath. He'd just taken a huge gamble, one that could cost Alexis her life—and the baby's. He leaned over, feeling light-headed. He thought he might throw up. Had he overplayed his hand?

Garwood was so arrogant he might think he could still get away with killing her.

He turned to look at Jana. She was glaring daggers at him from where he'd forced her to sit back under the overhang of the rocks. She'd heard the whole conversation. She knew how much he cared about Alexis. He shook his head that after everything she could be jealous.

"Come on," he said, seeing that she was shivering from the cold. He was shaking, too, but from anger and fear. He pulled her to her feet.

The first thing she did was make a run for it, and she tripped and fell face-first into the snow. He went after her, hauled her up and sighed.

Somehow, he got her off the mountain and into his pickup. Seriously, now what was he going to do with her?

He started the engine and prayed that Alexis was somewhere warm and safe and that he would get her back.

CHAPTER TWENTY-ONE

ALEXIS WORKED A hole into the thick, itchy fabric, widening it with her chin until she could breathe. She lay back, sucking in the fresh air, before trying to force her head through the opening. The fabric tore, and she shoved her head out and managed to push herself into a sitting position, her back against the wall.

Looking around, she took in her surroundings. She was in a room without any furnishings other than the mattress under her. Through a small window over her head, she could barely make out the lower part of a tree in darkness outside. Basement, just as she'd thought. There was nothing on the white walls. Her guess was that it was a new house that was still in the construction stage and she was in a basement bedroom. Earlier, she'd thought that she smelled fresh sawdust. Other than that, she had no idea where she was or how much time had passed.

Sitting there, she listened but heard nothing at first except the lower murmur of voices in the next room. At the sound of footfalls headed her way, she quickly ducked herself back into the fabric and rolled over on her side on the mattress, her back to the door.

She heard the door open. Holding her breath, she listened, knowing whoever was in the doorway was also listening. Then the door slowly closed. She heard it click shut but didn't move until she heard it being locked again.

"I think she's asleep," Deputy Terrance Cline said just outside the door. "How long do we have to stay here with her?" A mumbled response and then, "If it's going to be all night, then I'm getting some sleep."

She sat up again, coming up through the hole. As she tried to force her shoulders through the fabric, she could feel the straps binding her arms at her side slip a little. If she could just wriggle out...

But then what? She lay in the darkness. Her struggles to free herself and the past two days were taking their toll, but now that she could breathe freely, she felt better. She fought her bindings a while longer, before exhaustion got the better of her.

CULHANE HAD GOTTEN away, but now he didn't know where to go. Garwood had Alexis. He thought about the faux-gem necklace. Garwood needed it—just as he needed Jana. Because of that, he wouldn't hurt Alexis.

Unless it was already too late.

When his phone rang, he felt his heart bump against his ribs. Garwood with another deal? He'd half hoped it would be. He was ready to take any deal just to get Alexis back. He needed to hear her voice. He desperately needed to know that she was alive. He tried to hide his disappointment as he took the call. "Al?"

"I've got something. Not sure how much it might help. I kept wondering how Jana had gotten involved in all this and why the burglaries were happening in broad daylight. Jana was a housekeeper up at Big Sky. She had the run of a lot of expensive houses."

What a gold mine for a kleptomaniac, Culhane thought, wondering what else she'd taken. Knickknacks, things that hadn't been missed? There were just two things he needed to know. "Did she work for Atwater? And do you still have that soundproof music room in your house?"

Forty minutes later, Culhane was on his way to Big Sky sans Jana. She was locked in Al's music room.

The drive up the Gallatin Canyon to Big Sky took longer because of the winter traffic. He remembered a time when it hadn't been this busy. But that was before the ski resorts became so popular and the town grew and more people built homes and condos in the shadow of Lone Peak.

He'd found Atwater's address on his phone. The problem was the Atwaters lived in an exclusive, gated community—much like Lost Sunset Ranch. Culhane drove up the paved road and stopped at the guard gate. Only one guard came out as if they'd recognized the faded Cardwell Ranch printed on the side of the pickup. Everyone in Big Sky knew Dana Cardwell Savage and the former marshal, Hud Savage.

"Who are you here to see?" the guard asked and checked the clipboard in his hands.

"Mr. Atwater, but he isn't expecting me. I found something of his that I believe belongs to his wife." The guard looked at him quizzically. "My name's Culhane Travis."

Culhane watched the guard go back into the booth and make the call. It was late. Snow drifted down through the darkness, the flakes like fairy lights in the glow of the guard station. He felt the darkness and cold soul-deep, his emotions swinging from an aching fear for Alexis to a murderous rage toward Garwood. He'd gotten into law enforcement because, like Alexis, he'd believed in right and wrong. Justice, he'd known, was much more elusive, but it was something to strive for. Working for Garwood, he'd become disillusioned. He couldn't see himself ever going back to it.

"Mr. Atwater said for you to leave whatever it is here at the gate."

He shook his head. He'd been expecting as much. "If he doesn't want it…" He started to shift the pickup into Reverse, but the guard stopped him, just as he knew he would.

"In that case, take this. I've marked the Atwood estate on the map."

Estate, Culhane thought as the gate slid aside and he drove into one of the most exclusive clubs. He'd heard a person had to put up millions of dollars before they could be considered. Famous names were often thrown around as to who lived behind these walls. He could see mansions tucked back in the pines as he drove.

Atwater's estate wasn't as grand as some. But it was massive compared to a normal home. He drove up the heated driveway to the stone edifice, parked and climbed out. As he walked to an entrance wide enough to let a tank through, he wondered how long it had taken Atwater to call the sheriff—and how much time he had before the first cruiser got here.

As he went to push the intercom button, half of the double front door swung open, and he saw inside the house to a water feature he remembered too well. This was the house where he'd met Jana. The house where he'd attended the party almost seven years ago.

For a moment, he was too stunned to speak, but then all the pieces began to fall into place as the door was opened—not by Atwater but a boy of six or seven. It took Culhane a moment to get over his second shock of the night.

The boy looked up at him, his blue eyes and that shock of wheat-blond hair too familiar. Jana must have worked in this house as a nanny seven years ago. It was the oldest story of all. But how could Atwater's wife not notice the resemblance? How had Jana not seen it?

With a start, he realized she had. She'd stolen the necklace from this house. Or was this one of the houses Jana cleaned here in Big Sky? Was this why she'd returned to Big Sky, to be near her son?

"Hello," Culhane said to the boy, his voice rough with emotion.

The sandy-haired child glanced over his shoulder, but only for a moment, before turning wide, innocent blue eyes back on Culhane. In the background he could hear someone calling the name Joshua. "If you're here to see my father—" But that was all he managed to get out before a large dark-haired man appeared behind him.

"Son," Atwater said, placing a firm hand on the boy's shoulder. "Your mother's calling you. She has a treat for you before bedtime."

Without another look at Culhane, the boy turned and ran back inside.

"You have something for me?" Atwater said, his tone no longer cordial. Clearly this exchange was going to take place on the doorstep. He saw the man look past him. But no one was watching because there wasn't another house around even if anyone could see through the falling snow.

"You told the guard you had something for me," Atwater repeated.

"I do," Culhane said. "A message for the sheriff."

The man frowned. "I assumed you had brought something of value, or I wouldn't have told the guard to let you in."

"Oh, it's valuable. Tell Garwood to release Alexis Brand, or I will take the necklace to the FBI and expose not just your insurance fraud but everything else that has to do with

Jana Redfield. I suspect you fired her, and that's why she took the necklace. Did she figure it out? Or had she always known where her son was?"

"I don't know what you're—"

"A simple DNA test would prove—"

"Don't you dare threaten me or my family," Atwater said from between clenched teeth as if trying hard to remain under control. "You have no idea who you're dealing with."

"Oh, but I think I do. You and Garwood think you're above the law. But you're going down. I'll see to it," he told the man. "Just in case you try to have the guards stop me on my way out, I didn't bring the necklace. It's somewhere safe. If anything happens to Alexis or me, it goes straight to the FBI with everything Jana told me."

With that, he turned and walked back to his pickup. To his surprise, he had no trouble getting out of the gate. He was back on the main highway headed toward Bozeman when he got the call from Garwood. He sounded scared even as he threatened him. Culhane had figured that Atwater would put even more pressure on the sheriff. The man sounded as if the stress was taking its toll.

"Let me talk to Alexis. Now," Culhane said and waited with his heart in his throat.

"She's not here. You can talk to her in the morning. Unless you do something stupid like you just did." The line went dead.

It was going to be the longest night of his life.

GARWOOD MADE THE call as soon as he hung up from Culhane. Deputy Furu's phone rang four times before he finally picked up. "What's wrong?"

"Nothing. I was in the john, and I left my phone in the

other room," Furu said, sounding testy. "Are we making the exchange?"

"In the morning. Culhane wants to hear Alexis's voice first to make sure she's all right. She is all right, isn't she?"

"She's fine. Terry just checked on her. She's sleeping. I don't understand, though, why it is taking so long."

Garwood thought about telling the deputy about Culhane's visit to see Atwater and the subsequent furious phone call to him. But he didn't want the deputy to think he wasn't on top of this. He could hear something in Furu's voice that worried him.

"This whole mess will be over soon. It's Culhane's word against mine."

Furu didn't say anything as if he didn't believe him. Because he knew it wouldn't be that simple to clean up this mess. Did he also know that Willy had no intention of letting either Culhane or Alexis live? They'd put him through too much already. He'd take care of them himself. Furu was too squeamish to do the job, and Willy couldn't depend on Cline to do it right.

"You just get me the new people we need for the operation," he said. "Try to find someone better than the last ones." He was still upset over what Atwater had told him tonight. Jana had been working for a Big Sky housekeeping company so she would be able to see her son when she cleaned the Atwater house.

He said he hadn't known about it until his wife recognized her and fired the housekeeping company, saying that Jana had broken something. Apparently it was after that that Jana had gotten into the house and taken the necklace.

Willy had been furious but had to hold his tongue. If Buzz had been able to keep it in his pants seven years ago, this would never have happened. Willy had come up with a plan to buy Jana off by throwing her together with Culhane—until Atwater decided he wanted the kid. He'd found out that his wife couldn't have kids, and Jana was carrying a male baby.

Willy couldn't believe everything he'd been through for Atwater. He'd brought all of this on himself. Not that Willy had a choice but to clean up the mess that had been made. Atwater had introduced him to the right people, invited him to the right parties. Willy wasn't ready to give that up.

"I don't think it should be business as usual for a while," Furu said as if Garwood cared what he thought. "I would think you'd want to let things settle down for a while first."

That's why you aren't in charge and I am. "It's almost Christmas. This time of year there are a lot of people at Big Sky for the holidays. There are lots of parties, lots of drinking, lots of jewelry. I should have all the information soon." Another reason he had to kiss Atwater's rosy behind. The man provided what houses to hit, when and what to take. "We can't pass this up." Atwater would want his split. "Once the holidays are over, most of the really wealthy residents will be off to St. Barts or Monte Carlo or wherever they all go."

He waited for Furu to argue the point and was glad when he didn't. "What I need you to do is call Culhane in the morning. Just let her talk long enough that he knows she's all right, then tell him to call me. That's it. I'll let you know about the exchange."

"We are going to exchange her for the necklace, right?"

Garwood didn't like what he was hearing. "You getting squeamish, Furu? I thought better of you."

"Not squeamish. Just cautious. I think it's bad business if Culhane or Alexis get killed, especially with the lawsuit against the department."

"You don't have to worry. Culhane is dropping his law-suit, and both of them are going to keep their mouths shut because they will have no proof. It already looks like his case is just sour grapes over being fired. Once he drops it, all of this will go away."

"I hope you're right. I'll make the call." He disconnected, leaving the sheriff feeling anxious. Maybe it was time for Furu to have an accident. Garwood would miss him. But before he'd come to take the local-sheriff position, he'd realized that men under him often had an expiration date. Furu's seemed to be up.

In a perfect world, Furu would take Cline with him. But that would have to wait for a while. He couldn't have too many bodies turning up—and right before Christmas. Cul-hane's and Alexis's would be plenty. After all, they were both wanted for questioning and were considered armed and dangerous. Anything could happen.

CHAPTER TWENTY-TWO

ALEXIS WOKE TO the thin stream of light that bled through the basement window. She blinked and sat up to listen. No sound. The deputies must still be asleep. Which meant she had an opportunity. She considered the room for a moment. There were three doors. The one Cline had locked, one that was probably a closet and the third…a bathroom? A bathroom with a window that opened? If she was right and this was a basement, then under law it needed an egress window in case of fire.

She began to wriggle and felt the straps loosen from her efforts last night. A little more and she would be able to get an arm out. She felt stronger this morning, more clearheaded than she had last night. The sleep had done her good.

After freeing an arm, she quickly rubbed feeling back into it before she slipped down the straps that bound her and threw the dark blanket aside. She knew she had to move quickly. She heard a phone ringing in the other room. That meant something was likely to change.

She moved as quietly as possible toward the first of the two doors. She listened for a moment, then eased it open just enough that she could see inside. Closet.

Moving swiftly but as quietly as possible, she opened the second door. Bingo. It was a nice-sized bathroom with a window. She stepped inside, locking the door behind her.

If they came into the room and saw her no longer on the mattress, the locked bathroom door might buy her a few minutes tops. But she'd take them.

She hurried to the window afraid she was going to find that it didn't open. With a surge of relief, she saw the crank and quickly began to turn it. As the window opened, she saw that she would have to pull herself up and then fall out of the window onto a pile of dirt just outside.

But this part of the house backed up on forest. Once she was through the window, she could run into the trees. That was if she could run. The drop was more than she expected, considering that the window was in the basement.

She shoved out the screen, knowing that the noise she was making might bring them. But she had no choice. The screen came loose, she set it aside, then tried to pull herself up. Her arms still felt numb from being tied up for so long. But she managed on the third try.

Outside the bathroom door, she heard someone come into the room. There was a cry of alarm, then footfalls. Someone tried the closet door and then she heard the knob rattle behind her. Any moment, one of the men would knock down the door and be on her.

She thought of the baby growing inside her as she slithered up and out the window. In the distance, she could hear Christmas bells ringing and realized it was Sunday and the bells were coming from a nearby church.

THE SHERIFF HAD never been good at waiting. He paced his home office. Why hadn't Culhane called? Willy had been so sure that the man was in love with Alexis Brand and would jump at a deal. Was Culhane playing him, or did he really not care?

Atwater had called again, anxious to get the necklace back. Like Willy wasn't just as anxious?

When his phone rang, he felt such a sense of relief that his legs went weak, and he had to sit down. So much was riding on this. The crime-scene techs would be finishing their investigation of Jana Redfield Travis's murder. He would have to move on what they found, and yet, the last thing he needed was some law officer to pick up Culhane before the necklace was in his hands.

"Hello?" He knew he sounded smug, but now he had Culhane exactly where he wanted him. Once Culhane heard Alexis's frightened voice, he would bend, and this would be over. At least for Willy. Not so much for Culhane.

"We have a problem," Deputy Furu said. "Alexis got away."

Willy couldn't believe he'd heard correctly. Was this a bad joke? "How is that possible?"

"We had her bound up, but she got loose and went out the bathroom window into the woods behind the house. Cline and I are out looking for her now. She can't have gotten far. I'll call when we have her." He disconnected.

Gripping the phone so hard than his fingers ached, he wanted to explode. How could the fools have lost her? Everything was riding on this trade. Culhane was expecting a phone call from her. What would he do when he didn't get it? Take the necklace to the FBI?

Willy slammed down his phone, kicked his desk and sent his trashcan cartwheeling across the room. Were they trying to ruin him? Did they not realize that they were going down with him?

His phone rang. He snatched it up, hoping it would be Furu and that they had Alexis. But of course it was Culhane. He declined the call, knowing he would have to take the next one. But first he had to figure out how to play this.

ALEXIS HAD NO idea where she was as she ran through the pines. She needed to get to a road, to people, to a phone to call for help. Had there been a creek, she would have followed it down, knowing that was what lost hikers were advised to do. But the house seemed to have been in the middle of nowhere. From the bells she'd heard there was a church nearby. But she had no idea where. She couldn't double back to the road for fear of running into the deputies, so she kept going. Ahead she could see some rock outcroppings that rose up high enough that she might be able to see something from there.

She knew the deputies wouldn't be far behind, and there were two of them. Her chances of actually getting away weren't good. But she'd had to try. She was still dressed as she had been earlier in the mountains. But they'd taken her gun and her cell phone.

The ground was covered with dried pine needles beneath the trees. But no snow. That meant that they had to be in the western part of the valley away from the mountains. Breathing hard, her boots pounding the ground beneath her, she kept moving. All the while, she listened for the sound of traffic—and the men behind her. She heard nothing but her own ragged breath.

Furu and Cline would have a hard time tracking her in the needles, she told herself. She hoped they would split up to find her—and that might give her an edge.

At the high outcrop, she slowed and looked back. All she could see were dense conifers. But while she couldn't see men, she knew they were back there. Hurriedly she climbed up the rocks. At the top, she tried to peer over the trees. She could see the tops of mountains in the distance but little else.

She heard someone coming fast. Ducking down into a spot in the rocks where she could hide, she found a softball-size boulder she could use as a weapon if one of them got close enough. Crouched, she waited.

CULHANE CALLED THE sheriff's cell-phone number again, more than worried now. Something was wrong. He could feel it. Garwood had been anxious to make the deal, and now he wasn't answering his phone?

His heart thundered in his chest. Alexis. Something had happened to her. That's why they hadn't made the call to let him know that she was alive. He felt sick. He should have just made the deal. Maybe Garwood had been telling the truth about Alexis not having a lot of time.

If he could get his hands around Garwood's thick throat right now—

"Hello." The sheriff sounded chipper. Or at least wanted him to think he was.

"Is there a problem, Garwood?" He tried to keep both the anger and the fear out of his voice. "I thought you wanted this necklace. Maybe I should just turn it over to the FBI and let them deal with you."

"If you were going to do that, you would have already," the sheriff snapped back.

"What makes you think I haven't?"

"Because that wouldn't be healthy for your girlfriend," Garwood said.

"If she were healthy, I would have already talked to her." Silence. It hung between them too long. Culhane felt his stomach roil. The ache in his heart was unbearable.

"She's fine," the sheriff finally said. "We're having trouble with cell-phone coverage where she is. But we're moving her. Once we get coverage…"

He was lying, and yet Culhane wanted to believe it with all his heart. He heard something in the background. "Are you having an office Christmas party?"

"One of the dispatchers brought her baby in," Garwood said. "If you're asking if I'm taking this seriously, I am. Once you get the call from Alexis, let's get this over with."

Culhane couldn't agree more. He disconnected and prayed he'd hear her voice again. Soon.

ALEXIS HEARD ONE of them coming through the pines. Had to be Deputy Terry Cline, she thought. He'd always been like a bull in a china shop, knocking things over in the office, banging into desks, spilling his coffee.

It was no surprise that she heard him coming. He came crashing out of the pines headed in her direction. She peered around the rocks, saw him stumble over some downed limbs, twigs snapping under his big feet. All of it announcing him long before he reached the outcropping.

"Come just a little closer," she said under her breath as she watched him remove his Stetson to stop and wipe sweat from his forehead. She saw him glance back. Following his gaze, she saw nothing. The deputies must have split up, just as she'd hoped.

Not seeing his partner, Cline moved to the rock cropping and sat down just below her.

Alexis knew she would get only one chance. She didn't have much time, and if she made a sound, he would hear and stand up, and her chance would be lost. Worse, he would see her above him. Once he yelled and let Furu know that he'd found her…

She lifted the rock. For just a moment, she hesitated. If

her arc was accurate, the blow to the head might kill him. Or she might miss entirely. In which case he could turn and shoot her. She didn't want to kill him but reminded herself that these two had kidnapped her, and who knew what they planned to do with her. Letting her go didn't seem to be an option. She suspected Garwood was using her to lure in Culhane. Once that happened, she had no doubt that it was to end with both of them dead.

Rising slightly she hefted the rock. Her foot scraped on the loose rocks under her feet. Cline heard and rose, turning to look behind him.

The rock caught him in the side of the head. The blow made a horrible sound like hitting a pumpkin with a hatchet. But he didn't react. In fact, he remained standing, though dazed. She saw him fumbling for his gun, but she was too shocked to move.

Just as she found her feet and was about to take off, he crumpled to the ground.

Alexis stood staring down at what she'd done before shaking herself out of the shock of it and clambering from the outcrop. Furu was still out there. She had to get Cline's gun.

Earlier, she'd seen him carrying it. But as she hurried to his body, she couldn't see it. Was it possible he'd fallen on it?

The last thing she wanted to do was touch his body. She bent down next to him and tried to lift his dead weight. She was about to try again when she heard the crunch of loose rocks behind her. Before she could react, she was grabbed from behind and thrown to the ground. The deputy loomed over her, the weapon in his hand pointed between her eyes. She saw his gaze shift to Cline but quickly came back to her with a shake of his head. Reaching down, he grabbed her arm and jerked her up and onto her feet.

"Let's go," he said. "Your boyfriend is waiting for your call."

"Wait," she cried. "Aren't you even going to check for a pulse?"

Furu hesitated. "He's breathing. I can see the rise and fall of his chest." As if knowing what she was going to say next, he beat her to it. "I'll call for an ambulance once we get out of here."

CULHANE JUMPED AT the sound of his phone. He'd just hung up from talking to the FBI. He'd been so sure that Garwood was bluffing and that the real reason he couldn't talk to Alexis was that she was dead.

It was Garwood. He held his breath, debating what he would do if this was another lame excuse for why he couldn't talk to her. He accepted the call but said nothing until he heard her voice.

"Culhane?"

His heart soared. He felt tears burn his eyes, and his knees went weak with relief. "Alexis." All of his fears, his worries, his love came out in that one word. "Are you all right?"

"I'm fine."

He heard the phone being snatched away. "Now it is up to you if she stays fine," Deputy Furu said and disconnected.

For a few moments, he stood holding the phone, still hearing the sound of her voice and feeling both relief and fear. She was alive. But for how long?

He looked down at the phone in his hand for a moment before calling the FBI back. Garwood would be calling soon with the meeting place for the exchange. He would double-cross them. There was no way the sheriff was going to make the trade and let them go. He needed the necklace. Culhane needed Alexis. Which meant he was going to need backup.

Garwood sounded irritated when he called, as if he'd been trying the number and hadn't been able to get through. Which was probably the case.

"Do you know where those old silos are outside of Three Forks near the headwater of the Missouri?" Garwood asked. He did. "We'll meet there in thirty minutes. Bring the necklace. Come alone. We'll make the exchange and be done with this foolishness, although I didn't see anything in the newspaper this morning about you dropping your lawsuit."

"It was on the radio this morning. Won't be out in the paper until tomorrow or the next day." Culhane disconnected. After today, there would be no need for the lawsuit.

The silos were near the confluence of the three rivers. He could get there easily in thirty minutes. By then, it would be full daylight. It had snowed in the mountains last night, but by the time he got to Three Forks, the ground was bare and so was the highway.

He had no doubt he was walking into a trap. The FBI had been alerted and knew the location. All he could do was hope that it didn't turn into a shoot-out. Worse, that he might have made a terrible mistake by bringing in the FBI, a mistake that would cost him everything, including his own life.

THE SHERIFF WAS almost to the silos when he got the call. He saw it was from Furu and picked up, afraid that Alexis hadn't been found. Still, he planned to meet Culhane and get the necklace, one way or the other.

"Cline may be dead."

Willy realized he wasn't even interested enough to ask how. "The bad news?" he demanded as he drove toward the headwater.

Furu cleared his voice. "I have Alexis. She nailed him with a rock behind the house where you had us take her." The condemnation was in his words.

He wished that he'd stopped by the house where they'd been keeping Alexis and finished her before coming here. She would only complicate things further, he realized. But then, Culhane was just stubborn enough not to even show him the necklace until he saw Alexis.

"Is she all right?" he asked.

"For now," Furu said.

"Good."

"Apparently you let her talk to Culhane?"

"I did."

"He seemed satisfied, so we're all set."

Silence.

The deputy had never been one to blather on about anything, but still Willy found his monosyllabic speech annoying. He knew he should show some remorse for Deputy Cline, but letting a woman kill you with a rock? He wouldn't want that on his death certificate.

"I'm sorry about Cline. I've set up the trade. It isn't that far from you." He decided since Alexis was alive—after killing his deputy—he would make the trade, then arrest her and Culhane. He gave Furu directions to the silos. "All you have to do is show up with her and leave. I'll take care of everything else." He disconnected. He'd shoot Culhane and arrest Alexis.

As for Cline… He shook his head. The deputy may have done him a favor by dying while trying to bring Alexis Brand in for questioning. Good thing Deputy Furu had collared her. Then he'd used her to bring in Culhane. Unfortunately, Culhane would put up a fight and be killed. Willy could see how he could single-handedly solve the case. But Alexis would squawk. It might be simpler if they were both dead.

Ahead he could see the turnoff to the headwater. New snow turned the mountaintops glistening white and put a chill in the air. He'd wanted to beat Culhane here and apparently had. The former deputy would expect a trap.

Willy smiled at the thought, thinking how easily Culhane had walked into the trap at the cabin—and gotten away. That time, there had been Jana and four deputies. How Culhane had slipped the noose with Jana, he had no idea. At least Furu and Cline had been able to abduct Alexis without anyone being the wiser.

This time, he was on his own. As he pulled into the parking area near the silos, he checked his weapon. Loaded and ready. He holstered it.

Culhane would expect him to be armed and vice versa. It would be like the Old West. Just not at high noon, he thought, as the sun rose over the Bridger Mountains bringing daylight from behind a bank of snow clouds.

CULHANE THOUGHT ABOUT what he'd learned regarding Sheriff Willy Garwood while in his employ. He didn't think most of it would be hard to prove. He had the necklace, which he'd photographed and texted to the FBI. Insurance fraud might be the easiest crime to prove against Atwater and the sheriff.

Murder would be harder. Right now all the evidence pointed to Culhane himself. No matter how this went down at the silos, he was on his way to jail until it was resolved.

While he had Jana under wraps, he couldn't depend on her telling the truth.

He had to believe that eventually, it would all come out—the kidnapping and everything else—and Willy Garwood would be convicted along with his rich friends. They wouldn't get what they deserved, but at least Garwood would never be sheriff anywhere in the country again. Culhane figured that was something. If his rich friends bailed on him, the man might actually see some prison time—if he hadn't destroyed all the evidence against him.

Culhane tried not to think about Garwood not getting what he deserved. But he told himself no matter what, he wasn't taking the law in his own hands. That's why he'd called in the FBI. He didn't trust himself. But he didn't want the man's blood on him, either. He'd already decided he was done with the law. He wanted a different kind of life—with Alexis and his baby and the other babies he hoped they would have.

It was a vision of that life that he held onto as he slowed and turned off the interstate and onto the gravel road to the headwater. He could see the silos in the distance. A large black SUV was sitting in the nearby parking lot. Garwood. He'd come alone. At least it appeared so since Culhane couldn't see anyone else.

CHAPTER TWENTY-THREE

ALEXIS COULD TELL that Deputy Furu wasn't in the mood for trouble, but that didn't stop her.

"You know this isn't going to end well," she said as he grabbed her roughly and bound her hands behind her with plastic flex-cuffs. "When it goes down, Garwood will let you take the fall. He'll get his fancy friends to bail him out while you—"

Furu stuffed a glove into her mouth, making her choke. He grabbed her arm and shoved her toward his SUV parked nearby. She stumbled along with him prodding her if she moved too slowly.

What happened now? That's what she kept asking herself. She might have killed Cline. Just because he'd been breathing when they'd left him didn't mean he would survive without medical attention—and soon—given the temperature. Nor had she heard Furu make a call for an ambulance.

Was that why Furu was in such a bad mood? Was he worried about what the sheriff would do? What *could* he do? Earlier Furu had let her talk to Culhane—only long enough that he knew she was alive. They must be setting up a trade. Her for the necklace? What about Jana? Was she part of the deal?

She knew Culhane would never go for that. He wouldn't risk another life even to save hers and his own. Surely Culhane knew that he couldn't trust the sheriff not to renege on the deal. No way was Garwood going to let them live.

At the SUV, Furu opened the side door and shoved her in. She fell awkwardly to the floor face-first and became trapped between the front and rear seats.

"Stay there." He didn't have to say *or else*. The *or else* was in his tone, in the way he slammed the door.

He climbed behind the wheel to start the engine. As he pulled away, he turned on the radio. A Christmas song came on, reminding her how close it was to the holiday. She hadn't shopped yet for Culhane.

Tears burned her eyes at the thought of how excited she'd been. This was to be their first Christmas together as a couple. Culhane had talked about them getting a tree, but neither of their apartments was large enough for much of a tree.

"You've never gotten a tree for your apartment before," she'd said. "Why now?"

"Because I want to start the tradition with you and me."

She recalled that feeling that had rushed through her veins and warmed her all over. He'd moved closer, drawing her to him for a kiss. "This is the first year that I'm actually looking forward to the holidays."

That day now seemed like it had been months ago instead of only days.

The song ended as Furu turned onto what sounded like a busy highway and sped up.

CULHANE CLIMBED OUT of the pickup and into the cold morning air. The hard ground crunched under his boots as he stuffed his gun into his jacket pocket, curling his palm around the grip, a finger on the trigger. Gloveless, he put his other hand in his pocket with the necklace.

He knew Garwood would want to see the necklace before any exchange was made. He also knew that the sheriff wasn't above killing him for it.

As he approached, he could see his breath. The sun was at his back. Garwood stood in profile as if more interested in the river. Culhane wasn't fooled. Out of the corner of his eye, he kept watch for movement. He didn't trust this man any farther than he could throw him. Garwood wouldn't come alone. Then again, his boys probably had Alexis. Maybe the sheriff had run out of those deputies who would do anything for him—especially if murder was involved.

He stopped a good distance from the sheriff. He'd seen the man at the firing range. He was deadly with a handgun. But not at this distance.

"Culhane, I wasn't sure you would show up," the man called, turning only his head to look at him. "Did you bring it?" Was he afraid of turning broadside because it made him an easier target? Garwood had also seen him shoot at the firing range so he *should* have been worried.

"Where's Alexis?" he called, their voices echoing off the silos.

"She'll be here." The sheriff glared at him.

"In case you're worried, I'm not wearing a wire. I don't even have my phone with me so you can be honest. If you remember how."

"You really enjoy taunting me, don't you?" the sheriff said.

"You're a corrupt cop, so yes. You are everything I despise. It's my duty to try to get some justice—especially for Jana."

"Jana? So she is dead. I didn't know you cared," Garwood shot back.

Culhane was fine with letting the sheriff believe Jana was dead. He feared what the man might do if he learned the truth. That Jana was not in the custody of the FBI.

"Sadly, Jana didn't realize that making a deal with you was like making one with the devil. Have you ever kept your word about anything?"

The sheriff laughed. "You made a deal with me, Culhane. The necklace for your… Alexis. Let's see it."

"Not until I see Alexis. It's only fair—a word you aren't familiar with."

Garwood shook his head angrily. Clearly Culhane was getting under the man's skin. They both had so much to lose, but the sheriff was on his heels. If the necklace surfaced—especially publicly, then his life as he knew it would come crashing down. Garwood might be able to wiggle out of it. He was adept at lying. But Jana could seal his fate, putting the last nail in the coffin with her testimony. What Garwood didn't know was that Culhane had even more to lose.

ALEXIS THREW UP in the back of the SUV, making Furu swear as he drove.

"Carsick," she said, not wanting him or his boss to know what was really going on with her. "Sorry."

Furu didn't say anything for a long while. "I used to get carsick when I was a kid," he finally said, sounding almost compassionate. "It drove my father wild. He thought I should be able to control it."

She lay in the back between the seats wondering where they were going. To meet Culhane and make the exchange, but where? She'd heard enough of Furu's phone call to know that she was going to be traded for the necklace. But then what? Surely Culhane realized that Garwood couldn't be trusted to keep his word.

That meant she had to find a way to even the odds.

"There was this one time after a big Thanksgiving dinner driving home…" she said.

The deputy laughed. "I've been there. Miserable, huh?"

"Yes. The other kids made fun of me because I couldn't go on any of the carnival rides, even the ones for babies."

"The worst were the Twister and the Bullet," Furu said after a moment. "I upchucked all over my friends." He laughed again. "I hated the carnival. I loved the cotton candy—"

"Oh, no, that only made it worse."

"That and the corn dogs."

"You're going to make me sick again," she said but laughed to let him know she was kidding. This was the most conversation she'd ever had with the deputy, even though she'd worked with him for several years before she was fired. He'd always been so aloof that she'd thought it was arrogance. Maybe she'd been wrong. Maybe he was just ambitious. Too bad he'd grabbed onto the sheriff's rotten coattails.

Furu slowed. She suspected they'd been on Interstate 90, based on the sound of the other traffic and the speed with which it seemed they were traveling. The interstate speed limit in a lot of Montana was now eighty.

"You should keep your head down," the deputy said as he drove up a bumpy road, pulled over and cut the engine.

As if she had a choice, she thought, still trapped between the seats. Then she realized that he was referring to when she got out. It surprised her. As he opened his door, she felt the cold breeze and smelled water. Given the length of time they'd traveled, she knew it had to be a river. She wasn't all that surprised when Furu helped her out and she saw the silos.

As if on cue, Culhane had heard the sound of a vehicle engine. He hadn't turned around to look as it had grown closer, though. He'd noticed that the sheriff also hadn't bothered to look, which he took to mean that Garwood knew who had pulled in. He ached to see Alexis, to make sure she was all right, to find a way to keep her safe, knowing how dangerous this was going to get.

"The necklace," Garwood called, sounding both irritated and worried. A breeze had kicked up. It blew across the sagebrush-covered area, kicking up dust that whirled around them. The breeze, especially this close to the river, was chilling.

He heard the vehicle engine switch off. A door opened and closed, then another. Still Culhane didn't turn. He kept his gaze on Garwood, waiting for him to make his move—even as he worried that Furu or Cline might shoot him in the back. Probably Cline, since he was even more Garwood's puppet than Furu.

He watched the sheriff stomp his feet as if trying to warm them. But Culhane suspected he was mostly just getting impatient. This was taking too long. Garwood needed this over so he could start covering his tracks. He would frame this to make both Culhane and Alexis look guilty of Jana's death. The man had resources. Culhane didn't doubt that he would pull it off—unless stopped.

Behind him, he could hear the crunch of boots. He listened, surprised that he heard only two people approaching.

Just as his heart was about to drop to his feet, Deputy Dick Furu and Alexis came into view off to his right. He heard no other sound as they stopped some distance away. Garwood, Culhane, and Furu and Alexis made a triangle. None of them too close to the others.

"You can see that she is fine," the sheriff called. "Now, let's see the necklace."

"Not until he uncuffs her," Culhane said.

Garwood swore loudly. "You have pushed me as far as—"

The snap of the cuffs being removed cut off whatever else the sheriff had said

Furu pushed Alexis forward, then turned and began to walk back in the direction he'd come.

"Where do you think you're going?" Garwood demanded, but the deputy didn't answer as he kept walking. "Furu?" He'd told him he could leave, but now that he was here…

Culhane could hear the deputy continue departing. A moment later, a vehicle door opened and closed, an engine revved and tires threw up dirt and gravel as Furu left.

The sheriff looked as if he might have a coronary.

"I guess it's just you and me," Culhane said.

"And your girlfriend. Let's not forget about her," the sheriff said.

THE COLD BREEZE stirred her curls as Alexis stood out in the cold. Culhane was on her left, the sheriff off to her right by the river. She was afraid to move. Deputy Furu had cut the plastic cuffs off, leaning close to her. She'd felt the sudden weight in her right-hand coat pocket as he'd put something in there before he'd walked away.

She listened to him leave, seeing the sheriff's reaction to it. Clearly that was not what the sheriff had in mind. Was he suddenly afraid that he couldn't handle the two of them alone? He had no idea, she thought, as she slipped her hand into her pocket and felt the gun Furu had put there.

A ripple of excitement raced along her nerve endings. Of course, it might not be loaded. Maybe it was just a cruel trick to make her think she was safer than she was. She didn't think so, though. Furu had told her to keep her head down. He wasn't happy about this and wanted no part of it. He'd just evened the odds with the gun, she told herself, hoping she wasn't wrong.

He'd armed her with a gun, even if it wasn't loaded.

Because he'd known she was going to need it.

She ran her fingers over the cold steel and cupped the grip, her finger on the trigger for a moment. A Glock, if she wasn't wrong. It would have an ammunition clip. She felt... There was a clip in it. Still, that didn't mean it was loaded. But why else give it to her?

Then it hit her: so that when the sheriff shot her, he would be shooting an armed person of interest. But, she quickly told herself, he could just as easily plant a gun on her after the fact. She kept hearing Furu's words. *Keep your head down.*

"Looks like a standoff," Culhane said, his voice carrying across the expanse between them.

"You still haven't shown me the necklace," the sheriff said.

"Throw Alexis your car keys, and let her leave. This is between you and me, Garwood."

The sheriff seemed to consider it for a moment. "First you show me the necklace."

"I'm reaching into my left-hand pocket for the necklace," Culhane said.

Alexis readied herself, worried that once he withdrew it, Garwood would go for his weapon. She kept her focus on the sheriff, but out of the corner of her eye she could see Culhane pull the necklace out and hold it up. The morning light caught on the allegedly faux jewels, making them shimmer and shine.

"Your turn," Culhane said, still holding the necklace up with his left hand. His other hand was in his other pocket— just like Alexis's was. "No one has to die here today. Less mess for you to clean up. Especially when you don't know which side Furu is going to land on."

The sheriff had seemed mesmerized by the necklace reflecting the light but appeared to shake himself out of it. "I know exactly which side my deputy will fall on, Culhane. But you're right. Why shed more blood than necessary? You're still wanted for murder, and your girlfriend is wanted for aiding and abetting. When it comes to a question of credibility—"

"That's if Jana is really dead," Culhane said. "Your keys, Garwood."

The sheriff hesitated, then said, "I'm reaching into my pocket for my keys."

CHAPTER TWENTY-FOUR

"WAIT!" ALEXIS CRIED and began to walk toward Garwood. "Why don't you just give me the keys? I saw you throw at the company-picnic baseball game last summer."

"Alexis, no!" Culhane called, but she kept walking.

The sheriff looked surprised as she began to close the distance between them. "She's right. What was I going to do? Throw them to her? I'm not that good, am I?"

Garwood sounded pleased. He was smiling as she neared. She could almost see the wheels in his head turning. The moment she got within his reach, he would grab her and use her as a shield before killing both Culhane and her—and getting away with the necklace.

But Alexis already knew what he planned. She stopped six feet from him. "You should be able to toss the keys from there," she said.

The sheriff laughed. "Why don't you let me hand them to you? If I miss and they drop in the sagebrush—" He lunged for her an instant before she brought the weapon out of her pocket. It didn't matter, she realized, if the gun Deputy Furu had given her was loaded or not.

She grabbed the barrel and swung the moment his head was within her reach. He'd already latched onto her arm as the butt of the gun struck the side of his head. He let out a howl of pain. His fingers loosened but quickly found their grip again on her coat as he jerked her toward him.

"Where'd you get a gun?" Garwood said, looking confused.

"Your deputy thought I might need it." There was that moment of stark fear in the sheriff's gaze that she took satisfaction in before she tried to break his hold on her.

But off balance, she lost her footing even as she saw him reaching for the gun with his other hand. Seeing an opening, she kicked him in the crotch.

A loud *oof* escaped his lips, and he lost his grip on her arm. She swung the butt of the weapon again, but Garwood was already reaching for her. He blocked the blow with his arm and grabbed her, throwing her to the ground and knocking the weapon from her hand.

He was bent over, clearly in pain as he drew his own weapon and turned it on her. "You stupid bitch."

THE MOMENT CULHANE saw what Alexis had planned, he took off at a dead run toward Garwood. The sheriff was having trouble keeping his focus on both of them. Alexis had purposely stepped where she was blocking Garwood's view of him.

Alexis had to know what the sheriff would do—just as he did. When she pulled the gun, it surprised them both and gave her those extra few seconds to swing the butt at Garwood's head.

With the sheriff momentarily distracted, Culhane sprinted, weapon drawn as he closed the distance between them. He saw her swing the weapon, catch the sheriff in the head. The blow had to have dazed Garwood, but he didn't let it stop him. He grabbed Alexis and threw her to the ground.

Culhane watched in horror as the sheriff pulled his gun and turned it on Alexis.

After that, everything seemed to happen at high speed. The sound of a helicopter approaching was drowned out by the report of gunshots: Culhane fired as he rushed the sheriff, but Garwood had seen him coming and got off a shot before Culhane tackled him and knocked him to the ground.

From the corner of his eye, he saw four men materialize out of whirling dust in front of the silos. Dressed in black flak jackets and armed to the teeth, they rushed forward. "Drop your weapon!" one of the men was yelling.

He hit Garwood with the butt end of his gun with enough force to send blood flying, and then he dropped his gun, kicked away Garwood's and fell to his knees next to Alexis's motionless body.

The FBI swarmed over them, the blades of the helicopter sending the dust flying around them in a blinding whirlwind. He bent over Alexis to shield her from the flying debris and to feel for a pulse. *Please, God.* He felt one. Strong and steady. "That's my girl," he said. "I love you. Alexis. I love you. I can't live without you."

"FBI. Put your hands behind your head!" bellowed a male voice behind him. "You, too, Sheriff," the agent said. "Now!"

Culhane didn't want to let go of Alexis, but he had no choice. He put his hands behind his head. "Alexis is hit," he said but wasn't sure if anyone could hear him. The ground next to her was bright red with her blood.

"Get me an ambulance!" the sheriff was screaming. "I'm shot. Culhane Travis shot me. I was trying to take him in for murder! You can't arrest me! I'm Sheriff Willy Garwood. It's those two you want."

"On the ground," the FBI agent ordered.

"You don't understand," Garwood cried. "He murdered his wife Jana!"

"Jana Redfield Travis is alive and well and in custody," the FBI agent said as he grabbed him, rolled him over in the dirt and cuffed him.

"She's alive?" The sheriff shot a look at Culhane before the FBI agent pulled Garwood to his feet for his perp-walk to a waiting vehicle. Covered with dirt, the sheriff limped on his wounded leg toward the waiting vehicle. "You will pay for this, Culhane!" he yelled over his shoulder. "I will see to it."

In the distance, Culhane could see that agents had detained Deputy Furu. They'd surrounded his vehicle and now had him out and on the ground.

All Culhane cared about was Alexis. Not that he didn't hope that the sheriff lived to stand trial for murder, for attempted murder, for insurance fraud and whatever else the FBI dug up on him.

As he was cuffed and pulled to his feet, he stared at Alexis's pale face. Two EMTs raced up and began to see to her. "How is she?" But he got no answer as he was led away. He stumbled as he felt his heart break. She had to be all right. He'd seen her try to roll away as the sheriff had fired. He had no idea how badly she was shot. But she had to make it. And the baby.

He felt another chunk of heart shatter at the thought of the baby.

Two FBI agents led him to a waiting vehicle. Before they reached it, an ambulance pulled up. He looked back at the two EMTs on the ground with Alexis as they motioned for a stretcher, and then he was forced into the back of a dark-colored van with no windows.

All he could do was pray, something he hadn't done since his mother was alive.

CHAPTER TWENTY-FIVE

ONCE TAKEN INTO CUSTODY, Culhane was allowed one phone call. He could have called a friend. He could have called his father's lawyer. He called Earl Ray Caulfield in Buckhorn, Montana.

ALEXIS DRIFTED IN and out. When she finally opened her eyes and focused on the room, she realized she was in the hospital. Her mother sat on a chair next to her bed holding her hand.

"Mom?"

Her mother's eyes filled with tears as she squeezed her hand. "Hold on. Your father is out in the hall pacing. I promised to let him know the moment you opened your eyes. Don't close them again," she said and jumped up to hurry to the hospital-room door to call for him. "Harry, she's awake!"

"Don't yell, Imogene. It's a hospital."

Alexis felt her heart fill with love for her parents as she heard the joy in both of their voices. In an instant they were at her bedside, one on each side, each taking one of her hands.

"Now, don't accidentally unplug her, Harry," her mother warned when he took her hand hooked up to the IV.

"She isn't plugged in, Imogene." He smiled down at Alexis. "I won't hurt her." She saw her parents share a smile across her bed. For all their chatter at each other, she'd never known a couple more in love. They were inseparable and always had been. Alexis had been a surprise late in their lives, one that seemed to have brought them even closer together.

"Now, what's this we hear about you catching a bunch of crooks?" her father asked.

"Harry, I don't think this is the time."

"It's fine, Mom. Have you heard anything about Culhane?"

Her parents shared another look. "I'm sure he'll be by to see you as soon as he gets out of the hoosegow," her mother said.

The doctor came in and asked her parents to wait outside. They both hurried out, looking worried, though.

"The baby?" she asked the doctor once they were alone.

"Is fine."

She closed her eyes, tears leaking out as she let herself finally breathe. She'd been so afraid. The doctor was saying something about her loss of blood, a concussion and a future scar. Her hand went to a bandage above her temple.

"You'll have headaches for a while, but you were very lucky that the bullet only grazed your skull. We'll keep monitoring you and the baby, but I don't see any problems at the moment," the doctor finished and cleared his throat. "There is an FBI agent here, though, who would like to speak with you."

She opened her eyes and nodded. A few minutes later, the agent came into the room. "Are you up to a few questions?" he asked before setting up a video camera. She told them everything, from waking up to find out that Culhane was wanted for the murder of his wife to being abducted by deputies Terrance Cline and Dick Furu. "Culhane didn't kill Jana. He didn't kill anyone."

"Jana Redfield Travis is in custody. She confirms your story," the agent said when she'd finished.

Alexis let out a sigh of relief. "And Culhane?"

"He is still part of the ongoing investigation."

"And Sheriff Garwood?"

"He's been booked."

She thought of Dick Furu and the gun he'd slipped into her coat pocket. "Deputy Furu helped save our lives."

"He's turned state's evidence against the sheriff and has been helpful in filling in the gaps," the agent said as he turned off the video recorder and rose to leave.

"It's over." Her hand went to her stomach and the baby still there. Culhane's baby. Their baby. She had to fight back the tears.

The agent smiled. "The investigation is ongoing, but I think it is safe to say that your part in it is over. Shall I send your parents back in?"

"Please," she said and braced herself. She hadn't wanted to tell them the news until she'd told Culhane, but she couldn't keep it a secret any longer.

CHAPTER TWENTY-SIX

DAYS LATER, EARL RAY pushed Bessie in a wheelchair toward the door out of the hospital. The sun had come out and
shone bright overhead. He stopped her in a pool of golden
light and bent down to make sure she was all right.

"I'm fine," she said, not for the first time since she'd been
released. His love for this woman filled him to overflowing. Now that he'd finally admitted it to himself and to her,
he felt weak with it and yet stronger than he could remember. It made him want to laugh and cry at the same time.

He'd kept her at arm's length for so many years. Almost
losing her had been his undoing. Maybe he could have let
her move to Arizona and kept on living. But hearing that
gunshot and seeing her fall to the floor... The memory
almost dropped him to his knees. At that moment, he'd
known that he was through not just denying his feelings.
He was through living alone in the house he'd shared with
Tory. He'd kept it just as it had been, a mausoleum he'd built
like a wall around him and his heart. Yet Bessie had broken through that wall even as he'd denied it. Once he'd accepted the truth, he'd been waiting for a sign from Tory. He
wasn't sure if she was letting go or if he'd let go of her. He
liked to think that she would have wanted him to be happy.

His plan had been to wait until he and Bessie got back
to Buckhorn. But now he moved around to the front of the

wheelchair and placed his hands on the armrests to look down at her; he knew this couldn't wait.

Her gaze shot to his ring finger. There was a white band of skin, the wedding ring he'd kept on all these years now put away along with his memories of his first wife. He saw her eyes widen as she looked up at him again. Her mouth opened, but she didn't speak. An anomaly in itself.

Shock widened her eyes further as he dropped to one knee. Those beautiful blue eyes overflowed with tears as he reached into his pocket and brought out the black velvet box.

"I love you, Bessie Walker. I've loved you for years. I should have told you how much you mean to me a long time ago. I hope you'll forgive me and marry this old fool." He wondered if she still wanted to move to Arizona. He had no desire to winter there—let alone live there—but he knew if she had her mind set on it, he'd go. He'd go anywhere she wanted.

"If you still want to go to Arizona, then that's what we'll do." His voice broke, and he felt his own eyes mist. He'd come so close to losing her. He wasn't going to waste another minute. "Please say you'll marry me and make me the happiest man in Montana."

She laughed softly. "We've never even been on a date, Earl Ray Caulfield."

He chuckled. "Bessie, we've been dating for years over blueberry muffins, cinnamon rolls and apricot fried pies. You going to play hard to get, or are you going to say yes?"

She wiped at her tears. "Yes, you old fool. Yes."

Earl Ray slipped the ring on her finger, then rose and kissed her, sealing the deal. "I don't want to go to Arizona," she said when the kiss ended. She looked down at the ring on her finger, then up at him. "I can't think of anything I'd like more than spending the winter curled up with you in Buckhorn."

"That's the woman I love," he said, smiling down at her.

"Now, can we get out of this hospital?" she said. "I want to go home."

"Yes, home," he said as he began to push her to the exit. "I'm thinking we'll sell both of our houses and start fresh," he said. "It will have to be a house with a big kitchen."

She laughed and reached back to cover his hand with her own. "Wherever we end up will be just fine. We'll be together."

"You realize it will have to be a big wedding," Earl Ray said, thinking out loud.

"You're right," she said as the doors opened onto a beautiful day. "Everyone in the county has been waiting years for this. We can't cheat them out of a happy ending."

He laughed and looked up into Montana's big blue sky overhead. This time there was no doubt. He felt as if Tory was giving them her blessing. "Thank you," he whispered and stepped into this new life, feeling younger than he had in a very long time.

CULHANE WALKED OUTSIDE a free man and took a breath of the cold mountain air. He'd been cleared of all charges. The investigation of former sheriff Willy Garwood, however, was continuing.

If it went to trial, Culhane might be called in to testify. But with Dick Furu's testimony, the prosecutor didn't really need too much more. The former sheriff would be going to prison. For how long would depend on whether or not Garwood's rich and powerful friends helped him out.

Right now, all he could think about was going to Alexis. Thanks to Earl Ray, he'd been kept up to date on her con-

dition. She was being released today. The ex-military man
had pulled some strings and gotten him and Alexis out of
a legal mess much sooner than he'd thought possible. Even
better, Earl Ray had kept him informed of Alexis's medical
status. He'd been relieved to hear that the bullet had only
grazed her skull, leaving what Earl Ray said would be a
cute scar but that she and baby were doing fine.

But as he neared the curb, he saw Earl Ray standing beside his pickup waiting for him.

"What's this?" Culhane asked, suddenly worried that
maybe things weren't as good as he'd told him.

"Hop in and I'll tell you," Earl Ray said smiling.

Culhane balked. "I can't tell you how much I appreci-
ate everything you've done for me and Alexis. I owe you a
debt of gratitude, but I need to see her. I need to know that
she really is all right."

"I understand, but take my word for it, she's fine. Your
lawyer and I agree that this other matter needs to be settled first. Indulge me just for a little while. Alexis is being
picked up by her parents from the hospital as we speak.
She's going to their house for a while."

That set off alarm bells. Admittedly after everything
they'd been through, he could understand that she might be
having second thoughts about a lot of things—him especially. But what about the baby? Earl Ray had assured him
that the baby was fine. Still, he needed to get to her to see
for himself that she and the baby were really doing well.

"If she is all right, why is she going to—"

"They just want to spoil her for a little while. She's fine,
I promise."

"And the baby?" he'd asked, heart in his throat.

"The baby is fine, too."

Culhane finally let himself breathe. Still he couldn't wait

to see her, put his arms around her and hold her. "I don't know how I'll ever be able to repay you," Culhane said.

"I just did what I could." Apparently the man could do a lot. "I promise I won't take much of your time. Consider it a favor. It's something I promised to show you."

"You promised who?" Culhane asked suspiciously as he and Earl Ray climbed into the truck.

"I'm sure you're aware that your father's lawyer has been trying to reach you for some time," the older man said as he started the engine.

Culhane groaned under his breath. "I don't care about the money."

"So I've heard. Anyway, when I told him I was planning to see you today, he gave me something that I promised to pass on."

AS THEY DROVE out of town, Culhane saw Christmas lights and decorations adorning houses and businesses everywhere he looked. He'd almost forgotten about the holiday—something he purposely had done since he was twelve. Until this year. It would be his first with Alexis as a couple.

He wanted to start a new tradition with her—after years of believing he could never enjoy it because of the painful memories of his mother.

He'd been trying to come up with something special for Alexis for Christmas—something other than the engagement ring he'd been carrying around. Asking her to marry him was only part of it. He wanted to give her something that would make her brown eyes turn that warm honey color he so loved.

Culhane felt as if he'd wasted so much time digging his heels in about getting serious. The moment he'd met her, he'd felt that special something, and yet he'd held off even asking her out. He'd been afraid that she'd disappoint him. Or worse, that he'd disappoint her.

Alexis had turned out to be like no woman he'd ever met. With Alexis, what you saw was what you got. She was the most honest person he knew. So why had she kept the pregnancy from him?

Because, you fool, you'd said you wanted no part of marriage and babies.

That's because he had wanted to be honest with her. At that time, it was true. But that was before he'd gotten to really know her. All he'd been thinking about this past year was spending the rest of his life with her, making a home, making a family.

But you haven't told her that.

"How do I convince Alexis to marry me without her thinking it's just about the baby?" he asked Earl Ray as the two of them drove out of town twenty minutes later.

The older man laughed. "I've been such a fool myself, I'm probably the wrong person to be giving you advice. But I will, anyway, because I can see that you both love each other. Am I wrong?" Culhane shook his head. "A simple proposal won't do it. She needs to know what you have planned for your future together now that there are going to be three of you. I understand you aren't interested in going back to your job as deputy."

"No."

Earl Ray nodded. "Your father's lawyer and I had a nice visit. He thinks you've been avoiding him."

"I have."

"He said he's known you since you were a boy and that the happiest time of your life was living on the ranch before your mother died. He said you were a natural with the horses."

Culhane was surprised that the lawyer knew that.

"Now that you have your inheritance…" Earl Ray slowed the pickup.

Ahead Culhane saw a sign that arched over the entrance into what was called The Crooked Tree.

Earl Ray drove under the sign and down a narrow paved road in the direction of the mountains. A large red barn stood on the horizon near what appeared to be a stable. He caught his breath as the main house came into view.

"What is this place?"

"A horse ranch that has just come on the market. Apparently in your father's will, he'd asked his lawyer to find something extraordinary for you. Are you aware that your father has been involved in your life from the sidelines? He instructed his lawyer to find you a new home. Your father apparently in his later years regretted selling the ranch where you grew up. He regretted a lot of things before he died, I'm told, but like a lot of us, he hadn't known how to articulate those regrets to the one he loved." Culhane started to argue the point, but Earl Ray stopped him. "Before you see the property, I was told to give you this."

The man reached into his pocket and brought out a business envelope. "I'll take a walk and let you read it. Find me if you want to when you're done." With that he stepped out of the vehicle, leaving Culhane holding an envelope with his name written in his father's neat, no-nonsense script.

ALEXIS PLACED A hand over her stomach. It felt strange being here in her parents' home. So much had changed in such a short time. Maybe it was almost dying. Or maybe it was simply being pregnant.

"I don't understand your attitude," Imogene said as she placed the tea set on the coffee table between them. Her parents had brought her to her childhood home, insisting she needed their loving care.

They'd taken the news about the baby better than she'd expected. They'd been delighted. They'd just assumed, though, that there would be a wedding.

"Of course Culhane wants to marry you," her mother said. "He loves you."

Alexis shook her head as she accepted a cup of tea. "This is not the way I want things."

Her mother raised a brow. "Well, it appears this is the way things are. Are you telling me he doesn't want to marry you?"

"I haven't told him about the baby." Before her mother could ask why not, she continued. "Because that's the problem. Culhane will do the right thing. He proved that with his first wife. I don't want history repeating itself. I want him to want to marry me just for me."

Imogene rubbed her temples. "How can he, when there is no longer just you? Alexis, he deserves to know. You can't keep something like this from him."

"That's just it. Once I tell him, how will I ever know his true feelings?" She didn't tell her mother that she suspected Culhane already knew she was pregnant. Or at least had his suspicions. He knew her body too well.

"Well, you won't know unless you give him a chance to show you," her father said as he walked into the room. "He deserves that."

Alexis ached to see Culhane. There was so much unsaid between them. They'd both risked their lives for each other. Did she really doubt his love? "I know he loves me, and I love him. But sometimes love isn't enough."

Her mother's eyebrows shot up. "I highly disagree. Look at your father and me."

Alexis waved that away. "The two of you were made for each other."

"Not hardly," Imogene said with a laugh.

Her father came over and put a hand on his wife's shoulder. "Your mother wanted nothing to do with me when we met. I asked her to marry me three times before she said yes, and even then I could tell she had her doubts."

Her mother laughed again, nodding at the truth. "I still do," she said jokingly.

"So Culhane's gun-shy," her father said as he took a seat on the couch beside her. "I like him, and I'm a great judge of character." He chuckled. "Sweetheart, I think you can trust this man. But you have to give him a chance. He deserves that, and so do you and your baby."

"In this case, your father is right," her mother said and smiled at her husband. "It happens so seldom, him being right. But I agree with him."

CULHANE STARED AT the envelope feeling as if he'd been ambushed and resenting it. He hadn't wanted to deal with any of this, even though he'd known he couldn't keep avoiding it.

For a moment, he wanted to shred the envelope and whatever was inside. There was nothing his father could say. No excuse the man could make. No man should ever treat his son the way his father had him.

He fisted his hand for a moment, the letter crinkling in his palm as he fought his anger, his sense of betrayal, his hurt. Wasn't it bad enough to lose his mother? Why take away his home and the ranch that he loved before taking away his father as well?

Opening his fist, he looked down at the crumpled envelope and slowly tore it open and pulled out the single sheet of paper. He was expecting a typewritten letter like the few he'd received at boarding school. Short and businesslike, with his father's signature at the end.

What he hadn't expected was to see that this one was in his father's handwriting and appeared painstakingly done. Something about that clutched at his chest, making it hard to breathe.

Son, I'm so sorry.

The words blurred for a moment.

I should have talked to you, tried to explain the pain I was going through. When we lost your mother, I lost myself. I abandoned you, feeling I had nothing to give and you were better off without my bitterness and despair. I know you've never forgiven me for selling the ranch, but son, I couldn't bear living there. Everywhere I looked I saw her, I smelled her scent, I heard her voice. I don't expect you to understand.

The words blurred again, and he found himself choking on strangling emotions, because Culhane *did* understand. He wouldn't have before he met Alexis. He'd never known the kind of love that fills your soul, that makes you want to move mountains, that makes you want to run for fear you will lose it and die of it.

He wanted to quit reading but forced himself to continue.

I should have talked to you, but you were so young. It broke my heart to send you away. I love you, son. I always have. But I knew I couldn't be the father you deserved. All I could do was work hard and make sure you would be cared for when I was gone. I wanted to

go with her. I would have, if not for my love for you.
That's why I've worked so hard. It's all that has kept
me alive. I knew I couldn't be the father you needed.

He stopped reading and took a few deep breaths, feeling his father's pain and his own.

By the time you were older and I had learned to sur-
vive without your mother, you were no longer inter-
ested in me. I don't blame you. I hope someday you
can forgive me. I know that all the money in the world
won't make up for what you lost. What we both lost.
But it's all I had to give.
Just like buying another ranch won't fill that hole left
in your life, and I'm sorry. But it's the best I can do.
I hope you have that special someone to share it with
and will make your own wonderful memories. I'm told
that you might have found that person in Alexis Brand.
That's why I've asked my lawyer to find something
special for the two of you that you both might like as
my gift to you—and my way of saying I hope you find
the happiness you deserve. Your father.

Culhane clutched the letter in his hand for a long moment, tears burning his eyes, before he carefully folded it as he grieved the tragic loss of both of his parents. His father was right. The ranch where he'd grown up wouldn't have been the same without his mother. They both would have suffered because she was the one who'd made it so special. When she'd died, she'd taken the magic with her.

Folding the envelope, he put it in his pocket, opened his door and went to find Earl Ray. "Let's see this ranch," he said when he found him, and Earl Ray smiled.

CHAPTER TWENTY-SEVEN

CULHANE HAD NEVER been more nervous in his life. He stood at the front door of Alexis's parents' home afraid to knock. There was so much he wanted to say, but he feared that he either might not get the chance—or he would say the wrong thing.

"Just tell her what's in your heart," Earl Ray had suggested when he'd dropped him off at his pickup. "The words hardly matter. She'll see the love in your eyes."

Culhane hoped he was right. His lucky Stetson in hand, he took a breath and knocked. When Alexis answered the door, she'd looked surprised and uneasy. He told himself he should have called, but he'd wanted to surprise her. Also, he'd been afraid she wouldn't want to see him.

Now she had to at least tell him to get lost.

He smiled at just the sight of her, his heart aflutter in his chest. She was more beautiful than even in his memory. Earl Ray was right. She would have a small scar at her hairline. He wanted desperately to kiss it, to kiss her.

"I thought we could talk on the drive," he said.

She frowned, surprised no doubt that those were his first words after all this time apart. "On the *drive*?"

"There's something I need to show you." He hadn't wanted to like the Crooked Tree ranch. He hadn't wanted his father to be right about anything. But what struck him after seeing the ranch was how much his father had *known* him. Culhane had loved the place, and even more surprising, it was exactly the kind of place he thought Alexis would love as well.

He turned the brim of his Stetson in his hand. "The letter explains the rest."

She quirked an amused smile. *The letter?*

"From my father."

"Oh," she said.

He looked past her to where her parents stood together. He said hello before turning back to Alexis. "You up to a drive?"

She seemed to hesitate, looked over her shoulder and then said, "I'll get my coat."

On the way, he handed her the letter. He figured it could say it better than he could. He felt her glance at him occasionally as she read. When she finished, she wiped her eyes turning her head away so he didn't see and said, "Whew. Are you okay?"

He nodded. "But because of what happened after my mother died and then Jana, I really thought I wanted nothing to do with marriage and kids. I was afraid I'd mess them up the way my father had me." He saw her expression and quickly rushed on. "Until I met you. You, Alexis Brand, changed everything."

ALEXIS FELT AS if a helium balloon had just been attached to her heart. Seeing Culhane like this… It filled her with so much joy. He'd looked so nervous when she'd opened the door of her parents' house to find him standing there, hat in hand.

She'd been half-afraid of what he had to say. But then he'd said something about a drive and a letter. She'd been worried that the letter was from him. But from his father?

That, too, had been a surprise. So Culhane's father had known about her. Known about them.

They'd driven some distance out of town before Culhane slowed. There was something he wanted to show her. As he turned under an arched sign that read *The Crooked Tree*, she shot a glance at him. "What is The Crooked Tree?"

He looked nervous again. "You'll see."

She felt herself smile. As nervous as he was, she could feel his excitement. He looked happy, his blue eyes shining. She felt such a deep well of love for this man and what he'd been through. The letter from his father had gone a long way to heal some old hurts. In a perfect world, his father would have made those amends before he died, but they didn't live in a perfect world. Still, she could feel Culhane letting go of the past and embracing the future, so she had to thank his father for that.

Ahead, a wonderful red barn came into view and what appeared to be a stable. She looked over at Culhane again and saw that he was apparently waiting for her reaction.

That's when they dropped over a rise and the house came into view. She let out a cry of surprise and pleasure at the sight of the main house. It was three stories, white with tons of windows and a covered porch that ran the whole width of the front. It was framed with deep green pine trees and a mountainside with red rock cliffs above a creek.

"What do you think?" he asked as he stopped the pickup to take in the view.

"It's beautiful," she said on a breath. She couldn't help her excitement. The house was like something out of a magazine. All those windows… It was exactly what she would have dreamed of, if she'd ever dreamed anything like this was possible. She'd been too busy with her career to dream too far into the future—until Culhane.

"The owners set it up as a horse ranch," he was saying. "Over there is pasture enough for a couple dozen horses, and there is more land across the creek and back in the mountains for horseback rides." He turned to look at her. "Want to see the inside of the house?"

More than she wanted her next breath. "Can we?"

Grinning, he held up the key and drove on down to the house.

"The owners aren't home?" she asked.

"Not yet." He parked, and they got out and climbed the steps to the porch. He used the key to open the door, then turned to her.

Before she knew what was happening, he picked her up and carried her across the threshold.

"Culhane?" she cried, confused about what was going on.

"Welcome home—that is, if you like the place," he said as he kissed her and set her on her feet. "This ranch is what my father had his lawyer pick out for us. According to Earl Ray, who spent quite a lot of time with the lawyer, my father did research to try to decide what you would like. He added that to what he knew about me… Welcome to The Crooked Tree."

Alexis felt as if she'd walked into a fairy tale. The living room was spacious and yet warm and inviting with its beautiful stone fireplace and soft, comfortable-looking furniture. Over the hearth was an inlaid design of a beautiful tree with wide branches. Beyond the living room was a large, open kitchen, and beyond that was a deck that overlooked the creek and a fenced yard with a swing set and a small children's fort. As they moved through the house, Culhane was saying that he had had a fort just like it when he was a boy.

The floors were all hardwood, stained with a soft gray that went with the white woodwork. The whole place was filled with light from all the windows. Alexis took a deep breath as Culhane grabbed her hand and said, "Wait until you see the bedrooms."

"Wait, whose house is this?" she asked.

"Ours, if you like it."

Like it? She loved it. Everything about it fit her aesthetic as if Culhane's father had seen into her soul. She started to argue that maybe they shouldn't just tromp through someone's house, but she got caught up in his enthusiasm, and she desperately wanted to see the entire place.

The bedrooms were also bright and painted light colors. The owners must have had at least one boy and one girl. There was a blue room and a pink one, wonderfully whimsically decorated. The bathrooms were all tiled and elegantly appointed.

But it was the master bedroom that delighted her the most. There was a large king-size bed and two walk-in closets, his and hers, along with two bathrooms, also his and hers. As extravagant as that was, the room that stole her heart was off the bedroom. All windows, the sunroom had a large overstuffed chair and ottoman next to bookshelves that made her want to curl up and read right there.

"I thought you might like that part," Culhane said, standing back to watch her. "Look at this." On the other side of the master bedroom was another room, this one clearly a nursery.

"That's nice," she said, avoiding his gaze.

"Do you like it?" he asked.

"The house? It's beautiful. I love it, but—"

"Alexis." His gaze met hers and held it. "I made an offer on The Crooked Tree. It's ours if you want it."

"Want it?" she repeated.

"Want it and me," he said. She felt her breath catch in her throat as he took off his hat and dropped to one knee. She noticed that he was also wearing both his lucky hat and his lucky boots. Tears burned her eyes. "Will you marry me?"

She looked at this handsome cowboy she'd fallen so desperately in love with and felt her heart break a little. "There is something I need to tell you… I'm pregnant."

He let out a whoop. "I was hoping that was the case. We can start filling these bedrooms." He grabbed her by the waist and drew her forward to place a kiss on her belly.

"You're not just asking me to marry you because—"

"Because I love you? Absolutely! Because I want to spend the rest of my life with you? Most definitely. Because I can't wait to get you into that big bed over there? Oh, you have no idea how much I've missed you."

"Culhane, we can't. The place isn't ours yet."

He laughed. She did so love that sound. "My father's attorney had the place completely remodeled as per my father's specifications for us. Then he furnished it—complete with Egyptian cotton sheets and down comforters—not that we can't change it all, if you want."

She shook her head in disbelief. That he'd gone to that much trouble for them touched her heart. "I love it," she said, her voice breaking. "It's as if he knows us."

"It does feel that way, doesn't it?"

"I wish I had gotten to meet him," she said as she looked around. "Because everything about this place is exactly what I would have chosen."

He chuckled. "Believe me, I didn't want to like it. Just out of stubbornness, I tried to find fault with it when Earl Ray showed it to me. But, Alexis, I agree. It's perfect. Now, back to what I asked you," he said, reminding her he was still down on one knee. "Do you, Alexis Brand, take me with all my flaws, including my inability to plan anything? Will you marry me and have our babies?"

She met his gaze. The love in those eyes was what sealed the deal. She no longer questioned why he was asking her to marry him. He loved her. She loved him. And they were going to have a baby. Their baby. "You planned *this*," she said. "I think there might be hope for you yet. So yes, Culhane Travis, I will marry you and have our babies."

He reached into his pocket and brought out a small velvet box. Popping it open, she saw the engagement ring nestled there. The house and horse ranch were over the top, but the small pear-shaped diamond was perfect.

She looked up at him and smiled. "How long have you been planning this?"

He laughed. "I kept waiting for the perfect time. I almost blew it. As you can tell by the size of the diamond, I saved for the ring on my deputy salary."

"I love it all the more because of that," she said as he slipped it on her finger and rose to his feet. "But this ranch… It's so much."

He nodded. "I still haven't talked to my father's lawyer, so I have no idea how much my father left me, but apparently this ranch didn't make a dent in it. I love the property and want to raise horses and make a living doing that. If you're agreeable, I'd like not to touch the money I was left. Let our kids and grandkids deal with it. If we raise them right, they won't need it. What do you say?"

She reached for him. "I say I love you."

He laughed as he took her in his arms and kissed her. The kiss was sweet and tender and held a promise of what was to come—not just today but years from now.

"I wasn't kidding about that bed," he said, eyeing it and

then raising a brow at her. "Or about this place being ours. What do you say, soon-to-be Mrs. Culhane Travis?"

"Alexis Travis. I like the sound of that. You think that bed is as inviting as it looks?"

"Only one way to find out." He swept her up in his arms again, and in two long strides, he tossed her onto the bed and jumped in after her.

CULHANE BURIED HIS fingers in her short dark curly hair and pulled her down for a kiss. Her eyes flashed with desire filling all that warm brown in her gaze with firelight. Her lips, bee-stung full, brushed his before his mouth took possession of hers.

Slowly, he pulled back to look at her, still amazed that he'd found this woman, even more amazed that she loved him. He gently touched the soon to be scar at her hairline, then leaned forward and kissed it lovingly. She sighed and snuggled closer. In that moment, everything they'd been through seemed to meld them together in a way that not even lovemaking could.

As he drew back again, their gazes locked, then she cupped his face in her palms and drew him down in a kiss. Her tongue teased at the tip of his, making him ache as his body responded. He couldn't wait to feel her naked skin against his.

But still he took his time, slowly unbuttoning her blouse one button at a time. Her nipples pebbled as he drew the fabric back to look at breasts covered by only a thin layer of white lace. He thumbed one nipple, making her gape with pleasure before he freed her breasts and feasted on them.

"Culhane." His name sounded like a plea on her lips as she jerked his shirt open, making the snaps sing. Her warm palms went to his chest.

In a flurry of activity, they discarded the rest of their clothing and pressed their bodies together, both sighing with a kind of release and relief. But the moment didn't last. Desire had them stroking and kissing and responding to a need that had always been there between them.

Alexis rolled him over onto his back. A moan escaped her lips as she settled down on him, her full breasts pressed to his chest. Desire spiraled down through him. He groaned in pleasure at the familiar feel of her as she adjusted herself to take the heat and hardness of him inside her.

He froze for a moment thinking of the baby. "He's fine," she whispered.

"He?"

She kissed him, teasing him with her tongue as she gently rode him. He cupped her breasts, tweaking the hard tips of her nipples as she rocked her head back.

He watched her come, satisfaction softening her pretty features as she opened her mouth and let out a joyful cry. He couldn't help the smile that curled his lips. Pleasuring her elevated his own desire. She kept riding him, taking him with her, until he reached the crest and she collapsed on his heaving chest.

He buried his fingers again in her hair, drawing her into him with his other arm as they lay skin to skin. "That's not bad for a first memory."

She smiled as she tried to catch her breath.

"I want to make memories in this house with you and our children," he said as he brushed her hair back and looked into those wonderful brown eyes.

"How many children are we talking?" she said, lifting a brow.

He grinned. "As many as we want. I want this baby to have brothers and sisters, something I never had," he said, gently placing his hand over her protruding abdomen. "We can always adopt too."

She smiled and nodded. "This is going to be such a wonderful place to raise them." Then he kissed her, and they spooned together as a breeze stirred the pines and the sun traveled across Montana's big sky.

CHAPTER TWENTY-EIGHT

THE NEXT FEW days were a whirlwind of activity as they moved out of their apartments and into the house on The Crooked Tree ranch. Alexis hardly had time to worry about what was happening legally with the sheriff's department or Garwood himself.

Her life had changed in an instant. With each load, she would put away her things in the huge closet and bathroom and marvel that this amazing home was theirs.

Culhane laughed and said that him having his own closet was a joke. "All I need is a place for my lucky boots." They were like two kids in a candy store as they moved into the house. They'd never had this much room and really didn't know what to do with it. Alexis knew it would fill up in time.

With each day she could feel her body changing. The day she felt the baby move, she called Culhane in from the stable.

"What's wrong?" he asked in alarm.

She shook her head, crying with joy, as she took his hand and placed it on her stomach. She watched his face as he felt their son move. The joy and wonder she saw there thrilled her more than he could ever know. Soon they would be a family. She told herself that all the bad times were behind them.

While she had made a point of not paying attention

to the news, she'd seen Culhane on the phone with Deputy Al Shaw numerous times. She'd overheard enough to know that the undersheriff, Larry Owens, had stepped in as acting sheriff for the time being. Owens, an older man who'd been with the department for years, had stayed in the shadows as if waiting to retire during Garwood's reign.

It sounded like Al was going to apply for the undersheriff position since Owens would be retiring when a new sheriff was hired.

Alexis was happy for him. Al was a good guy and would help whoever they hired for interim sheriff until the election.

It was no surprise to anyone but Garwood that everyone turned against him—including his rich and powerful friends. He was denied bail for his own safety, the judge had said. His trial was scheduled for next year.

Often when Culhane's phone rang, it would be Al with news. Alexis had been expecting Jana to call, and she was sure that Culhane had been as well. When his phone rang one evening, she'd thought this was finally it. Jana would need money to start over. Of course, she would lean on Culhane.

Had he asked her what he should do, she realized she would tell him to help her. Maybe it was the season. Or maybe it was all the blessings she and Culhane had, but she wanted the two of them to be generous—even though Jana would have been anything but with Culhane.

They were settling in to their new home, their new life and putting the past behind them. Even the boxes from their apartments had been unpacked.

That's why later that afternoon when she came downstairs, she was surprised to see Culhane standing before a huge pile of boxes.

"I thought you didn't have anything more to move," she said in surprise.

"My father's attorney dropped them by. They're Christmas decorations," he said with a wave of his arms. "My mom's. I guess my father saved them thinking..." He looked at her. "As I told you, my mother loved Christmas, and she had a lot of decorations. If you want, we can just haul the boxes away and not even open them."

"Are you serious? Not open them?" She scoffed as she moved to one of the boxes. "These are from your childhood. Of course we'll keep them." She held out her hand. "I'm going to need a knife to cut this tape."

He dug out his pocketknife and handed it to her. As she cut open the first box, she felt her eyes light up. "Oh my, these are beautiful," she said as she brought out two large deer adorned with ornate wreaths around their necks. "Wouldn't these look wonderful over there?" She opened another box with delight to find elegant wreaths for the doors and a whole family of geese for the mantel.

"And these lights! We can string them over there." She pointed to a spot by the window overlooking the creek before she saw his face.

He was staring at the deer, and there were tears in his eyes.

She quickly went to him. "Is this too painful?"

Culhane shook his head. "It brings back such cherished memories. I love that you love it."

"I do. Our children will love all of this," she said with a wave of her hand.

Culhane kissed her, and they both began to dig through the boxes.

"Shall we start putting things up?" she asked when

they'd taken the decorations out of every box. "You know how your mother had them, so just tell me and—"

He was shaking his head. "You decide where things should go. I'll help. But this is our home."

"I won't get it right."

He laughed. "Look at all of this. You can't get it wrong." He picked up a large beautiful crystal angel. "Without thinking, where would you put this?"

"Over there so the crystal picks up the firelight." She started to correct herself since there were so many other places it could go.

"Perfect," he said and carefully handed it to her. "Tomorrow we'll go buy a tree. It's a little late to be tromping into the woods for one." He considered the twenty-foot ceiling. "A large tree. Would you like that?"

"I would love that." She leaned in to kiss him, and he encircled her in his arms. "Our first Christmas."

Together they began to decorate the large main-lodge living room. Culhane put on holiday music. Alexis made hot apple cider. At the sound of a vehicle, they looked out to see one of the neighboring ranchers pull up. As he climbed out, he pulled a huge evergreen Christmas tree from the back of his pickup.

"I thought with all the moving, you might not have time to cut your own tree this year," the rancher said. "I'm Bob Barnhart from down the road." He extended his hand.

"Please come in and have a cup of coffee to warm up," Alexis offered.

But Bob declined. "I have to get on home, but I would love to sometime during the holidays. My wife is anxious to meet you," he said to Alexis. "Just wanted to welcome you to the neighborhood."

They hauled the tree into the living room. It was huge but would fit quite nicely.

"We're going to have to buy a tree stand," Alexis said after Culhane leaned the tree against the wall.

He laughed. "I'm sure there's one here," he said, motioning to the rest of the boxes they hadn't looked in yet. Sure enough, there was, along with dozens and dozens of ornaments that his mother had collected.

When Alexis's parents called to see how they were doing, she invited them over. Her mother brought a cranberry-orange coffee cake and some ornaments from Alexis's childhood.

"You are not climbing that ladder," Culhane said when he saw Alexis starting up it with more ornaments. She smiled down at him, shook her head and let him spoil her.

It was nightfall by the time Culhane put the star on the top of the tree. Her parents had gone home, leaving the two of them to enjoy their hard work. They stood back in awe, Culhane's arm around her, as they admired the results.

"It's...amazing," Alexis said, her voice breaking. "It's so...beautiful." She could see the Christmas lights reflected in his blue eyes along with the sheen of tears.

"Mom would have loved this." He turned to her. "She would have loved you and this little one."

"I know I would have loved her."

He nodded. "And she would have loved how happy we are."

"I think she knows," Alexis whispered. "A guardian angel has been watching out for us both. And now your father is with her."

CULHANE COULD ONLY nod around the lump in his throat.

He pulled her close, his gaze locking with hers. As each box had been opened and each decoration carefully lifted out, he had remembered happy memories from his childhood, the ornaments especially representing the best of his childhood Christmases.

"I feel like your mother isn't the only one here tonight," Alexis said. "This ranch is such a blessing. Your father wanted it to be perfect for us, and it is. He must have been so happy with you and your mother on your ranch."

Culhane nodded. "Looking back, I realize that all of this reminded my father too much of her. I don't think I ever realized how much he loved her. I think I, too, was a reminder of her."

"We know that he loved you," she said. "He just didn't know how to show it."

"He threw himself into his work," Culhane said. "After the first Christmas, I didn't ask to come home. Nor during summer vacation. Maybe he thought I didn't want to see him, either." He shook his head. "He would write me a check and tell me to get something I wanted."

"I'm so sorry," she said, pulling him close.

"It wasn't all bad. Christmas at the Cardwell Ranch with Ford was so much fun. He has all those cousins. We used to sled and have these humongous snowball fights." He laughed. "They treated me like I was one of the family. No one could be luckier than that."

"He knew you loved ranching," she said, motioning to the ranch they now owned. "You do realize how special this gift actually is, don't you? My mother said that your dad's lawyer came over to the house and asked them all kinds of questions about what I liked. Your father hadn't forgotten you. The Crooked Tree proves it."

He looked down into her beautiful face. "Do you have any idea how much I love you?"

"Do tell," she said, laughing.

"I prefer to show you," he said. "Every day of our lives. I want to make you my wife. I want to be your husband." He loved the sound of that. "I can't wait to marry you and raise our children here." He glanced around the room. "I've never wanted anything more in my life. My father *did* know me. This place… It's exactly what I would have chosen. We can have an amazing life here. You can still track down bad guys. You can do whatever you want. Just be my wife and share your life with me and our children. Let's not wait. Let's get married on Christmas Day."

ALEXIS LOOKED OVER at him to see if he was serious. "A Christmas wedding? You do realize that Christmas is coming up really fast?"

"Tell me what your fantasy wedding is like," he said later in bed. He'd leaned on his side to give her his undivided attention. "I'm thinking it would be here, downstairs. We have plenty of room. Can you see it?"

Alexis had to think for a moment. Had she ever let herself even fantasize about it? Slowly, she did begin to see it. She smiled and, closing her eyes, told him what she saw.

Culhane laughed as he kissed her, forcing her eyes open again. "Leave it to me."

That sounded a bit frightening, but she kissed him back and said, "I could help."

"No, I have it. Trust me." He grinned at her.

"All right. I'll call my mother. I'm sure she'll be excited to go with me to find a wedding dress."

"Just give me a list of who you'd like to invite," he said, sounding excited.

"HE'S PLANNING THE WEDDING?" her mother said when they met at the bridal shop. "I thought he never planned anything ahead of the next few minutes."

Alexis laughed. "He didn't. Doesn't. I'm sure it will be fine."

Her mother looked skeptical. "Maybe I'll offer my help."

"I'm sure he could probably use it." But the next day, after they'd found what had been the perfect wedding dress at the first shop they tried, her mother called to say that Culhane apparently had everything under control.

"You'll have to stay at your parents' house the night before the wedding," Culhane had informed her.

"You have to be kidding," she'd said.

"Not for that reason." He'd laughed. "You can't see the venue until that morning when we get married. I want to surprise you."

Her mother had raised a brow when she told her.

"No matter what, I'm going to love it," Alexis assured her.

Nothing was going to spoil their wedding day.

CHAPTER TWENTY-NINE

ALEXIS SAW THE expression on Culhane's face and knew something was wrong the moment she walked into the kitchen. He was on the phone. At first she'd thought it was Jana, but when he said, "It's fine. Thanks for letting me know," and disconnected, she knew it was much worse news than Jana.

She waited, wondering what could have upset him. Something about the wedding? When he said nothing, she broke the tense silence. "You don't have to worry. If we don't get married Christmas Day—"

"We're getting married Christmas Day," he said, putting on a quick smile that just as quickly disappeared. "That was Al." He took a breath and let it out before he spoke again. "Cline disappeared from the hospital."

She'd actually forgotten about Cline, once she'd heard that he was alive and doing better in the hospital. He'd awakened in the trees, walked to a neighboring house and got them to call an ambulance since Furu hadn't. She'd just been relieved that she hadn't killed him. After that, she'd forgotten all about it. Moving, getting settled here on the ranch, preparing for Christmas, thinking about their wedding... She swallowed, feeling guilty since she was the one who'd put Deputy Cline in the hospital.

As if reading her mind, Culhane said "Do not feel guilty about hitting him with that rock. He kidnapped you."

"I know. Where do they think he went?"

"That's just it," Culhane said. "Al's worried. Cline has some neurological problems, and as wrong as it is, he might blame you."

She felt her eyes widen. "You think he'd come out here? Threaten me?"

"I didn't want to tell you, but just in case... Not that I intend to let him near you."

She nodded. "The law's looking for him, right? They'll probably pick him up before we have to worry about it."

"I hope so." He turned to her, taking her shoulders in his hands and looking into her eyes. "I don't want anything to get in the way of our wedding. Nothing is going to keep me from marrying you Christmas Day. Certainly not Terry Cline."

CULHANE HAD LEARNED that bad news usually came in threes. After Al's call, he'd figured Jana was next. So he hadn't been surprised to get her call. The past was determined to drag them back—even at Christmas. He'd heard that she had been released on bail, so it had only been a matter of time before she'd be calling.

"Jana," he said and braced himself, expecting she was going to hit him up for money. He hadn't decided what to say. It wasn't like he didn't have it. But he also knew that no matter how much he gave her, she'd be back for more again and again. He figured if he said no, she would threaten to sue him. He wasn't sure he wanted to be dragged through that, either.

"I just called to thank you," Jana said. "You really did save my life."

That took him by surprise. "You're welcome."

"I have some news that I wanted to share with you," she said.

He waited, still bracing himself.

"You know about my son, Joshua. Well, I'm going to be his nanny again for a while until Buzz Atwater and I get married."

"What? I thought he was going to jail for insurance fraud."

"It wasn't him," she said. "It was his wife. She'd been taking all the real jewels out of the jewelry he'd given her and replacing them with fake ones, then working with the sheriff to have the most expensive ones stolen. Buzz had no idea until the emerald-and-diamond one was stolen a second time. That's when she confessed what she'd been doing with the sheriff. They're getting divorced. Buzz and I are moving to Houston and starting over—once my legal problems are behind me. Buzz has hired me a good lawyer. We're going to be a family."

"Jana…" He started to warn her about getting her heart broken but realized it would be a waste of breath. "I'm happy for you."

"Thank you. And I'm sorry for…everything," she said.

He disconnected and hoped Jana had a happy ending— for her son's sake—and went to tell Alexis the news.

ALEXIS HAD WAITED until almost the wedding to have the final fitting for her dress since her body seemed to change daily. She'd already packed to spend the night with her parents. Culhane had insisted so he could surprise her tomorrow when she arrived at the ranch. She loved his excitement about the wedding. Added to her own, they were both almost giddy with it.

"I'm all packed," she announced. "Are you sure you

don't need help with the wedding plans?" she asked Culhane, seeing that he looked worried.

"The wedding is coming along fine," he said and seemed to hesitate. "They still haven't found Cline. Please be careful, okay?"

"I will." She hated to even mention her last appointment with the seamstress. "I have a dress fitting in an hour." She splayed her hands over her stomach. "Your son is to blame."

"In an hour? I'll go with you."

"Culhane, you can't go with me. You can't see the dress before tomorrow."

His phone rang. "I have to take this." He stepped into the other room and closed the door. When he came back out, he said, "I have several deliveries coming that I have to sign for. Maybe you can get your mother to go to the fitting with you."

"Mom's busy getting dinner ready for tonight, remember? Culhane, I'll be fine."

He moved to her to take her shoulders in his hands. "Promise me you'll be careful and that you'll call me when you leave the bridal shop."

She smiled. "I promise." But she could see that he was still worried.

"Take your gun," he said.

She pulled back to look at him in surprise. "Culhane—"

"Do it for me and Junior."

She smiled. "Junior?" He shrugged and gave her a shy grin. "All right. But I'm not sure how my shoulder holster will look with my wedding dress," she said jokingly. She went to the closet, reached up on the top shelf and pulled down her weapon. Strapping it on, she reached for her coat. "It won't be long before I call you."

"Good," he said. "You'll go straight to your parents' house, right?"

"Yes, and I'll see you there. Don't forget, Christmas Eve dinner is at six."

"I won't forget." He drew her close. "Stay safe."

"You, too," she said and kissed him and left. It worried her that he was so worried about Cline. As neurologically injured as the deputy was, it surprised her that he hadn't been picked up yet. What if he'd gone off somewhere and died? She shuddered at the thought. That would mean that ultimately she had killed him.

Alexis parked down the block from the bridal shop and joined those still shopping on the crowded sidewalk. She could hear Christmas music and bells ringing. As everyone scurried past, there was excitement in the air. She breathed it in, smiling to herself. She couldn't remember ever being this happy. She was getting married tomorrow. To Culhane Travis. Her smile broadened as she reached the shop. She couldn't wait to try on her dress.

CULHANE WENT TO work getting the house ready for the wedding. He wished more than ever that his mother was here to tell him what he was doing would make his bride happy. He was winging it. For a man who didn't plan, he had a plan. That always made him nervous.

With such a tight deadline, he had to scramble to get the cake and the band and the flowers—and offer double the cost. He didn't care. It was worth it. He wanted Alexis to have her dream wedding.

As it started to come together, he began to breathe a sigh of relief. He really might be able to make this happen. It took his mind off Garwood and what might or might not be happening.

"Deputy Dick Furu is singing like a canary," Al said when he called. "We had no idea of all the illegal stuff the sheriff was involved in. But Furu did. Not just that, the deputy kept track of all of it with receipts and photos and recorded phone calls."

"He was either covering his behind or—"

"Or planning to take Garwood down from the first. I thought at first he might have been working with the FBI all along."

Culhane had let out a low whistle. "What about Garwood's rich friends?"

"Dropping him like a hot potato," Al said with a laugh. "Rumor is that Garwood has had to sell everything he has just to pay his criminal-defense lawyer. I heard that a lot of lawyers wouldn't take his case."

Culhane felt such an overwhelming sense of relief. Maybe he did still believe in justice. "Now I can drop my lawsuit."

"Are you sure you don't want to come back? I wouldn't make any hasty decisions."

"I'm going to raise horses out here on the ranch. I'll tell you all about it when I see you. By the way, there wasn't time to send out proper wedding invitations. Alexis and I are getting married tomorrow in the afternoon. I hope you can come."

"That quickly?"

"I couldn't wait," he said and laughed. "I'm not letting that woman get away. After I almost lost her…" He had to swallow down the lump that rose in his throat. "I'm just not taking any chances."

"I think it's wonderful. Just tell me when to be there."

"One more thing. Still nothing on Cline?"

"Sorry, he hasn't turned up, but I'm sure he will."

That's what I'm worried about, he thought as he looked out the window at the dark pines along the creek. The ranch was isolated with lots of places to hide. Culhane told himself that by tomorrow, this house would be teeming with people who'd come to wish him and Alexis well.

He tried to shake off the bad feeling he'd been carrying around with him since Al's call about Cline escaping the hospital. As he disconnected, he checked to see if he'd gotten a text from Alexis yet and had just missed it. Maybe the fitting was taking more time than she'd thought it would.

He checked his watch, surprised that she hadn't been gone that long. When was he going to stop worrying about her? When Cline was caught. But then, he told himself, he would probably never stop worrying about her, and soon there would be a baby to worry about as well.

FOR A MOMENT, Alexis was afraid the bridal shop was closed. She felt a wave of panic. Her heart began to pound at the thought of not getting her dress today—especially with Culhane working so hard to make this happen.

But when she reached the front door, she pushed, and the door swung open. Her pulse began to slow a little. Still, the main lights in the front weren't on.

As she started toward the back, she heard the door lock behind her and felt a moment of alarm until she realized they must have stayed open only for her. "Hello," she called as she walked toward the rear.

"Back here."

She followed the voice, thinking about her dress. She couldn't wait to see Culhane's expression when he saw it on her. She came around a rack of dresses and saw the seamstress and owner of the small shop, Helen, look up. She was in her late fifties, an elegant woman with a gray bob that framed a classically beautiful face and bright blue eyes.

"I hope you didn't stay open on my account," Alexis said.

Helen waved that off. "You're my last fitting today, so I've locked up for the day. Not to worry. I still have things to do before I go home. Want to see your dress?"

Alexis clapped her hands together. "I can't wait." The last time she was here, they'd made some changes that they both were excited about.

"Step in the dressing room. I'll bring it to you," Helen said.

Alexis took off her coat and hung it on the hook by the door before stepping in the dressing room. Once inside, she took off her shoulder holster and laid it down on the upholstered bench before she began to shed her sweater, jeans and boots.

"Here you go," Helen said and reached through the curtain to hand her the wedding dress. "You need help?"

"No, I'm good," she said as she held it up to her and looked into the mirror. She broke into a huge smile and hurried to put it on. It wasn't until she stepped out to show Helen how perfectly it fit that she saw him reflected in the triple mirror.

Cline had his arm locked around Helen's throat and a pair of scissors in his other hand pointed at her face.

CHAPTER THIRTY

CULHANE HAD BEEN pacing the floor. He'd tried to call Alexis, but his calls went straight to voice mail. He'd told himself that she was probably still at her fitting and had turned off her phone.

He started to call her again, but instead called his father's lawyer. Thomas Quinn answered on the second ring. "I need your help."

A low chuckle. "That's what I'm here for. Tell me what you need."

He did. Ten minutes later, Thomas drove up at the ranch and Culhane left him to sign for the deliveries while he drove into town. He told himself he was on a fool's errand, but he didn't care. He'd been waiting for the other shoe to drop. He feared it had.

Driving too fast, he was afraid he'd get pulled over, which he decided might be all right, too. If his fears were warranted, he could use some backup from the law. He parked behind Alexis's car and ran down the sidewalk through the dwindling shoppers to the bridal shop.

She was still in the shop? It was getting dark. It wasn't that long until they were supposed to be at her parents' for dinner. He felt his concern jump when he reached the front door to find it locked.

He thought about breaking the glass but decided going in the back might be the smartest thing he could do. At this point, Alexis might not even be in trouble, he told himself even as his heart argued just the opposite. Something was wrong. He could feel it. He should never have let her go alone.

"DEPUTY CLINE," ALEXIS said, surprised how calm her voice sounded since her heart felt as if it was about to burst from her chest. Helen looked terrified and with good reason. "You really shouldn't be seeing me in my wedding dress."

He looked confused as if Alexis hadn't quite realized what was going on. He tightened his hold on Helen's throat and shoved the blades of the scissors closer to her cheek. "I'll kill her." Helen began to cry, tears rolling down her cheeks, her lips quivering.

"Why would you do that?" Alexis asked. "Helen's never done anything to you."

"You almost killed me!" he cried, his voice shaking with anger. "You messed me up big-time. I... I can't think straight. The doctor said I might never be able to think straight again."

Alexis wondered if Cline had ever thought straight. "You kidnapped me."

"Yeah, but I didn't hurt you."

"But now you're threatening to hurt this woman who never did anything to you. Why don't you let her go so you and I can settle this?" She saw him considering whether it was a trick. "I have no weapon. I'm in my wedding dress. What could I possibly do to you?" She could see that he still didn't trust her. Maybe he wasn't as injured as she thought.

His arm seemed to relax a little around Helen's throat, the scissors not quite so close to her face. "They're going to put me in prison because of you. They had me cuffed to a hospital bed."

She hadn't noticed the metal at his wrist until then. It made a tinkling sound, reminding her of the Christmas bells she'd heard ringing earlier. She had to swallow the lump in her throat at the thought but refused to let herself think of everything that would be lost here if this didn't go her way. She couldn't let him harm Helen. She thought of her gun on the upholstered bench only feet away in the changing room. But if she made a move for it, she couldn't trust what Cline would do.

"This is between you and me, Terry," she said as calmly as she could. "Let her go so we can finish this."

WHEN CULHANE REACHED the alley entrance, he stopped to catch his breath. He could see where the lock had been broken. Pulling his weapon, he slowly eased the door open, hoping it didn't make a sound.

It was dark back there in the storage area, but he could see a light in the distance. As he slipped in, he let the door close silently behind him. It took a moment for his eyes to adjust. He didn't want to fall over any of the boxes stacked along each side as he moved cautiously forward.

He hadn't gone far when he heard voices and someone sobbing. His heart dropped. He'd been right to come here. He'd been right about there being trouble. He knew who he'd find in the next room. He just prayed he could get Alexis out of it alive.

As quietly as possible, he crept toward the sound of the voices as he tried to make out who was talking. He was rewarded by hearing Alexis's. It was strong and assured. He smiled inwardly at the thought of her.

It was the other voice he heard that had anger welling up

like lava from inside him. He told himself he couldn't blame Garwood for this, even though he did. Garwood cultivated men like Terrance Cline for his dirty work. He brought out the worst in them and then cut them loose on society.

He stepped closer until he could see through a gap in the doorway into the dressing-room area. Cline had his back to him, one arm locked around a gray-haired woman's neck and a pair of large scissors in his other hand that he was using to threaten both women.

What Culhane couldn't see was Alexis. She must have been in one of the fitting rooms beyond his view. He understood now why Alexis's voice had sounded so reasonable. She was trying to get Cline to release the woman.

"Let Helen go," Alexis said. "Your problem is with me."

"Why don't I just kill you both?" Cline asked. "My life is over. What do I care?" He tightened his hold on the older woman making her cry out.

Culhane realized he couldn't get a clear shot from where he was. He could try to get closer, but if Cline heard him coming, there was no guessing what the man might do. Clearly he had nothing to lose at this point.

He frowned, wondering if Alexis had her gun. He told himself that he knew this woman. She would have done what he'd asked her. She'd have the weapon. But if she were wearing her wedding dress right now, she wouldn't have it on. However, if it was within reach… She would have already gone for it, possibly.

But maybe she couldn't reach it without a distraction.

Culhane knew he was gambling on knowing his bride-to-be. If she had her weapon with her in the dressing room like he suspected, then she was just waiting for an opening.

Praying he was right, he looked around for something he could use to give her that opening.

ALEXIS COULD FEEL everything going south. Cline was starting to lose it. He was realizing what his future held. He was already in so much trouble that his injured mind was telling him that another two deaths wouldn't matter.

Helen seemed to realize it as well. She'd stopped crying and had grown very pale. She looked as if the only thing holding her up was Cline's arm around her throat. Alexis knew she had to do something, but in the time it would take her to get to her gun, Cline could kill Helen. And yet she knew she had to take that chance unless—

The sound of boxes toppling somewhere in the shop caught all of their attention. Helen's eyes had widened in alarm—and so had Cline's. He'd half turned to look behind him—and Alexis made her move, knowing she might not get another chance. She grabbed her weapon and, leading with the barrel, swung back into the doorway of the dressing room to point it at any part of former deputy Terrance Cline that she could put a bullet into. With him half-turned, he'd given her clear access to his side.

She didn't have time to think, to worry or to fear that she might hit Helen. She pulled the trigger.

THE MOMENT CULHANE heard the shot, he was moving, rushing Cline. He told himself that Alexis was one hell of a shot. She wouldn't have fired until she had a target she thought she could hit.

As he came around the corner, he saw that Cline was still standing, still had a choke hold on Helen, still held the scissors too close to her face. Worse, he saw that he didn't have a clear shot.

Alexis's second shot took the legs out from under Cline. Culhane saw the man begin to slump. All that seemed to be keeping him upright was his hold on the older woman in front of him. Culhane closed the distance quickly, going for the scissors. He wrenched them out of the former deputy's hand and tossed them away before he grabbed Cline's arm and unlocked it from around Helen's neck.

Helen stumbled a few feet away before her knees buckled and she dropped to the floor. Cline fell back, crumpling on the floor in his own blood. His eyes were wide with both anger and terror as Culhane stood over him. Had the man tried to do anything, he would have shot him, but he didn't have to worry. Cline wasn't going anywhere.

"Alexis?" Culhane called. He looked away from Cline to see that the dressing room curtain was closed. "Alexis?" Just as he was ready to go rushing in to check on her, she stepped out in her T-shirt and jeans. He let out of a sigh of relief. "You scared me."

"Sorry, I had to change out of my wedding dress," she said, sounding so wonderfully reasonable. "It's bad luck for you to see me in it until the wedding."

He shook his head as he heard the sound of sirens and turned to see Helen propped up against the wall with her phone in her hand. She was crying again, but they were tears of relief, he saw as Alexis went to her.

"Nothing is going to keep us from getting married tomorrow," Culhane told Cline. But he realized that the former deputy was no longer listening. He was dead.

CHAPTER THIRTY-ONE

"KEEP YOUR EYES CLOSED," Culhane said as he guided her up the stairs to the ranch house and across the porch. "Ready?" He'd met her at the bottom of the stairs when she'd arrived with her mother and father.

She would never forget the look in his eyes when he'd seen her step out in her wedding dress. She'd tucked that memory away for safekeeping as he'd taken her hand. "You are so beautiful," he'd said, his voice breaking with emotion.

Her parents had hurried inside to join the other guests. She could hear Christmas music playing and smelled something sweet and warm on the air as they disappeared inside.

Now at the front door, Alexis could feel herself shaking, and not from the chilly December day. They hadn't gotten their white Christmas, but there was a bite to the air that promised it wasn't far behind. She swallowed and told herself she'd never been more ready for anything in her life.

Last night had been a late one at the sheriff's department. It was the middle of the night before they made it to her parents' house for Christmas Eve dinner. Her mother had filled plates for them and popped the food in the microwave, and they'd all sat around the table talking.

"You've both been getting arrested a lot lately," her mother had said.

"Well, that is all behind us," Alexis had promised as she

looked over at Culhane. "We're going to raise horses and kids. I'm going to bake and cook and decorate and maybe even have a garden in the spring."

Her father had looked skeptical. "That certainly sounds like a change of pace." Her mother had agreed. Then Culhane had left for the ranch to finish up getting everything ready for the wedding, and Alexis had taken her dress out of the box, hung it up and climbed into bed. She'd dropped off instantly only to be awakened this morning by her mother's cheerfulness and her father's blueberry cream cheese stuffed French toast.

It was her wedding day, and she was now about to see what her future husband had planned. She looked into his very blue eyes and nodded. "Ready."

Culhane opened the door, and Alexis caught her breath. He'd promised that it would be a small wedding, with just friends and family. He'd also promised that the ceremony would be quick.

But she'd never been prepared for this. He'd made the huge living room into a winter wonderland for the most beautiful Christmas wedding ever.

"Oh, Culhane," she said on a breath as she took it all in. "It's amazing."

"You like it?" he asked sounding worried.

"I love it," she said, throwing her arms around him. This from a man who'd never had a plan? She smiled over at him. "You've thought of everything."

"I tried," he said with a grin. "You know me."

Oh, she knew him. Could a woman ever love a man as much as she loved this one? "Let's do this," she said as he took her hand and led her through the guests gathered to the podium framed in the window overlooking the creek.

"Earl Ray?" she said when she saw who would be officiating the wedding.

"I am a man of many talents," he said humbly.

"You certainly are. Is Bessie here?" she asked and looked around, spotting her in the crowd. She waved, delighted to see her.

"She wasn't about to miss this," Earl Ray said.

"Bessie made our cake," Culhane whispered. "Wait until you see it."

Alexis felt tears sting her eyes. "You really have thought of everything. Thank you."

Earl Ray cleared his voice. The music died down, and the ceremony began. Throughout it, Culhane held her hand right up until Earl Ray said, "You may now kiss your bride." And he did.

As HE LOOKED AROUND the room, Culhane couldn't believe that he'd pulled it off. Christmas music played in the background as friends and family visited. He'd kept to some wedding traditions and skipped others. Bessie's cake was a huge hit. So was his mother's punch. Alexis had seemed pleased, and that's all he really cared about.

"I can't believe what the two of you have been through," Al said shaking his head. "Are you sure you won't be bored stiff raising horses? Alexis told me that she's closed her bounty-hunting business. That she's looking forward to child-rearing and the domestic life." Al looked skeptical. "You really think you can keep her on the ranch?"

Culhane laughed as he looked across the room at his lovely bride. "I do like the idea of a houseful of children," he said with a chuckle. "But you've known Alexis long enough to know that she will do what she wants to do. Whatever it is, it's fine with me."

"Modern marriage," Al said and laughed. "I never thought I'd see you succumb to it."

"Me either," Culhane agreed. "But when you meet someone like Alexis…"

ALEXIS FELT AS if in a dream. Everything had happened so quickly, and yet there were moments that were imprinted on her memory as clear and in-focus as if they had just happened.

"The wedding was so wonderful," she said to Culhane as the last of the guests left. She'd insisted her parents take some of the cake. Her mother had gotten the recipe from Bessie, something Earl Ray said was nothing short of a miracle.

"I'm glad you liked it," Culhane said as they stood on their porch. "It was a bit unorthodox."

She shook her head. "It was perfect. All of it." She was so glad that she had trusted him. She couldn't have come up with a more beautiful wedding.

Twilight had settled over the ranch, turning the pine-covered mountains a midnight blue. It reminded her of other evenings in the mountains, but none this vivid. The smells, the colors, the sense of the solid earth beneath her was so intense that it made her heart soar.

"But I didn't give you your white Christmas," he said as he put his arm around her and led her back inside.

"You gave me all of this," she said, stopping in the doorway to take in the room again. He'd added just enough to the decorations they'd already put up to make it enchanting. The man had style, something he and his lucky hat and boots would have never let her imagine. The wedding had brought out even more Christmas spirit in both of them.

Like him, for years she'd opted to work the holidays

rather than face her empty apartment. The first few years she'd gotten a small tree and decorated it with tiny lights. It had looked so forlorn that she'd ended up taking it over to an elderly neighbor's apartment.

The man had looked at it, then at her. "What am I supposed to do with that?" he'd demanded.

"Plug it in," she'd said and thrust it at him. A few nights later when she'd stopped by his apartment, she'd seen the tree in his window, the tiny sparkling lights glowing. She'd smiled, glad it had given someone a little cheer.

Now, Culhane pulled her close. "Pretty night."

"Beautiful," she said. "It's so…peaceful here. Do you hear the creek?" She felt him nod.

"I hate to pull you away from this, but you must be freezing," he said and stepped back to turn her to face him. "Come inside. I need your help."

She raised an eyebrow, but he gave her no clue as they entered the house. Once in the large living room, the blaze in the fireplace a welcoming warm crackle, she saw that he had alcohol-free champagne chilling and two glasses.

"Merry Christmas, Mrs. Travis." He poured her a glass and one for himself. "To us."

She clinked her glass against his and took a sip of the bubbly. It tickled her tongue. She smiled at her husband. *Husband.* Would she ever get used to that?

He was so darned handsome. She hoped their son looked just like him.

As she felt him moving, she put her hand on her belly. Culhane came up behind her and encircled her with his arms to place his hand over hers.

"Your son is kicking up his heels," she said as something outside caught her eye. She turned toward the large window.

"Culhane, it's snowing!" Huge lacy flakes drifted down, growing thicker as she watched them in the outside lights.

He hugged her as they watched it snow. "I promised you a white Christmas, didn't I?"

She snuggled against him. "You're a man of your word."

He laughed softly. "I sure hope Santa can find us."

"You aren't one of those people who can't wait to open presents, are you?"

"Today I got the best present anyone could ask for," he said and nuzzled her neck. "But I might have shaken a couple of the ones under the tree with my name on them."

"You're incorrigible. What am I going to do with you?" she said, laughing.

"I'm sure you'll think of something." Together they stood there watching the snow fall as the fire crackled in the stone fireplace. Safe and warm, they talked about the future.

FIVE MONTHS LATER, Culhane took his infant son in his arms. He looked down into that perfect little face with awe and felt his heart fill with love for his son. *His son.*

He looked at Alexis and smiled through his tears. "Thank you."

"I didn't do it alone," she said with a laugh.

"You are amazing," he said to her, meaning every word. The last few months had been the best in his life. He couldn't imagine anything topping them until now. "I never dreamed of the kind of joy that you've brought to my life, and now this?"

She chuckled. "So you like him?"

"Oh, Alex." He tried to swallow the lump in his throat as he pushed aside the blanket a little to look at his son's tiny feet with their ten perfect toes. And those hands! As he touched one, the little fingers opened only long enough to wrap around his finger. "Hey, this kid has a grip! And he just smiled at me."

"Of course he did," Alexis said grinning. "You're going to be a great dad."

"I hope so." He looked at his wife again. *His wife.* "I love you," he whispered as he handed her their son and sat down on the edge of the bed to put his arm around her.

"He's going to need a name," she said, smiling down at the infant. "He looks like you."

"We could name him after your father."

"Harry? I think not," she said with a shake of her head. "Anyway, Dad already vetoed that idea. What about naming him after your father?" He could tell that she'd been hesitant to even suggest it.

"You would be all right with that?" he asked.

"I see your father's love every day in our home and this ranch." She nodded. "I would be more than all right with it."

Culhane tightened his hold on her. "How did I get so lucky? All right, then, son. Nathaniel Culhane Travis. Boy, that's a mouthful for such a little guy. How about we call you Nate after your grandfather for the time being? Hey, he smiled again."

Alexis laughed. "It's gas, Culhane. But Nate it is."

"When can we start trying to make another one?" he asked with a grin.

"Culhane." She shook her head, but she was smiling.

* * * * *

Look for the next book in the
Buckhorn, Montana series coming from
New York Times *bestselling author B.J. Daniels.*
Read on for a sneak peek.

THE SATURDAY EVENING the crows came, Jasper Cole had been standing in his ranch kitchen cleaning up his dinner dishes. He heard the rustle of feathers and looked up with a start to see several dozen crows congregated on the telephone line outside.

Just the sight of them stirred another memory of a time dozens of crows had come to his grandparents' farmhouse. The chill he felt at both the memory and the arrival of the crows had nothing to do with the cool Montana spring air coming in through the kitchen window.

He stared at the birds that now all seemed to be watching him. There were so many of them, their ebony bodies silhouetted against a cloudless sky, their shiny dark eyes glittering in the growing twilight. As this murder of crows began to caw, he listened as if this time he might decode whatever they'd come to tell him. But like last time, he couldn't make sense of it.

Laughing to himself, he closed the window and finished his dishes. He didn't really believe the crows had come to warn him this time – anymore than they had the last time. His grandmother had though. He remembered watching her cross herself and mumble a prayer as if the crows were an omen of something sinister to come. As it turned out, she'd been right.

At almost forty, Jasper could scoff all he wanted even

as a bad feeling settled deep in his belly. That feeling only worsened as the crows suddenly all took flight as if their work here was done.

Over the next few days, he would remember the evening the crows appeared. It was the same day Leviathan Nash came to Buckhorn, Montana, to open his shop in the old carriage house and strange things had begun to happen— even before people started dying.

"If need be, I could run my way out of these woods. You can't run," Linnea added.

"No, but I can return fire if we get into trouble," Jace argued. "And I stand a better chance of hitting a target than you do."

It was a good argument. Well, it would have been if he hadn't had the gunshot wound. It wasn't on his shooting arm, thank goodness, but he was weak, and any movement could cause that wound to open up.

"You could bleed out before I get you out of these woods," Linnea reminded him. "Besides, I'm not sure you can shoot, much less shoot straight. You can't even stand up without help."

As if to prove her wrong, he picked up his gun from the nightstand and straightened his posture, pulling back his shoulders.

And what little color he had drained from his face.

Cursing him and their situation, she dragged a chair closer to the window and had him sit down.

"The main road isn't that far, only about a mile," she continued. Linnea tried to tamp down her argumentative tone. "I can get there on the ATV and call for help. Your deputies and the EMTs can figure out the best way to get you to a hospital."

That was the part of her plan that worked. What she didn't feel comfortable about was leaving Jace alone while she got to the main road. Definitely not ideal, but they didn't have any other workable solutions.

Of course, this option wouldn't work until the lightning stopped. She could get through the wind and rain, but if she got struck by lightning or a tree falling from a strike, it could be fatal. First to her, and then to Jace, since he'd be stuck here in the cabin.

He looked up at her, his color a little better now, and his eyes were hard and intense. "I can't let you take a risk like that. Gideon could ambush you."

"That's true," she admitted. "But the alternative is for us to wait here. Maybe for days until you're strong enough to ride out with me. That might not be wise since I suspect you need antibiotics for your wound before an infection starts brewing."

His jaw tightened, and even though he'd had plenty trouble standing, Jace got up. This time he didn't stagger, but she did notice the white-knuckle grip he had on his gun. "We'll see how I feel once the storm has passed."

In other words, he would insist on going with her. Linnea sighed. Obviously, Jace had a mile-wide stubborn streak and was planning on dismissing her *one workable option*.

"If you're hungry, there's some canned soup in the cabinet," she said, shifting the subject.

Jace didn't respond to that. However, he did step in front of her as if to shield her. And he lifted his gun.

"Get down," Jace ordered. "Someone's out there."

Don't miss
Pursued by the Sheriff
by Delores Fossen, available January 2022 wherever
Harlequin Intrigue books and ebooks are sold.

Harlequin.com